DRAGONKILLER

Arthur Butt

Cover Art:
Michelle Crocker
http://mlcdesigns4you.weebly.com/

Publisher's Note:
This is a work of fiction. All names, characters, places, and
events are the work of the author's imagination.
Any resemblance to real persons, places, or events is
coincidental.

Solstice Publishing - www.solsticepublishing.com

DRAGONKILLER

Arthur Butt

Chapter One

Hope paced. She sat, sprang to her feet, hesitated, and checked the sky.

The rain clouds had parted, revealing a weak sun setting over the mountain peaks. A chill wind blew, tousling her hair.

Not yet. Soon.

She hurried to her pack. Satan watched with interest and nudged an arm. "Don't be greedy," she laughed, the pressure inside her small body diminishing. "You know the rules, no treats until *after* the killing."

The great black stallion nuzzled her hand, and receiving nothing, resumed cropping grass.

Still chuckling, Hope withdrew her copy of the *Shaddrad*, the Demon Book of the Dead, from her bundle and resumed her seat by the fire. Squatting, the manuscript fell open to a well-worn page:

"Seek not the monster in his lair when he sleeps, or is awake, but rather when the inner eye is closing, and the outer not yet open."

Wise words. She had forced herself to memorize each word in the book. They had kept her alive for eight years so far.

Hope leaped up again and returned the manuscript.

Stretching, she prepared herself, stripping off sodden riding cloak and tunic down to chain mail armor. With a light touch, she wiggled the hilts of her swords. Assured they were loose in their scabbards, she measured the progress of the sun one more time. It had disappeared, leaving a ruddy glow in the sky.

It was time.

The squeezing in her chest vanished, dismissed as a nuisance. She strode up the mountain trail, skirting pools of lava and smoking rocks, until the mouth of a cave arrived into view. Hope drew her long sword and took a deep

1

breath.

A fetid blast of air mixed with the smell of brimstone hit her in the face. She choked.

Damn. Apprentice mistake. Good way to get myself killed. What would the monks at the monastery say? If she had been born a man it wouldn't have mattered, but… The constriction inside built again. Hope fought for control and won. More cautious now, she stepped inside.

It was not dark. The amber glow of fires cast dancing shadows on the walls and floor. In the rear of the cavern a darker shape stirred, short tongues of flame shooting from the nostrils.

The dragon was awakening. The inner eye closing, it's outer not yet open.

Like a cat stalking a bird, she took short steps, creeping up to the monster until she stood by his side. Hope leaped, landing on his back, sword raised high.

The massive head stirred, eyes wide, jaws gaping to seize her. With a look of triumph, the blade plunged down, cutting through iron scales, skin, and muscles, driving into the heart.

Hope dove backward. Six-inch teeth snapped where she'd stood. The tail caught her behind the legs, flipping her over. Slapping the ground to absorb the impact, Hope rolled and stooped low as the tail reversed. A stream of flames traced her movements. She dodged right, ricocheted off a boulder, and ducked behind the rock's safety as another blast of fire swept above.

The sinuous neck reached back, teeth grasping at the handle of the sword. Unable to seize the blade, the dragon bellowed in rage. Jets of flame lashed the cavern roof. Rocks and dust pelted down on Hope as the massive tail struck the walls.

The thrashing grew slower, the flames diminished. A convulsive shudder rattled the body. The neck sank lower. With one last spasm the dragon's head sank to the ground, faint trails of fire leaking from nose and mouth.

The monster lay still.

Hope rose and emerged from hiding. "Easier than I thought," she muttered, sated. For the moment, the thrill of revenge replaced the emptiness within. *Filthy beast, you'll never attack anyone again.*

She strolled to the monster's side and climbed on the wide back, withdrawing her sword. Leaping down, she walked to the neck.

Hope enjoyed some parts of killing, and others she viewed with distain. This portion was detestable. The monster was not dead. A dragon would regenerate its heart given enough time and return to life. Humanity only knew of one way to guarantee they never revived to plague the world again.

With a sigh, she got busy.

A long, weary time later, the head dropped away from the neck to roll at her feet. Lifeless eyes stared up, the red glow glazed over. Covered in sweat, scales, and blood, Hope put her long sword away and withdrew the short blade.

"Okay, you bad boy," she cooed, "let's see how old you are." Hope cut through the tough scales and skin on the dragon's side from the wishbone to the anus, gutting the beast completely. The wet intestines slipped onto the floor of the cave.

Fishing around in the entrails, her fingers grasped an organ. A quick flip of the sword sliced the prize loose. *Heavy,* she thought, gauging the weight of the warm mass. *Must be an old one.* Holding the flesh like a dead mouse, she strolled down to camp.

Satan shifted nervously at her approach, and snorted, his eyes showing white.

"I would think you'd be used to the smell of dragon blood by now," Hope chided. She reached into a saddlebag and extracted a piece of fruit. The horse sniffed and the reward disappeared.

Hope pulled an empty leather bag from the pack, dropped the dragon flesh in, and secured the pouch to the saddle horn.

"Well, what do you think boy? Ride to the castle or camp for the night?" Satan pawed his hoof and swished his tail, hoping for more fruit.

"You're right. Castle it is, no sense wasting our time around here." She brushed long brown hair back from her too narrow face, trying to comb the knots out with fingers. An adrenalin rush still boiled within. No way she'd fall asleep for a while.

A screech sounded overhead. The shape of a night flyer crossed the moon and swooped into the cave. Soon there'd be more, and the creeping grey vermin everyone hated. Hope didn't want to wake on this slope and discover one of *those* sitting on her chest.

"Maybe I can beg a hot meal and a bed after I've been paid," she lifted an arm, sniffed suspiciously, "and a bath. I stink."

The time was well past midnight. She mounted Satan and rode.

Six hours later, New Valley drifted into sight. Dawn was breaking and the cobblestoned main road jammed with foot traffic. The crowd parted in hushed silence as Satan clomped up the street. Whispers followed her:

"That is the Dragonkiller..."

"... a mere slip of a girl. How...."

"She is covered in blood."

Hope gritted her teeth and forced herself to relax. She was used to the remarks, conscious changing people's views was impossible. It didn't matter. She carried the proof with her. She concentrated on the castle atop the hill. Hurrying up the grade, she discovered the drawbridge down, as well as the portcullis.

"Hey." Hope waved at the guard on the parapet.

"Open up."

The sentry was the same who stood watch yesterday when she left. He signaled down and the iron bars rose. Entering the courtyard, she grabbed the leather sack.

Soldiers ran up. Hope tossed Satan's reins to one and ordered, "Make sure he's feed, watered and groomed. I have business with your lord." Without glancing back, she marched into the castle and sought the great hall.

Hope heard the babble of people long before entering the room. She strolled between the lower tables, and the voices dropped to murmurs. Mounting the raised platform where the king and queen breakfasted, the noise ceased altogether.

"King Hela," she announced, standing opposite the pair, hands on the table, "I have returned. The beast is dead as you requested. I ask for payment."

The queen recoiled from Hope's grim appearance, her nose wrinkling in disgust.

Hope regarded the woman with an expression of contempt. *You gallop through a storm, fight a dragon, and see what you look like.*

A stray breeze stirred, carrying Hope's odor to the king. He jerked back too.

One of the nobles, a baron, sitting at a lower table, scrambled onto the platform and stood beside the king.

"How do we know the beast is slain?" he asked Hela. The baron surveyed Hope's gore cover, slight frame, grimaced at her rank hair, and waved, "Except for the appearance."

Hope shifted her gaze to the noble with malice, shooting hate, and then fixed on the king. Without a word, the sack dumped on the table and the flesh spilled out, the meat shimmering dark with clotted blood, the gizzard of the dragon.

Hope granted a disdainful smirk to the baron, yanked out her belt knife, and slit the organ apart. Pressing down, half-digested food and different colored gems splattered. Diamonds, rubies, and emeralds spilled on the dining board.

"Your proof, Sire," she said, sticking her palm out. "My payment."

The king, queen, and baron craned their necks forward gazing at the stones. The rest of the assembly from the lower tables hurried to stare in amazement.

"Y–Yes, Dragonkiller," Hela stuttered. He nodded to his steward, who dashed away, scurrying back with a leather pouch. The king emptied it on the table. Yellow coins rolled out. "Twenty gold rounds as you requested," the king said. "But I do not…"

Hope scooped the coins into her pouch without counting them. She reached into the pile of jewels and selected a ruby from among the scattered baubles. "If I may," she asked, "a souvenir of the killing?"

"Of course," the king answered, confused. "I still do not…" He waved at the precious stones. "You do not want the rest of these?"

The sense of exaltation left, replaced by a desire to hide and relax. She didn't want to give long explanations. "I received my payment, that's all I require." Her body ached. "If I may, however, ask for some food and a place to sleep?" She gave the queen an abashed look and said in a soft voice, "A bath would be nice, too."

The queen's eyes snapped wide at this unexpected change in attitude and request. Recovering, the woman replied, "Of course my dear. That is the least we can do for you." Rising, she snapped her fingers and waved the steward back over. "Quick, ready a chamber. Fetch a bath, and whatever food the dragonkiller desires." Her expression softened. "Is there something more we may do for you, my dear?"

Hope gripped the edge of the table again, trying not to sway with fatigue. "That will be sufficient, Your Majesty. I won't need anything else."

Lackeys jumped and the steward guided her up a staircase in the keep to the highest chamber. Men dragged in a brass tub. They returned hauling bucket after bucket of boiling water, filling the bath to the top. The servants hurried away and a young woman and man entered. They stood quietly waiting.

Hope was about to remove her clothes. Attendants were not employed in her household, and while not critical of those utilizing personal valets, the presence of these two watching made her uncomfortable. Nothing else was required anyway.

Both received a curt nod. "You are dismissed. I do not need your help." She waited for the pair to leave.

"Please, if you will, Dragonkiller, this is our job," the woman answered. "The queen has assigned us for bath," she inclined her head to the tub, "food, and bed."

The girl appeared so expectant, Hope decided to let them remain for a while. She had no wish to raise the ire of the queen against these two for not performing their tasks.

A thought struck her. "Bed?" Hope raised an eyebrow. The girl couldn't possibly mean what Hope thought she meant. Their expressions said otherwise. "Either of you?"

The woman smiled. "Either, or, your choice. We are here to please."

Startled, Hope inspected the two closer. They appeared to be brother and sister, maybe in their late teens or twenties. The man grinned and flexed his chest muscles. Hope smiled back and shook her head no. The dragon had already pounded her enough. The woman underwent a closer inspection.

The girl had high breasts, white teeth, and startling green eyes, dark wavy curls brushed and perfumed in a pageboy cut. Hope lifted the woman's hands and examined them. "Soft," she murmured, "clean with manicured nails."

"We are of the household staff, and our lord employs

7

us to entertain his guests," the girl replied with a coy smile. "My brother and I are extremely skilled."

Hope was tempted. A sharp pain shot up her back, like a hot nail running up her spine. "Not tonight, little one," she said with real regret, "bath and food only."

The woman's expression made it unclear if the girl was disappointed or not. The happy smile never wavered.

Shrugging, Hope stripped off clothes and armor, dropping both in a pile at her feet. "These can be cleaned and washed."

The two servants gasped. Not because of Hope's figure, it was average. Naked, her body was a mass of old scars and bruises. She looked like a purple doll ripped apart and sewed back together.

She gazed down at herself. *Yes, I'm a mess, aren't I, comes with the trade.*

The tub beckoned. With a sigh, Hope eased her sore body into the hot water, feeling the aches begin to fade away. She gulped air and dunked under, holding her breath as long as possible. When she surfaced, the man was gone, so were the soiled garments.

The woman worked *swabu,* scented ash and vegetable oil, into Hope's scalp, building lather, shampooing the thick mass. Afterwards, she combed it, picking out bits of dragon scale and bone with her fingers. When done, the girl produced a sponge, adding additional fragrant soap, and washed Hope, starting at her face and scrubbing down.

After a minute, Hope called a halt. "I'll do the rest, my dear," she giggled. The girl tickled in all the right spots, and she really wasn't up to playing tonight. Hope finished the job herself with minimal fuss.

The young man appeared carrying two pails of water, a bundle under his arm. Behind him hurried cooks carting a table and food. He placed the containers down and handed the bundle to his sister. "Bed clothes for the dragonkiller." To Hope he said, "Shall I rinse you?"

Hope stood. "Yes please." She smiled at the girl, "I think we are done here."

Water cascaded as the man poured the buckets over her head. Hope stepped out of the bath, while the servants drained the tub and totted it away. With breakneck speed, the cooks set the table. The girl covered Hope with a soft towel, rubbing and making sure Hope was quite dry.

The smell of the food drew Hope's attention. Except for a few handfuls of dried fruit and nuts, she had not eaten since yesterday. Hope debated whether to ask the two attendants to stay and dine, and decided no. She had accomplished her duty, besides she was terrible at small talk.

After everything was finished, she ordered, "You may go now, tell the Master of the Stable I will depart before dawn and to have my horse ready."

She ate, yawning, and fell into the bed, sleeping the day and night. The sun had not yet risen when she awoke. Her clothes and mail were cleaned and sitting at the foot of the bed, the weapons shiny and hung on a peg.

Must remember this valley. She stretched. *Nice people. I could deal with the merchants in the future.* She dressed, found Satan saddled and ready, mounted and departed.

Leaving the valley, she spied two soldiers hanging the mutilated remains of a body from a tree. She paused to watch as they wrapped a rope around the corpse and let it swing freely.

"Murderer?" That was the usual punishment for people displayed in such a fashion.

"No." The two climbed onto their wagon. "Half-breed."

The men spat on the ground. Hope did, also. It was custom. "We caught him an hour ago, lurking around the houses in town," one replied. He wiped his face and squinted at the morning sun. "Claimed he was searching for food, but no doubt he hid himself last night, waiting to attack someone."

Hope felt her insides twist. "Do you know what species?"

The soldier shook his head. "Small wings hidden under his shirt, demon red eyes. We do not know what he was, but does it matter?" He shrugged. "As soon we discovered the monster, he was stoned." The man said proudly, "We keep the old traditions here, Dragonkiller, you can be sure of that."

"Did you kill the bitch that spawned him?" Hope asked casually.

"No," the soldier said, disappointed, "but if she's around we'll hang that whore too." He touched his nose. "I have a knack, I can smell the scum."

Hope painted a smile on. "Anyway, good job, that's one less to worry about." She raised a fist, saluting, and hurried off.

***

In three weeks, Hope made three quick stops at different valleys, collecting signed contracts as she headed up the mountain chain. A hundred years ago a trip like this would have been impossible. Even fifty years ago, the journey was dangerous. Now traveling on the plains involved no more than a long and tedious trip.

Nevertheless, after reaching the divide leading to her valley, her back and neck muscles tightened. It always happened arriving home. Hope was used to the feeling and ignored the pain.

The gap through the pass was empty. The guard towers, which defended the opening since she remembered, had long since crumbled, the stone carted away for construction of new buildings.

She ventured down the lane leading to town and spied a wagon train approaching. The caravan drew closer, and she recognized the first driver as one of the neighbors, a young man who owned a small farm next to hers. Hope drew abreast of him and halted Satan, greeting the farmer with a wave.

"Mistress Nearwood, back from your trip?" he called, yanking on the reins of his team. "Business good?"

"Excellent," she acknowledged, "signed three contracts for my grain and a Letter of Intent for my melons in the fall." She studied his wagons. "And you? Are you leaving?" Tension levels rose.

"Going onto the plains, lay out a farm as far as the eye can see," he boasted. "One day I'll be a rich planter like you." He dealt the swords and chain mail peeking out from beneath her tunic a dubious stare. "You still feel it necessary to travel as if preparing for war? What do you fear?" he asked, raising his arms wide. "The time of the monsters, half-breeds, and the bitches that spawned their kind is long gone." He spat.

Hope spit, too. "Sir, I may be old fashioned, but my father always said to go armed. You know my father, he was..."

The farmer held his palm up. "Yes, yes, yes, last captain of the free companies, first settler of Nearwood Valley. Declined the kingship and started the council. I've heard the tales a dozen times in the tavern." He snapped the reins of his wagon. "Well, this is not getting me my plantation. Good business for the rest of the year."

Hope chuckled. "If I stay here chatting, I'll be a poor planter," she agreed. "May the gods be with you, also."

The wagons roll by with a farewell from the farmer's wife. Hope liked those people, never snoopy, always minding their own business. The woman even crocheted an afghan for her as a thank you present, after Hope lent her husband seed for the spring planting, and presented it at the festival of Eostre. They were good folks. She wished the next owners were as unobtrusive, or buying the property was an option, and not worry about nosey neighbors.

The town was unchanged, prosperous and bustling. Hope noted with pride another half mile of aqueduct was finished. A vision of her father's, pushed and paid for by Nearwood money, to transport running water from the mountains to the valley residents.

A few acquaintances shouted her name in greeting. Hope rode by the market, curious to know who browsed. Diane was not present, but the overseer running their produce stand lounged outside the office, watching the townspeople hunt for the best vegetables and fruit to buy. The man snapped to attention when he spied Hope, and then relaxed as Satan sped past without stopping.

At the pace the horse established, the town rapidly shrank in the distance. Soon they treaded on her property, riding down a tree-studded lane. On the right spread acres of grain, while to the left, rows of plants, vines, and orchards sprang up. Beyond, mountains filled with lumber for export to the growing towns of the plains filled the horizon.

Hope noted with a farmer's eye, they would need to hire pickers for the orchards. She hated that. Besides the cost of extra workers, you never knew what they saw or said afterwards.

The manor house rose into view. Tension escalated. She scanned the yard. *Good. No strange activity, a few people conducting their duties.*

She rode in. Servants rushed from the house yelling greetings. Hope put a finger to her lips. "Hush, I want to surprise Diane."

Grins and nods answered her. A groom snatched Satan's reins as Hope ran up the steps into the hall.

"What in the world is happening down there?" Diane's boots tramped into view on top of the staircase. "Hello? Is anyone here? Of all the…" The remainder of the young woman materialized and she saw Hope. With a cry of joy, the girl ran down the rest of the steps.

"Hope?" Diane hit her big sister with a bear hug that almost knocked both over.

"Diane," Hope couldn't stop laughing.

"When did you get back? How have you been? Did you survive? Of course you did, you're here aren't you?" Diane tittered.

She released Hope and stepped back. "We need to have a big feast in your honor. I'll let the hands know. Cooky. COOKY? Where are you? Hope is home." The cook was standing at the doorway beaming at both sisters. "Oh, there you are next time answer when I call. We're going to throw a big dinner. I was..."

"Hold on." Hope put an arm around her sister. "I've been gone almost two months. The last thing I want is more people."

Diane pouted. "But..."

Hope said to the cook, "Some wine, cheese, and bread. If the grapes are ripe, I'll have those too. I've been dying for a grape. We'll have brunch in the office." She guided Diane along the hallway. "I want to check the books. Let's see if we made any money while I was away."

The food arrived at the same time Hope settled into the soft, high-backed chair behind her desk. Diane sat opposite her sister. Hope set the account ledger in front of her and commenced flipping pages.

"What's the matter, do you think I've been stealing from us?" Diane griped when Hope frowned and double-checked figures.

"Of course not, dear," Hope murmured, flipping a few leaves of the book in rapid concentration, "but you know how you are with math."

Diane muttered something under her breath.

"What, I didn't hear you." Hope flicked another page.

"I said we had the same teacher."

Hope closed the book and looked up. "Yes, but I wasn't busy thinking about boys."

13

They both laughed.

"So tell me, how did the killing go?"

Hope poured herself a goblet of wine. "Typical." She tasted the drink with satisfaction and bit a wedge of cheese. "Easy in fact, for once."

"I can send a messenger to the mountains, then?"

"Of course. I'll write out a report of the killing in the morning." She untied the purse from her belt, and emptied coins onto the table. "Here, we're rich." Hope picked up the ruby and dropped the bauble into a jar with seven more of the jewels.

Diane barely glanced at the gold. "Why do you continue…?"

Damn. That again? Hope jaws clamped shut. *We're starting this so soon? I haven't been in the house ten minutes…* "You know why." Hope eyes blazed.

"It was eight years ago." Diane reached a hand across the table. "Surely you can forget…"

"Forget? Forget? I will never forget. I don't believe you said that." Hope tried hard to regain her temper.

Diane flushed pink. "I chose my words poorly. Why can't you accept it?"

"I have."

Diane pointed to the jar with rubies in it. "If you must continue this, at least keep the jewels. They're yours by right."

"I don't do it to become wealthy. We're rich enough already," Hope scoffed. She straightened her shoulders, took a deep breath, and said, "Is he here?"

A soft smile spread across Diane's lips. "Of course, in his room, where else would he be? He's waited since you left. Should I fetch him?"

Hope raised a hand and stood. "No, I'll go by myself. You needn't bother."

She strode down the hallway, paused at a door, eager for the confrontation with the half-human, half-dragon

14

monster that lurked within.

She knocked.

The door opened.

"Mommy, *you're home.*"

"Yes, son, I'm home."

Chapter Two

Apophis threw his arms around Hope's legs in a tight hug. "I've missed you, Mommy." He gazed up with bright brown eyes, the forked tongue flickering in and out of his mouth in excitement. "Did you bring me anything?"

Damn. In the excitement of the killing, and the trading afterwards, she'd forgotten the promise. Hope squeezed him closer and exclaimed, "Yes, but it's in town right now. I'll ride first thing in the morning and pick it up, okay?"

Apophis stuck out his lower lip, but answered, "I can wait." He released Hope and grasped her hand, tugging his mother eagerly inside his room. One wall held shelves and nooks lined top to bottom with books and scrolls, another with cupboards filled with games and toys. A large rocking horse and stuffed bear dominated the floor next to a four-poster bed. Floor to ceiling windows with heavy drapes let in a trickle of afternoon light.

Apophis sat on the edge of the bed and asked in a grownup tone, "How was your trip?"

"Oh, fine," Hope replied, ruffling his stiff black hair and sitting beside him. "I couldn't wait, though, to return, see you and Aunt Diane."

"Can I make a trip with you next time?" He added in a wishful voice, "I never go anywhere."

Hope cringed. If people saw him, if anyone knew, it would mean his death. The stoning she would receive, or the hanging afterward, didn't matter. He was her son. He must survive.

"We'll see," she replied. "Mommy doesn't plan on taking any more trips for a long time. Too much work to be done here at the farm." Hope squeezed him tight, savoring the warmth of his small body. "What have you been doing while I was away?" A chalk sketch rested on an easel by the window. She wandered over to study the picture. The mountains and sky rising behind the house shone in beautiful colors.

He couldn't view those hills from his room. "When did you see these mountains?"

Dread of discovery knotted Hope's stomach, the pain in her neck rising high. The household staff was safe enough as well as the farmhands. They'd worked on the plantation for years, most before her parents died. Still, sometimes strangers wandered onto their land, or unexpected visitors arrived from the town or neighboring farms. What if…

There was that one occasion with the worker who became talkative at the tavern. Afterward Hope spread the story he'd been fired for stealing, became disgruntled, and ran away.

No one would discover that body.

Diane was so careless sometimes. Hope understood her sister was trying to do right for the boy. He couldn't hide in the house *all* the time. She would have words with Diane about when and where Apophis went.

Hope realized the boy had spoken. "What?"

"Yesterday Aunt Diane and I rode to see the syrup trees," he explained again.

Hope squeezed her eyes shut. Definitely talk to Diane. That grove was in the mountains. The two must have ridden during the day. She gnashed her teeth thinking how dangerous that was. "We're having a special dinner tonight because I'm home," she said. "Do you want me to ask Cooky to make something you really like?"

The boy put his finger to his mouth. "Blood pudding?"

Hope smiled with an indulgent chuckle. "Of course."

***

Even though it was summer, and the spring planting finished before she left, the plantation still demanded attention, fowl plucked for feathers or food, herd animals

17

marked with the Nearwood brand, or fences mended.

Hope resumed her old routine with a sigh.

After the excitement of the hunt, Hope's day-to-day work of supervising the farm bored her, but she applied herself with determination as if engaging in battle.

It wasn't right to leave this to Diane. That girl did become confused at times. Produce for signed contracts must ship to the closer valleys, and that Letter Of Intent. Had they planted enough melons to provide the merchant the quantity he professed to need? Better check here in the valley for a secondary supplier, in case. Hope needed to know that when the monks contacted her for a killing, her sister had as little work to do as possible. Hope couldn't have her too exhausted to take care of Apophis.

The bookkeeping was a mess as usual. Diane claimed to have developed her own system and understood the figures perfectly. Hope couldn't, and she sweated for a month re-recording sales, accounts of pay for the workers, and scribbled copies of bills-of-ladings, before she was satisfied the books reflected the current dates.

Hope swung between amusement and irritation each time she was forced to call Diane into the office asking what two dots and a question mark meant, or a heart drawn over a buyer's name. Finally, her sister exploded and exclaimed, "You know, if you spent more time with Apophis, and less time worrying about every little detail, we would all be happier."

Hope thought about it. Her sister was right.

She stopped tolling away in the office, crossed the farm on Satan, examining crops, directing the hands to the harvests immediate needs. She set aside time however, to play with Apophis, teach him his lessons, and late at night, when no one else stirred, wake him to stroll outside. Sometimes they even saddled horses exploring the fields and woods together. Hope cherished these moments. She wished bitterly she could give him more.

Two months after returning, Hope drove a cartload of crops to town. Three wagon trains of vegetables had already found their way outvalley, and tomorrow the chief wrangler was organizing a herd drive onto the plains for delivery to a rancher. Business was good.

On the second day back, Hope purchased a bird for Apophis, an exotic one from the Southern jungles. Excitement ran wild, different seeds and fruit shoved into the cage, and a list of names proposed, but the wonder died.

First stop, the stand, she decided. The next couple of days were too hectic to spend time with Apophis, and a distraction was needed so he didn't mope in his room, complaining he had nothing to do. Besides, she enjoyed seeing the anticipation on his face, and eased the guilt of not paying attention to him as much as possible. She unloaded quickly so she could snag something to keep the boy entertained.

The market was crowded. Planters from the rest of the valley hauled in their produce also. Hope didn't mind competition. The rivalry excited her. Besides, the farm sold the best vegetables in the region and the whole town recognized the fact. She drove the wagon to the rear of the office and workmen leaped to unload the crops.

"Be back," she shouted to the overseer with a wave and sauntered into the crowd, ready to shop.

The toymaker fiddled away in his shop as always, since Hope was young herself. Painted dolls, miniature figures of monsters, and the free company heroes who slayed the demons, littered the corners. Puppets and carved animals dangled from the ceiling. The toymaker himself was busy sitting at his counter, hammering away. He glanced up, startled as Hope bustled up to his counter, and parted the other bystanders watching him.

"Why, Mistress Nearwood, how glad to see you." He glanced at the others standing near. "You can always tell when a Nearwood woman is on the prowl." He laughed at his own joke and put his hammer down. "What brings you to my shop today? Not another plaything to keep your sister amused, is it? I've never know a grown woman to collect so many toys. You would think she was furnishing a room for a child."

"I'm looking for something to bring on my next trip abroad," Hope replied in a confidential whisper with a wink, "always a good idea to take a bribe along for children. It makes dealing with the buyers easier, a good impression, if you know what I mean." A puppet might be nice. Apophis could plan shows during the day and perform whatever he concocted at night. He would like that. The boy had a flare for pretending.

The man nodded. "I've got just the thing." He ducked under the counter and reappeared with a gadget that reminded Hope of a spider. The object, cradled in soft cloth, wobbled as the toymaker placed the thing in front of her to admire.

"Does it do anything?"

The old man nodded. "Watch this."

He fished a flat piece of steel from his breast pocket, picked up the toy, and shoved the key into a slot. Twisting it a few times, he released the spider on the counter. The gadget began to dance and walk across the board on its spindly legs.

"*See,*" he exclaimed. "It moves."

"Well, I'll be." Hope reached out. "Do you mind?"

The toymaker shook his head. She picked up the spider and held the gadget in her palm. The toy danced a few more times, slowed, and stopped. "How does it work?" She upended the strange object and examined the thing from all angles.

"Wind it with the key," he explained. "There's a spring inside. As the spring unwinds, it spins gears, which moves the legs." He made a twirling motion with his fingers. "Isn't that amazing, huh? I purchased it from a trader of the plains. Clever folks out there. Those people are always trying something new." He paused, thinking. "That reminds me, a different fella wandered in. I think he was asking for you." The toymaker frowned and rubbed his chin. "It couldn't have been you though."

"Huh, what do you mean?"

"The man described a woman resembling you, long brown hair, chainmail, swords, riding a black horse. Sounded like you when you go a trading. But..." he chuckled, "he was asking for a dragonkiller." The toymaker studied her up and down with amusement. "Imagine our gentle Hope Nearwood being a dragon slayer."

Alarm bells rang in Hope's head. She laughed along with the old man. "Yes, gentle. That's me, but are you sure he didn't say grain seller?"

The toymaker shrugged. "Sounded like dragonkiller to me. He was asking at all the shops. If you're curious he said he'd be in the tavern having something to drink."

Hope frowned. "Humph. That explains it." This was a totally unacceptable situation. The identity of each killer stayed a strict secret. "Wrap this up, will you," she said, handing him back the mechanical spider, "I'm going to discover who this stranger is. Probably a misunderstanding, but I don't want to pass up a sale. I'll pick it up on my way back." She hurried away.

There must be a mistake somewhere. Clients never searched for her. They trekked to the monastery. The monks dispatched a courier to the closest and best qualified.

Whoever this stranger was, it meant trouble.

Even though it was the middle of the day, men drifted in and out of the tavern. Hope paused. She had no qualms about stalking into the building, but that was completely out of the character cultivated for so many years. In this valley, Hope was not the dragonkiller. She was Mistress

Nearwood, First Family, a woman of gentle birth. For her to walk into a room full of drunken, gossiping people accompanied by a man was cause for wild rumors, to enter by herself was unthinkable. She already had to fend off questions about her comings and goings by some of the more prominent members of the council. The fact that few visitors received invitations to the manor house always sprouted talk about the Nearwoods. She didn't want to start another round of speculation.

Hope waited by the door for someone familiar to enter or leave. The minutes ticked by. She grew impatient.

"*Damn,* I'm going to hear about this for the rest of my life," she muttered under her breath. Steeling herself, she pushed the door open.

The room fell quiet as the patrons scrutinized her. The interior was dark. The smell of smoke, beer, and urine filled the air. Hope ignored the few nods that came her way, hoping to finish as quickly as possible.

In one corner by the massive fireplace, a scruffy man in a dirty blue tunic hunched over a table, a black riding cloak thrown over a chair beside him. Set before the stranger was a half-finished plate of food and a tankard of ale. Hope strode over, placed her back to the curious patrons, and glared down.

"I understand you asked for a woman of my description?" she rasped in a low voice.

The man lounged back and sipped from his tankard. He folded his arms. "If you are a dragon killer, yes," he answered in an amused tone, as if she'd said something comical.

In the quiet room, his voice echoed too loud. Hope replied, "I am a provider of vegetables, grains, and meat, but you asked for a woman who rides a black horse and goes armed. I ride a black horse."

This time the stranger grinned at her in delight, his dark eyes flashing with laughter. "That's a start, anyway."

He pushed a chair out with a booted foot. "Sit."

An undercurrent of anger surged through Hope. What does he think so funny? Summoning up all the scorn possible she replied, "I do not cavort with strange men in bars, nor do I conduct my business there." She growled so all could hear, "If you wish to buy melons, or wheat, I will be in my office." She spun on her heels, and without waiting, or to see if he tailed, stormed out of the tavern.

The door banged and the man fell into step beside her, his black hair tousled from haste in donning his cloak. "Are you the one I seek?" His expression held no glee now. Concern darkened his face as he hurried to keep pace.

Hope did not look at him. "Office," she snapped.

The overseer sat behind his desk, writing, when they entered. He saw her expression, the stranger hurrying behind, and left. Hope threw herself into the empty chair in a huff. "Now what is this all about?" she demanded.

The stranger sat opposite her. "I am seeking a dragon killer. People spoke of one living in this valley. If that is you, let us talk. If not, we are both wasting our time."

He watched her, and when no reply appeared forthcoming, rose as if planning to leave.

Hope was thinking. Who told him? Anyone knowing her real persona also knew how to make contact in the proper way. "Wait." The man acted like a rogue, but an honest one. She said in a lower, guarded tone, "How did you find me? This is most unusual."

An expression of chagrin passed over his face. "I did not know one obtained dragon killers in a proper fashion," he admitted. "Many years ago a man, half dead from fighting an *Ahuizotls*, wandered into my valley. Before he died, he told us of a far-off land, a place of few demons. When we asked what happened to make the beasts leave, he told of monster hunters who slew them all. Then he passed away."

"He is the one who told you where I was?" Possibly a

demon killer, dispatched to some far-off region became disoriented, and died from battle? Hope tried to recall who never reported in. Perhaps she could retrieve the bones, and send his spirit to the gods in the proper way.

"No," the man denied, "Only of a land where monsters no longer dwell." He leaned forward, resting his forearms on the table. "We dismissed his tale. He was delirious and we thought he raved, until an evil dragon roosted in our mountains. My king bid me hunt from valley to valley, seeking someone to assist us. My search led me here."

"If you ever seek one of my trade again, go to the monks in the Western Mountains," cautioned Hope. "They will convey your request."

He pursed his lips and nodded. "Hopefully we will never need but one of you. Can you help us?"

Hope drummed her fingers on the table. For some reason this tale didn't ring true, or he was leaving important details out. His story was possible, but improbable. The *Ahuizotls* had been extinct for years. She'd studied their breed, even seen stuffed and mounted creatures, dog-like demons with hands and mouths growing on the tails, said to be vicious man-eaters. No report of those brutes had surfaced for more than twenty years. Still, one or two might survive in the far corners of the world.

For all her misgivings, his words rang true. She probed his dark eyes and saw no sign of deceit. "How much will you pay?"

"Pay?" He uttered the word as if he hadn't thought that far ahead. "I, err…"

"My fee is twenty rounds of gold," Hope stated, "plus lodging and food."

"I carry these." He reached into his pocket and withdrew a handful of black opals, laying the gems on the table. "I did not know what money you carry in this land, however, I have employed them as currency. You must tell me their worth in gold."

That was odd, too. Gold passed for currency all over the world, even poor kingdoms hoarded small quantities for emergencies. Maybe he derived from some far off valley isolated across the plains from everyone else.

On occasion reports drifted in at the monastery of pockets of humanity so inaccessible even their language was odd. This man didn't speak that differently from her, but some of his expressions were peculiar, more archaic, and he pronounced words strangely. That might account for the demons still surviving near his home.

Hope pushed the jewels around with a finger, studying their luster. *Carrying gems and passing handfuls out like water, probably every merchant and tavern keeper he met became rich by swindling this poor bastard.*

She made a quick calculation and selected three of the biggest and darkest, scooping the baubles up and dropping the jewels in her purse. "I will take these." Hope pushed the rest back into his hands, committed to a new job now. "What's your name?"

"Brian." He rose and gave a slight bow. "You?"

She didn't hand out her name to clients, preferring to be addressed as dragonkiller. Nevertheless, she judged she'd be traveling with this odd stranger for a while. She might as well make the journey on familiar terms and finish with the matter. "Call me Hope." She stood. "We leave in the morning. Where do you lodge?"

He rose also. "At the inn, of course." He bowed again and Hope realized he still smiled behind the politeness. "I shall await you."

That night she conducted a tearful farewell with Apophis.

"Mommy has to go away again for a bit, but I'll be back. Okay? You be good and listen to your Aunt Diane." Hope's throat tightened.

He wrapped his arms around her neck. "Promise? I'm

going to miss you."

"Promise." Hope hurried out of his room.

Diane was waiting in the office. Hope entered sniffling back tears and sat.

"You know you don't have to leave," Diane said. "Chase this stranger to the monastery. The monks will locate someone else." She shuffled through papers on the desk, making a mess of the neat stacks Hope left. Her brown hair hung down in tangles. She brushed a strand back and sat up straight, revealing a harried expression.

"I can't. This is my job. I promised." Hope shifted in her seat, fighting back the urge to slap her sister's hands away from the contracts and notes arranged with care.

A night breeze blew in the window, mixing the papers even more. Diane threw her hands up in disgust and leaned forward. "Your *job* is to stay here and raise your son." Her knuckles turned white from gripping the edge of the table.

Hope rose and hurried to the window, shutting it with a bang. "You're too young to remember the time when…"

"Too young?" Diane's eyes blazed, making no pretext of studying the paperwork. "I wasn't too young to raise Apophis and run this farm after our parents took their lives and you ran off to train with the monks. At fourteen?" She snorted. "Too young? I was never young." She breathed hard.

Hope's mouth worked soundlessly. She stared at her sister in shock. "Diane, I had no idea, I never thought…"

Her sister was not finished yet.

"Of course you didn't." Tears squeezed out of the corners of her eyes as she blinked hard. "Someone says dragon and off you go. Need a contract signed in the next valley? Hope's on Satan, riding away. Do you realize I've never been out of this town?"

"If it's a holiday you want…"

The young woman trembled violently. "I don't need a holiday. It's you, me, this whole mess."

26

A burning started in Hope's chest, moving into her throat to choke her. "What can I do?" she pleaded. "If I knew of someplace to take Apophis, I would. Maybe out on the plains…"

Weariness filled Diane's voice as she shook her head. "What help would that be? As soon as someone saw him, you'd both be dead." The girl massaged her forehead. "It's just, I can't have friends. Marriage?" Diane released a hoot of hysterical laughter. "Heaven forbid I let another person enter our inner circle, and they learn the family shame."

Suppressed frustration boiled up inside Hope, bubbling over. "DO YOU THINK I WANT THIS? I AM AS MUCH A PRISONER AS YOU, MAYBE MORE SO."

"Mommy?" Apophis stood at the door, eyes wide. "What's the matter? I heard shouting."

Hope and Diane rose, hurrying to the child.

"It's okay, Mommy and Aunt Diane were just talking." Hope knelt and threw her arms around Apophis, hugging his scaled body close, not noticing his talonned fingers digging into her sides as she pressed her cheek fiercely against his.

"There's nothing the matter, Apophis. Everything is all right." Diane patted the boy's back, and tried hard to smile.

Hope squeezed Apophis once more and kissed him on the cheek, looking up at Diane. "I'll take him back to bed." She ruffled his hair. "Come on, little man. Let's get you tucked in."

The morning found Hope lost in thought as Satan trailed behind the stranger, Brian.

"Why so quiet, Lady Hope?"

Brian had slowed and rode beside her. "Thinking," she replied, "and call me Mistress, I'm no Lady." Never will be either. Diane was right. They both had to keep the secret, much too hard to explain away an unhappy missing

27

lover of their station.

She tore her mind away from the family troubles, the fact her father deserted her when she need him most. She realized for the first time she didn't know the distance they traveled, or for that matter, where they ventured. Her breath made puffs of steam in the air. It would soon be fall, and she hoped to be home before then. They must plant the winter wheat soon or the ground would freeze and be too hard to work. "Where is this valley of yours?"

Brian gestured to a mountain range with high peaks. "Across these purple plains, to the highest alp."

Hope narrowed her eyes. Snow already covered the summits, the riding treacherous for those in a hurry. If the passes closed before the job concluded, she'd be stuck in his valley until the spring. Regret for this assignment multiplied.

Again, something didn't feel right. No people risked that portion of the range. Maps displayed an expanding series of stark mountains. No humans dwelt there. The hills he identified comprised the epicenter of demon activity in the past. Her father told stories, the place of the last great battles of the free companies.

Hope studied Brian out of the corner of her eye. Unrest for this mission stirred within, supplanting the problems she fled. He didn't know about the monks who trained demon killers. *Everyone* knew about them, and he no idea what gold was.

He called the Vigrid Plains 'purple plains'? They were crimson red, soaked from the blood of demons over the centuries. Even his mount was different. The head squarer somehow than a normal horse.

Brian, on the other hand, appeared normal. Skin darkened by the sun, husky shoulders, needed a shave, though. His clothes had dark spots of grease and dirt, but the fabric showed they'd once been of good quality not so long ago.

An enigma, Hope decided. A man from a valley so remote, time itself had forgotten his land, a mystery to solve while carrying out this task.

Out on the savannah, the riding was easy and they made good time. Brian kept shifting in his saddle, sometimes standing in his stirrups to view the whole landscape in all directions. Hope watched with mounting annoyance. Obviously, nothing stalked the plains.

"What are you looking for?" she sneered. "Afraid the birds will swoop out of the air and peck your head?"

Brian chuckled and sat. "No, it is odd, that is all," he murmured, "to transverse a plain without fear of attack by beast or man."

"Why would you worry?" Hope asked in surprise. "The monsters that roamed these lands were killed off before I was born, and the men of the valleys have not yet repopulated the area."

"Still." He checked the mountains ahead.

"Your valley must be remote indeed," Hope probed, "if it is still besieged by demons. I guess your people don't trade much? I've never heard of a place like that."

"We trade some," Brian admitted, "with the nearer valleys. The plains, however we keep our distance from as much as possible."

"Odd, you said your valley was in those mountains," Hope gestured to the peaks ahead, "but I know of no towns there. These plains are your plains but no demons roam here. How do you explain that?"

Brian hesitated and chose that moment to study the landscape again. "My valley is not on this side of the mountains. I meant to say we must cross the divide at that peak, and travel to the far side," he mumbled. "I am sorry if you misunderstood me."

Mistake nothing. This man was holding information back. Mystery or not, Hope hated being lied to, nor entering a situation untrained for.

She cursed herself while weighing her options. She could've been back on the farm playing with Apophis, or preparing for the harsh winter months. Opportunity still existed to back out, ride home, and refund this man's money. No one would fault the decision. He hadn't conformed in the proper fashion anyway. This was the reason people sought the monks to start with. They would have wrung out every detail of whom, when, and where, until they knew exactly what they were dealing with.

Still...

Oh, hell. He wouldn't have searched this long if his people didn't require assistance. She'd stay on guard, be alert. Her father ventured into situations like this and survived. She would too.

They entered the foothills, blasted for centuries by dragon fire and the weapons of the men who killed demons. In hollows, bones of beasts so ancient Hope was unable to put a name to their species, littered the earth, piled higher than a tall man stood. Hope estimated they'd washed down from above, since no single area could sustain such a large population.

Higher up the mountain, bitter wind made Hope thankful for her heavy travel cloak. Flecks of snow pelted her face and melted. Later they stuck to the fur-lined hood. The faint trail they traveled disappeared under a blanket of white.

"Are you sure your valley lies this way?" Hope gasped as a cold wind snatched the breath from her mouth. This was a fool's mission. No valley existed in these parts of the mountains, or on the other side either. A churning radiated up from her chest and lodged in her throat as they hiked on.

"Yes," Brian shouted back to make himself heard over the screaming of the wind. He pointed a frozen hand upward. "That is the break I seek. We are nearly there." He waved her forward. "Hurry."

They entered the divide. Sheer cliffs of ice towered over their heads. The glare from the snow caused Hope's eyes to water, feel itchy, and blur her vision. The surrounding mountains funneled the air until it sharpened into a gale, deafening her. Sound mounted, roaring into a high-pitched shriek.

The cut narrowed farther. Hope and Satan plowed on until the track steepened, forcing her to dismount and lead the stallion by the reins.

The man in front did the same. Within a dozen steps, the animal halted. Brian cursed, grabbing the bridle and pulling the stubborn horse along. Hope guided Satan around the two, fearing if the stallion stopped, they would freeze to death on the spot.

Brian shouted and she pointed to her ear, unable to understand whatever he said.

"What?" If the fool needed to have a conversation, he could talk to his horse until they both turned blue and stiff. She waved him off in disgust and kept urging Satan ahead.

Brian tramped behind, tugging his mount when the animals balked. As they entered the defile, the light dimmed and they trudged in semi-darkness.

Hope spied an arch where the two tops of the cut merged before widening again. Some play of the dim light against the snow caused the notch to shimmer and change color. As they approached, Satan paused and then stopped altogether, refusing to go through.

"Move it, you." Hope yanked the horse forward. He responded with a snort, flanks trembling, and managed a few hesitant steps. "If you don't start walking we'll die in this place," Hope fumed, glaring back a Brian. "Do you want to become a block of ice? They'll dig up our bodies a thousand years from now."

Stupid. This is what fate devised for nice people, a crazy mission heading into death's teeth. She should have known better. If the weather didn't kill her first, the feeling of wrongness this place emitted would.

The walls and frozen earth of the pass reeked of ancient evil, loss, and terror. Hope felt eyes, petrified into the ice walls, staring at her as they trudged by.

Satan slowly placed one hoof in front of the other, ears flattened. The two inched forward, Brian and his horse pushed close behind.

Hope tugged again, and her coaxing paid off. They hit the arch and stumbled under the cap.

Nausea welled up inside her. The world spun.

Hope took another step.

As sudden as the sensation started, it stopped. The snow-capped mountains that loomed had vanished. She was in a cave. Through the entrance, vertical walls marched upward to the sky. Beyond, a faint path led to trees that clumped down into a small green vale.

Dazed, Hope walked Satan to the cave mouth and into a grotto.

The crash of falling rocks and cursing issued from the inside of the cavern. Brian emerged, leading his horse. He managed to coax the reluctant beast beside Hope and mounted.

"Are we ready to ride?" His voice held no indication anything unusual had happened.

"What...?" Panic stabbed her.

"Two days travel, maybe three if we do not strain the horses, and we will be at my valley, but we must away," Brian replied. He startled at a weird hoot that issued from the savannah. "To stay in one spot too long is dangerous."

"Where...?"

Brian grimaced. "Welcome to my world."

Chapter Three

Anger replaced fear.

"Where have you taken me?" Hope fumbled at her waist, withdrawing her long sword. "Explain yourself," she demanded, seizing the bridle of his horse. "What witchery is this?"

"That," Brian hooked his thumb back to the cave, "is a doorway between our worlds."

Hope stared at him in disbelief. It wasn't true. Brian fabricated a yarn spun for children and the dim-witted on festival days.

His face spoke different. *"You lied to me."* Hope leaped on Satan, meaning to retrace her steps to the cave.

"No, Mistress Hope. *Hope*. No, I did not." Pain reflected in his expression. "My valley needs you."

"Why didn't you tell me this before?" she rasped clutching her sword tight, her expression set in danger.

"I did not mean to deceive you. I was afraid you would think me mad, or a fool." Brian flushed red, the corners of his mouth bending down. He rode close. "You will still help us? You must," he pleaded. "You accepted our payment."

"Well..." Damn, they were here now. It had been a mistake not to ask where his valley was. Did it make any difference if this was her world or his? A killing was a killing and she wanted to return to Apophis and the farm.

A thought struck. "When the dragon is slain, how do I return?" She gestured to the cave. "That way?"

"Of course," Brian answered at once with relief. "As I entered into your world, you will revisit yours." Worry filled his voice again. "We must move. This land is not as gentle as the one we have left. It is not wise to remain anywhere long, unless protected. Demons still roam here. We are in danger already." He herded her down the rock-strewn vale. "Let us go."

The savannah reminded Hope of the yellow plains of her world. "What dangers do we face I do not already know?" Her thoughts traveled back to the monsters described in the *Shaddrad*. She smirked. Those she could handle, the demons her mind conjured the first few weeks at the monastery would be tougher.

Brian shook his head. "Many, and I cannot put names to all the creatures, but demons in plenty still abide on the high plains here, and travelers are never safe. Even in the valleys where humans dwell in numbers, attacks occur on occasion."

Hope nodded and relinquished her apprehension to that place where she kept guilt about Apophis, and concentrated on the job at hand.

They progressed halfway down the vale when Brian froze. "Be still Hope. Now you will see one of the monsters we face."

Two creatures on short legs scurried toward their position. As long as a man was tall, part crocodile, part fish, they had mouths at every joint. One paused, raised itself up on its legs, humanlike, and sniffed the breeze.

"What are they?"

"*Cipacti*," Brian whispered. "They have caught our scent. Now we must fight. Thank goodness there are only two of the beasts." He vaulted from his saddle and drew his sword.

"Why are you dismounting?" challenged Hope. "If they're that dangerous let's flee back to the cave." She watched the approach of the creatures. "Or let's outrun them. They don't appear that fast."

Brian shook his head. "Escaping to the portal is futile. They would track us into your world." He held the bridle of his horse. "In this terrain they need only attack the horses' legs. Cipacti spit powerful vitriol that eats the flesh from bones."

Hope nodded and dismounted. "We shall fight then."

They advanced, swords drawn. Hope read about beasts like this, but never anticipated meeting one. The thought dissolved as the anticipation of battle swelled. Fire or acid, it made no difference, the idea was move before the danger struck.

The monsters spied the two. With more speed than Hope credited, they scurried forward. When they drew within striking distance, black fluid shot from their mouths.

Hope sprang sideways, avoiding the liquid by twisting at the last second, and as if hitting a springboard, leaped toward the creature. The tail stabbed forward, the mouth ready to spew poison. Hope's sword flashed and the tip flew away.

The momentum of the charge carried her on. Twirling, she landed astride the cipacti as if riding Satan, knees clamped around the monster's sides. A hammer blow smashed her chain mailed back, the butt of the tail slamming her forward.

Hope drew her short sword, hammering the point between the two bulging eyes. The impact of the blade drove the head downward, pinning the skull to the ground, and she scrambled away.

The last beast backed Brian against a rock, smoking earth showed where the demon struck and missed. He licked his lips, eyes darting right and left as he sought a way of circumventing the demon's guard.

Screaming in rage, bloodlust rising, Hope advanced on the monster with long sword high. In one swift stroke, the blade swung down severing neck from body.

"Th-thanks," gasped Brian. "For a moment I thought he would kill me." Wisps of ash dropped from his cloak, evidence of the acid splattering him.

Hope couldn't help herself. She said, "He almost did." She pointed to the burning cloth. "You're on fire."

Brian issued a low oath, brushing at the spots in anger with his hand. He strode back and retrieved his horse. "Let us ride," he snapped.

They finished traveling down the valley onto the flat plains, galloping knee-to-knee through the tall amber grass.

"How do you survive in this place?" Their first encounter with the monsters of this land left Hope more shaken than she revealed.

Brian laughed. "Poorly," he admitted, "as you saw." He stopped and surveyed the surrounding territory. "We live, though."

In spite of his remark, Hope smiled. At least he had a sense of humor. "Are there many dragons?" She searched the sky hoping no demonstration of monster killing was in order.

"More than you wish to see," he said. "Usually they present no problem, staying to the high peaks. I wish our world was more like yours."

"Is it possible the demons from your world wandered into mine, or mine to yours?"

"Perhaps," Brian admitted as they rode. "When I learned of the portal that was the first thing I considered. You understand my surprise when I discovered none after traveling through." He waved toward the grotto. "Of course a full grown dragon would not fit through a small slot as that, unless the monster arrived as an egg or adolescent."

Coldness gripped Hope. Could it be? The teenage dragon that attacked her had traveled from this land, slinking back here afterwards? Smoldering joy overwhelmed her. Perhaps the time finally approached to avenge the burning disgrace.

To hide the excitement she said, "In my land we had free companies who swept the land of demons. After that, trained individuals such as me upheld the tradition, rooting out the last of the evil."

As the sun set in the western sky, they encountered a shallow river, parted in the middle by a low-slung island. Trees clung perilously to life in the center.

"We will camp here tonight," Brian announced as they splashed through the water. He sprang from his horse. "This is a safe place."

Hope examined the spot. The island rested in clear view of anything that chanced upon their location. "How can you be sure?" More preferable was one of the copses of trees they'd passed that would conceal them from predators.

"Evil will not willingly cross running water," Brian explained as he removed saddle and bridle from his mount. The horse wandered off to crop the short green blades of grass. "See there?" He strolled down to the river's edge and pointed to a series of blue, water-washed stones that circled the beach. "These rocks will protect us from whatever flies above."

He straightened one to align with the rest of the small markers. "Someone of power has camped here before," he commented.

"Power?" Hope watched as he sauntered to their camp and rummaged through his pack. "What power?"

"The ability to call those who live beyond." Brian withdrew a long polished stick of oak carved with strange runes. He proceeded to walk along the shore, tapping each stone with the wand as he passed. In response, the rocks glowed faintly. Hope shadowed on his heels. "You are a warlock?"

"Wizard," he replied, his expression locked in concentration. "In this world *warlock* has a bad connotation. It means, 'Oath Breaker', one who is deceitful. Someone who cannot be trusted."

"Oh." A flash of anger crossed her mind. Obviously, he didn't consider his omissions a lie. Hope shoved that aside for the moment and watched him cast his spells.

Magicians and mages performed in the marketplace on holidays and festivals. They amused, and all professed to have links with higher powers. Hope had never lent stock to their claims, but this was something different. With each touch of his wand, a blue spark flashed into the sky. A sense of peace filled the island, and the noises of the plains grew muffled.

Brian finished making a circuit of the island in silence, while Hope collected wood for a fire. They broke out travel rations. As they ate, Hope studied Brian's eyes. They were as dark as the opals he'd offered for payment.

"If you possess true magic, why do you need me to kill your dragon?" She leaned forward and fed more wood into the fire, hoping the increased light would diminish the gloom from his face.

Brian scowled. "Magic doesn't work on all creatures," he said. "Especially mine." He warmed his hands. "On dragons it has no effect." He grinned in the darkness. "I would think, being a dragon killer, you would know that."

Hope felt embarrassment without understanding why. "We have no workers of magic in my land. Besides, if witchery has no consequence, why should I care?" she answered, offended. "I only know what works." She touched the hilts of her swords. "This and this." Her jaw muscles tightened. "I have heard it said they talk. I would not know that either. I have never given them a chance. The beasts make some manner of noise, but for all I know, it's the jabber of birds."

What right had this Brian to question her abilities? He sought a trained and proven dragonkiller. Against her better judgment, she'd granted him a favor and gone with him willingly.

"What do you mean by, 'especially mine'?" she snapped back. "Are you a wizard or not?"

Her words brought something unexpected. The cords in his neck bulged and he slumped, studying the fire. "Sometimes my magic works, sometimes not. I am told I have the ability but not the will." Hesitant, he said, "Rely not on me for magic in a crisis, for I cannot guarantee it will be our salvation."

Hope tried to stay indifferent to his expression, but a pang of compassion resonated. She started to reach out and stopped. He was a client, nothing more. They all suffered adversity, her family did, and they handled problems their own way. Let her kill this dragon, revisit her struggles, and allow Brian to deal with his.

"I will take first watch," Hope grunted.

"No, let me," Brian said. "If any beast attacks, it will be in the evening. They kill, feast, and then sleep." When Hope began to protest, he held up his hand. "Be assured, Mistress Hope, if there is danger, I will call you. Whatever breaches our defenses I have no wish to stand against it alone."

Content with this statement, she settled down to rest, but sleep came slowly. Weird howls and moans of strange animals rang out, the cries of beasts fighting crashed through the night, and once, dragon fire lit the sky.

Hope saw the flash of brilliance and ran, panic gripping inside at the sight of the monster. Knife-like talons seized her, drawing her back, tearing along ribs and stripping off trousers. She twisted, kicking and screaming, and tried to scramble away. A heavy weight descended on her back, bearing her down, smashing her face into the hard earth.

She screamed, the iron taste of blood filling her bruised mouth, with the putrid smell of the monster's breath fouling her hair. Half unconscious she whimpered as the beast found her, entering in a brutal lunge, penetrating deep within. He plunged again, and again, his roars mingling with Hope's cries of pain. With a last thrust, he released and withdrew from her.

Long after she heard the heavy footfalls of the beast leaving, Hope lay on the ground, too stunned and panicked to move. She ached, both inside and out, her body on fire. When she finally discovered the energy, she rolled on her back, gazing at herself through swollen eyes: dirt, mingled with blood and semen, covered her stomach and thighs. She sobbed, her cries turning into wails no one heard.

She was still screaming wordlessly when Brian shook her roughly awake.

"Hope, are you alright?" He peered down at her. "You were moaning."

"Must have been a bad dream, can't remember what it was." Sweat covered her.

"It is dawn," he said. "If we ride hard today we will sight my valley in the late afternoon tomorrow."

Hope yawned and stretched. "Why didn't you wake me? That wasn't right." Brian stifled a yawn, and she felt a pang of tenderness for his sacrifice.

Brian was busy saddling his horse. He yelled over his shoulder, "I could not sleep. Too excited returning home, I guess. For two months I searched before locating you, and I have never been away from my native valley that long before."

"It is a hardship to be away from family and friends," Hope muttered.

The way she said this made Brian look at her sharply. "Yes," he agreed slowly, "but with luck this will be over swiftly and we can return to the ones we love."

At midmorning, they halted at a wide river. "We search for the ford," Brian apologized as he rode up and down the length of the water. "When I traveled this way before, the shallows were denoted by piles of rocks. I do not know if this way is too deep to cross."

He hunted along the beach, stopping at various points along the shoreline. After a few minutes, he stopped and ambled back, annoyed. "Maybe the other way," he said to Hope with a weak smile, and muttered to himself, "If they have not washed away in a flood." He set off again.

Hope watched him go with escalating impatience. *At this rate we'll be here all day*. Finally, the delay grew laughable as Brian continued to storm about in frustration. "Hey, wizard," she yelled. He swung around. "The water is this deep." She urged Satan forward into the murky river until the stallion stood belly deep in the middle.

Brian galloped back and splashed his horse into the water, meeting Hope on the opposite side. "I had not thought to do that," he admitted, chagrinned.

Hope flashed a haughty smirk. "Dragonkillers are trained to adapt. Let us go, we waste enough time."

By noon the next day, they crossed the plains, and started an ascent up a well-worn path into the mountains. At the summit two towers loomed, one on either side of the trail. Both fortifications jutted from the cliff face, cut from the virgin rock of the mountains.

Grim-faced guards watched their progress, bows at the ready, as they rode into the pass. Brian threw his head back and hailed the soldiers with a loud hoot, and the weapons lowered.

"This is my home," Brian exclaimed. He waved to the valley. "Mictian."

Spread below, green fields with farmhouses stretched to the distant mountains on the far side. Herd animals grazed in pastures, while a brooding castle dominated the center. From the top of the keep fluttered a banner with a bird of prey clutching a spear.

Clustered around the fortress a town spread fingers for a mile in every direction. Towers and manor houses, well defended by walls, dominated the higher elevations, each one flying the flag of their baron or lord.

Brian led them along a paved road winding its way between the farms that ended at the castle entrance. The portcullis was up, but soldiers marched out to block their path until they recognized Brian.

"Sir Brian, you have returned." The guards crowded around with questions and cheers.

"Yes," boomed Brian. "A long trip, but a fruitful

one." He answered the babble of queries tossed in his direction. "Is the king in residence?"

"Aye," a sergeant replied. He pointed to Hope. "Who is that?"

"The one I was sent to seek." He made a flourish with his hand. "Meet Hope Nearwood, Dragonkiller."

"Her...?"

Hope hit the man with a stare that froze him in his tracks. "I will try to live up to your expectations, Sirrah." She straightened her shoulders. "Brian, let's meet this king of yours." Without a glance at the soldiers, she nudged Satan and ambled into the courtyard.

Brian smirked at the sergeant, bent low, and winked. "You have done it now," he whispered, nodding to Hope's stiff back. "You had best run ahead and spread the word we have arrived."

The abashed soldier gulped and nodded, rushing away to announce their appearance.

Servants hurried to take their horses. The steward himself materialized and greeted Brian and Hope, escorting them to the great hall.

King Gregory stood at a table, two well-favored men, nobles by their dress, with him. Spread out between the three was a map. Hope caught a glimpse of the features. A long mountain range shaped like a J. Little red dots denoting human settlements nestled in the valleys, while an enlargement of Mictian dominated one corner.

The king's wife, Queen Adrinna, sat on a carved wooden throne, a silent witness to what they discussed.

None looked happy.

They have argued. She and Brian strolled up to the table on the platform.

"Sir Brian and Mistress Nearwood, Dragonkiller." the steward announced.

The king smiled gratefully and rolled up his map. Two chairs stood empty, and he waved to the seats. "Come, sit," he said quickly. "Mistress Nearwood…"

"…Hope…"

Gregory's eyes widened and he regarded her with warmth. "Ah, yes. Hope. You could not have reached us at a better time. We were discussing our, uh, problem."

The two nobles measured Hope with contempt. The shorter with a black beard and fat stomach said, "This is what you fetched us, Brian? You have been absent long enough to discover the underworld. You think this twig of a girl can kill a dragon?" He glanced from the king to Hope and back again. "You are a dolt."

The queen gasped. The king's jaw tightened. Before Brian replied, Hope said, "You sound like a brave man here in the safety of the King's hall." She granted him a contemptuous sneer. "I'm surprised you have not sallied forth and destroyed the beast yourself, or are you such a craven then?"

The noble sputtered. He laid his hand on the butt of his sword. Hope reciprocated with a smirk. The other lord was silent, his attention split between the two.

"Baron Wolf, cousin…" Brian strode forward and placed a restraining hand on the wrist of the baron, holding his arm down. "Is this how we greet a guest?" His eyes bore into Wolf's and flicked to the other man. "You Baron Weber, your hospitality is known throughout the valley. Surely you will welcome Hope in friendship."

Baron Weber ran his fingers through his grey hair and nodded. "You are right." He made a short bow. "Mistress Nearwood, I am glad to meet you."

King Gregory was right behind him. "We greet you, Dragon Killer." The Queen Adrinna was out of her seat and put her arm around Hope. "You must be famished, my dear, and dusty, too. We will see to your needs."

Baron Wolf remained mute until everyone glared at him. He finally stepped forward and muttered under his breath, "Forgive me, Dragon Killer, sometimes my temper overrides my senses. I loose herd animals every day, and one of my sons is missing." He bowed, but Hope sensed resentment still boiling under the surface.

Two young girls entered the hall, holding hands.

"Rehana, Maralene." The queen bestowed each a tender smile and beckoned both over.

"Word has spread through the castle that we have visitors," the older girl, Rehana explained as they approached, "and Cousin Brian was one of them."

Rehana exchanged quick grins with Brian and released her sister's hand, taking a quick step to wrap arms around the man, and rest her head on his shoulder. Straightening, the princess pushed yellow tresses back and smiled at Hope, waiting for an introduction.

"Mistress Nearwood," Gregory said, "these are my two daughters, the Princesses Rehana and Maralene."

Hope smiled at the older girl. "It is my pleasure to be in your father's house."

The two barons Hope dismissed without a second thought, but an instant liking for the king and his family bloomed. She said to everyone, "Please, do not call me Mistress. I am Hope, plain and simple."

The younger girl, perhaps Apophis age, goggled at Hope in amazement. "You're a dragon killer," the child blurted out. "For real?"

Hope laughed, squatting on her haunches until she was nose to nose with the little princess. "Yes, that's what I do," she answered solemnly. "It's dangerous work."

Maralene's mouth opened wide. "Aren't you afraid?"

Hope replied in a hushed voice. "Very." She raised her hands to her mouth and wiggled her fingers. "Dragons have *big teeth.*"

The little girl squealed in delight and hung tight to her mother's robes.

King Gregory jumped on this opportunity to say, "We will show you to your chambers, Hope. I will call in the neighbors and tonight we shall have a small feast in your honor."

The king hurried off before Hope could protest, the steward led the way to a spacious room where her packs awaited. Hope sat on the bed with a groan.

"Damn, rather be relaxing instead of preparing for a party. Don't know anyone. Want a good night's sleep," she grumped. With a last surge of energy, she kicked the pack. How to dress?

Her attire for the last three days would never do, mud-splattered riding cloak, sweat-stained tunic and breeches. The rest of the apparel bundled away was not better; clean, but well-used, suitable for hard work and dragon killing. That was enough. The people who employed her didn't want to entertain. They needed a monster slain as quickly as possible. She'd never before had an invitation for a banquet prior to, or after, a killing. No one wanted to get to know her. They wanted her gone like the problem she solved, not to remind them of it again.

Hope pawed through the pack, hoping Diane had hidden something appropriate inside without her knowledge. All too soon, the bundle lay scattered on the bed and she stared glumly at the clothes, selecting a tunic with a bloodstain on the back that wouldn't soak out, a torn undershirt, and leather pants with a small rip in the crotch she'd been planning to mend.

Well, this isn't a gathering to impress anyone. Listlessly she stripped, dumping the rank clothes in a heap. *If they don't like the way I look, no one has to kiss me.* A knock on the door interrupted as she slipped the blotted tunic on.

"Yes?"

Princess Rehana entered, balancing two ball gowns over her arms. "I am sorry to disturb you, Hope," the girl said and placed the dresses on the bed, "but I thought you would fit into one of these." The princess smoothed the gowns out. "We are the same size and..." Rehana stopped at the incredulous expression on Hope's face.

"Why, thank you." Hope gestured to the tattered outfit she wore. "I was going to dress in these."

"Oh, no." Rehana's hands flew to her mouth with a gasp. "Those would never do." The girl retreated a pace. "I mean, those are presentable, but..." The princess blushed, confused, and took another step back. "I knew you couldn't have fetched much with you. I hope these are suitable. You are too pretty for, uh..." Without finishing her sentence, she fled.

For a long minute, Hope stared at the empty doorway, suppressing chuckles that continued to rise in her throat. Apophis would love living with these people. After assuring herself Rehana was nowhere in earshot, she released a stream of titters. "Sweet girl," Hope said aloud. "Thoughtful."

She fingered the two dresses, picked each up, and measured them against herself. One was maroon, the other violet.

The violet, she decided, was too revealing. Not that she minded people seeing her scars, but it didn't match her dark hair and brown eyes. The gown hung wrong on her. Slim by nature, working on the farm, and killing dragons, had left her sinewy rather than curvy. She selected the maroon and dressed.

Brian met her on the staircase and exclaimed, "Beautiful," with such enthusiasm, that Hope laughed.

"You are too kind," she replied. "I am far from pretty."

"No, really," he said. "You clean up nice. Maybe we should rename you Heart Slayer." Brian chuckled at his joke.

Hope blushed. "You are handsome yourself, sir," she replied as he presented an arm. The disreputable ruffian had emerged as a gentleman. He'd shaved the straggly beard, making him appear years younger, almost boyish. He dressed in forest green tunic, ruffles protruding from the cuffs. Embroidered up the sleeves was his coat of arms: a sword over a wand.

A small group of people were already gathered in the main hall when they strolled in. Hope stayed close to Brian as he pointed out people. "You remember the Baron Wolf," he chuckled as the noble scowled at them in the way of greeting. "That woman is his wife, the Lady Rebecca." A stern faced woman with a long nose nodded their way over a goblet of wine.

An older man with a short grizzled beard approached with a tankard of beer in his hand. "Glad you are back, boy," he exclaimed. He slapped Brian on the back, and addressed Hope: "You are a dragon killer, huh? Maybe now we can stop the slaughter."

"Hope, this is my uncle, Baron Braun," Brian introduced him. "And yes, indeed, we hope this is the end of our dilemma."

As the baron wandered away, Hope asked, "Cousin, Uncle? Are you a noble?"

Brian studied his feet with a sheepish grin. "I am the nephew of the king, a second son of a second son." He waved to the milling crowd. "That does not mean much, though. Most of the nobility of Mictian are related in one way or the other."

A servant girl passed by, handing out drinks and sweet meats to the guests. The server approached and held out the tray to Hope. "Food... drink?" she offered.

Hope gasped. Faint scales traced up the girl's arm. Still staring, she reached out and clutched a goblet of wine, bringing it to her lips and gulping without tasting. As the servant walked away, a slight bulge showed beneath the dress.

"Brian, that woman," Hope whispered, not believing the king allowed such a one to walk free, "she's a half-breed. Dragon blood flows through her veins."

Brian watched the girl disappear into the crowd. "Maybe," he said, "is there something amiss? Can you use that breed to help kill the dragon? Should I call the woman back?"

"No, but how could she...? Why hasn't Gregory condemned that girl to death?" Brian acted as if nothing was amiss.

If his first remark caused confusion, Brian's second amazed more. "Death?" He raised his eyebrows. "Who would wish to kill a servant who has done nothing wrong?"

"That woman is a half-breed, an abomination. Creatures of that blood are disposed of at birth." The woman surfaced briefly carrying an empty tray, hurrying toward the kitchen. Brian and Hope watched her progress until she vanished.

"Is that what happens in your land?" For the first time, Hope heard disapproval in his voice. "Your world is more savage than it seemed," he commented. "Even the beasts and demons of the outer plains do not kill without reason."

"Of course we have a reason!" Hope said, flustered. "The race must be kept pure. Both mother and child is killed, otherwise humans will disappear forever."

"Nonsense." Brian pursed his lips. "Humans are human, half-breeds are half-breeds, and the demons are demons. One does not naturally breed with a different species, but if it happens, it is usually a case of rape. Who would fault either the mother, or the child? If it is otherwise and there is no offspring..." He shrugged. "That is their affair."

What he spoke was unbelievable. Hope studied the crowd gathered in the main hall, trying to guess how many more people were tainted. "Are they common, here in the valley?"

Brian rubbed his chin. "No. Most live on the plains, I think, between the towns of demons and the valleys of the humans. I have never found need to identify which cities are theirs."

"You mean they have their own villages, too?" Hope gasped. Her whole vision of how things worked was falling apart.

Brian leaned forward and said in a low voice, "Like anyone else they prefer to be ruled by their own kind. Most fear the prejudice of being a minority group within a full demon, or human, community."

"I thought you said it doesn't matter to humans," Hope replied. "Now you speak of prejudice."

Brian shrugged. "It matters not to us. Although I will admit, we do not trust the half-breeds and demons of the plains as much as we place confidence in our own kind. This is something they fear. I do not blame half-breeds. How would you feel surrounded by creatures not of your type?"

"I guess when you put it that way, you're right," she replied, "but that is more," Hope searched for the word, "sympathetic?"

A strange feeling of warmth spread through Hope for this land and Brian. They understood. Mictian valley was a refuge for Apophis. A place where her son could grow up to be a man. They would both be safe. The threat of death hanging over their heads would vanish forever!

Barely able to make it through the banquet, Hope sought her room, the world spinning upside down. She undressed and prepared for sleep, starting to make plans. Tomorrow, kill the dragon, leave, make her way home in no more than four days. Diane might balk at Apophis going, but her sister would want this as much as Hope did.

Some place to live? A job? That would all work out later. Until she established herself, perhaps the king would take her in, or she would purchase a farm and start all over again. Brian used opals for money. Hope knew a merchant that traded gold for gems. People would ask questions, but what did it matter?

Still lost in dreams, she blew out the candle and settled down in bed.

Her door creaked opened. A beam of torchlight stabbed into the room, revealing a female figure. The Princess Rehana. Hope fumbled for her short sword.

"What's the matter? Is there trouble?"

"No." The door closed and Hope heard the soft tread of footsteps creeping to the bed. Rehana sat on the edge.

"Why are you here then?"

The princess whispered, "I am a virgin, and may not lay with a man until I am wed. I thought, maybe…" Hope felt the girl stand, heard the gentle rustling of her dress as she removed it. The next moment Rehana slipped in between the sheets next to Hope. "You will not send me away?" the girl breathed into Hope's ear. "Please? I am so lonely."

Hope knew how Rehana felt. She'd been alone all her life, too.

On impulse, Hope reached out. The next moment lips pressed against her lips, a warm tongue entered her mouth. Hope stroked Rehana's back from shoulders to legs, receiving soft groans of enjoyment.

In the dark, hands traced along Hope's body as lips traveled down, pausing below her navel to nibble on the little hairs, and then moved lower.

Rehana's long tresses tickled Hope's thighs, calves and feet. The lips inched up again.

Hope's toes curled in enjoyment and she moaned with pleasure.

Chapter Four

She awoke the next morning more relaxed than in many days. Hope rolled over, stretched and opened her eyes. Rehana was gone. The memory of the princess leaving with a swift kiss sometime during the night still lingered. Hope smiled. Sweet girl. Living in this world was proving enjoyable. She sat up straight. However, today demanded serious play.

Today a dragon would die.

She strolled down the staircase humming a tune remembered from a summer fair. At the time, the song sounded silly, but all the young men and women danced to it now. Hope never danced. She attempted to learn once when young, but events intervened and the opportunity to practice never presented. No doubt, training was necessary. Maybe Rehana would help. It couldn't be any harder than dragon killing. In fact, it might be fun.

Except for Brian and King Gregory enjoying breakfast, the great hall had emptied, the rest of the household having eaten and gone.

"Hope." Brian rose, as did the king. "You look happy this morning." Brian patted the bench. "Eat. I would have expected you much earlier than this."

"The dragon will still be there waiting, I suspect," she replied, archly, taking a plate and piling on eggs and ham from a platter. She speared a roll and smeared on butter, drawing a pot of jam close. "Where is the monster anyway?" Hope mumbled through a mouthful of eggs.

"Five hour's ride from here in the Southern Mountains," Gregory replied. He picked up a tankard and poured a goblet for her.

Hope sipped. "Oh, this is marvelous," she said, taking a deeper gulp. "What is it?"

"Dama. It awakes and refreshes you. You will need the energy if you are to hurry."

"Plenty of time," Hope said, attacking the ham. It was good. Hunger gnawed at her middle. "It is best never to attack dragons during the light of day or at night."

"Really?" Brian watched in amusement as she demolished the food. He poured himself dama and said, "Why is that?"

"Dragons have four eyes," Hope replied, working on eggs, "the inner watch while they sleep. The outer watches when they're awake." She chewed, swallowed, and quoted, "'Seek not the beast when he sleeps or awakes, rather when the inner eye is closed and the outer not yet open'." Dama emptied from the goblet. "That's dusk."

"Of course dragons hunt day or night, but," Hope shrugged, "those are the chances you incur when you stalk a dragon." A roll smeared with butter and jam disappeared.

"It is wise we brought you here," Gregory said, "for there are many things we did not know about the beasts."

Hope smirked. "I don't have to understand dragons, Your Majesty, just how to eliminate the monsters." Were the dragons of this world different from hers? Better ask, best to familiarize herself so no surprises materialized. "Tell me about your dragon."

The king took a deep breath and a deeper draft of wine. "This dragon is new to us. Our old one..."

"You had one before?" Hope said, flabbergasted, "Did he offer you much trouble?"

"Not really. He lived in our mountains since my father's day." Gregory frowned, surprised at the remark. "Most valleys have dragons at one time or another." He scowled. "We had a truce with this one. On occasion, he would snatch a herd animal, and we overlooked that. He also killed the demons and beasts from the plains who attempted to invade our valley. Then he left, and a young one occupied his cave."

That was new. Conducting alliances with dragons was unheard of in her world. To hear the king talk, the valleys actually benefited from having the monsters around.

The answer why the old lizard left and the new one assumed his place was apparent, however.

"Probably a younger male drove the old one away. Once a dragon reaches maturity, the first thing he does is challenge another for a lair, unless he can ferret out an unoccupied cave. They have wide territories and mountains are desirable locations."

Gregory nodded. "No doubt," he replied. "We tried to reaffirm the truce with the new one, but he refused killing and devouring the envoys. Since then, he has raided our herds, and attacked people in alarming numbers. That is when we dispatched Brian to seek you."

"I have wondered about that." Hope gulped dama and sat back, crossing her legs. "How is it you do not have free companies to kill these monsters, or people of my profession? In this whole world humans must have banded together, if not for revenge, then for profit."

"Free companies we have," replied Brian. He leaned across the table obviously upset by the thought of those warriors. "They are few, however, and the price they charge would pauper the valley for years afterwards."

The king nodded in agreement. "That was the first thing we sought."

Annoyed, Brian added, "Nor are they the bravest. The ones we talked to requested more than a thousand men to help kill the beast, catapults and the ammunition. When we were unable to supply what they requested, the rascals scattered and ran." He raised his goblet to her and tipped his head, with unabashed appreciation. "Dragonkillers such as yourself we have none, only those who claim to kill dragons."

Hope couldn't tell if he issued a compliment or made a joke. It didn't matter. She'd been hired to do a killing. That was her job.

"No sense wasting time here," she said taking a last

bite of ham. Hope pushed away from the table and stood. "Have my horse readied, provide me directions to this dragon of yours, and I will be on my way."

She could finish this up, and leave by tomorrow morning, Hope decided, planning the rest of the week. Better break the news to Diane gently. Her sister had a tendency to cry easily.

King Gregory and Brian stood also. "Your mount is prepared. Brian will guide and assist you in the fight."

Hope groaned. A portion of her good mood vanished. The last thing needed was unskilled help. An excellent way to get both of them killed. "Your Majesty," she said, gazing seriously at him and trying to remain tactful, "It is not wise to have two people attack such a beast unless they have trained together. If you insist, I will take him as a guide, nothing more. He may remain outside the dragon's lair while I do the killing."

Brian issued a muffled oath. Hope ignored him and kept her gaze fixed on the king.

"So be it." The king extended his hand. "Good luck to both of you."

They rode south. The planter in Hope noted with curiosity the crops as they passed holdings. Most she knew. One however, which flourished in great profusion, caught her attention. "What is that?" Acres of shrubs with narrow green leaves flanked the lane. "Something to eat?"

"Bola," Brian replied. He swept his hand at the sea of emerald. "People chew the leaves to strengthen their bodies. It is also dried and smoked. This is the chief export of our valley," he said with pride. "Only in Mictian do the right temperature, humidity, and altitude exist for it to flourish."

They approached a castle, or rather, a tower surrounded by a wall. Fields of grain struggled to live in the parched earth. "That is my home," Brian said, "Hawk's Watch."

Seconds later, they ambled over a bridge spanning a narrow river and the cutoff leading to the tower.

"Aren't we stopping?" Hope asked, "At least to check?" The property showed years of neglect. The wall was in ill repair, the grain sewed unevenly in rows. She pictured how charming it would be with a firm hand, needed a small boy fishing in the river to make it perfect, though.

"Not today," Brian said as he kept riding. "Maybe on the way back we can visit. I sent word ahead last night of my return, but I do not wish to upset my steward." He let out a laugh and grinned. "It allows him a chance to put everything right and hide whatever he has stolen."

Hope laughed along with him. The ways of servants who weren't watched, even faithful ones, were well debated. "You are a wise man."

"Maybe," he hedged. "The king granted me this tower and land five years ago for services over the years, but I doubt I have spent a year in total here since," he admitted sheepishly. "In truth, I am as poor a farmer as I am a wizard. One day I shall live here permanently, settle down, and raise a family, but I fear I have a lot to learn about farming before that time."

Much of the land was untilled. Patches of the bola plants sprang up in haphazard fashion. "Your steward needs some teaching also," Hope joked, with a knowing smirk. The river was right there. He could install a water wheel, and dig irrigation ditches. No reason existed for the poor condition of his crops. As for the crooked rows, Hope shuddered. A drunk must have plowed those furrows.

The castle shrank into the distance. The cobblestoned road faded to a dirt trail. "I was told at the inn you are an excellent planter," Brian said as the horses picked their way into the hills. "Maybe after you have taught me how to kill a dragon, you can instruct my steward the correct way of tilling a field."

The mountains continued to swell. They entered the foothills and Brian guided Hope toward a high peak. The vegetation dissolved, replaced by smoldering rock.

Hope recognized the telltale signs, typical dragon lair, marking his territory, nothing new so far.

Farther on, they hit a level spot. The sun was sinking. "From here we walk." Brian gestured through the puddles of lava to a dark hole in the mountainside.

They dismounted. Hope removed her riding cloak and checked her weapons. "You will remain here," she commanded. "If for some reason I do not survive, inform King Gregory I have failed."

Brian's face changed to surprise. "And your family? These monks you talk of? Should not they be notified also?"

He was right. Always before her location was known, and the thought of death, or the people she left behind, hadn't bothered her.

Never to bring Apophis here or see Diane again, if she should fail? Hope pushed that thought aside. *She would survive.*

"Bring word to the monastery of what has happened. They'll inform those who need to know."

Brian nodded solemnly and took a deep breath. "Rest assured, Hope, I shall carry the word myself. I will *never* let your death go unnoticed."

She fought to keep the emotions that threatened to engulf her from showing. She replied gruffly, "Let us proceed."

"I have brought torches, I can light your way," Brian offered softly.

"No, the light will reveal us."

Hope frowned. She meant to say, will reveal me. He was trying to be helpful, she understood that, but why couldn't he shut up. This man was like an over friendly puppy dog.

Brain shuffled his feet. "Are you sure you do not want…"

"Stay," she ordered. His mouth drooped. She smiled tightly. "Guard the horses. We'll use the torches after the killing."

Hope cleared her mind, concentrating on the task before her, and started her ascent.

The cave was larger than most, she noted, with a good view of the valley on one side, and the amber plains across the peaks curving away into an arc. This was a prime location for a dragon. Black marks on the mountainside showed where the battle for the den between the older and younger monsters occurred. Additional splotches Hope didn't recognize lined the walls, glowing a sickly red on the stones.

Hope's senses expanding in every direction. Whatever was unusual was suspect. Could the dragons in this world be different, perhaps spouting a transformed flame? Damn. Too arrogant! Should have obtained more information when the chance offered itself.

Should she halt, quiz Brian? No. The sun had faded. If she didn't strike soon it would be too late, *assuming the dragons of this land slept by the same rules as they did in her world,* Hope amended with another curse. They had talked about the sleeping habits of the monsters, too. Double damn. Since this Brian arrived, she'd made too many wrong decisions.

Perfect timing, she cautioned herself, *in and out,* repeating this mantra like a prayer. The knotting in her guts eddied. Hope drew her long sword, and crept into the cave.

The monster was not in sight. Then a low rumble alerted her to a darker blotch among the shadows. Muscles tensed, she made small mincing steps toward the noise.

"HOPE, BEWARE."

A soft scraping whispered. She dropped to the ground as a flash of red light shot over her head. In front, answering gout of flames emerged.

The beast was awake.

Wild streams of dragon fire and beams of light slashed her way. Hope wiggled behind a rock, bracing herself to dodge as she gulped air. The boulder glowed red as a ball of flame hit the stone, the same color as the mountainside flanking the entrance.

A gold brilliance engulfed the boulder. The scarlet hit the yellow, deflected, and the shield burst.

The red changed course, aiming at the source of the gold. They clashed, illuminating Brian in the resulting brilliance, wand out.

Hope had no time to wonder. The dragon's head was up. The neck weaved back and forth, searching. She gripped her sword tighter and leaped forward.

The monster spied her and fire filled the cave. Before the flames hit, Hope dodged sideways, still advancing with a burst of speed. The tail swung. She jumped again. The tip passed under her feet, struck a rock, shooting a thousand chips in every direction. The shrapnel stung her shoulders.

Before the tail veered back, Hope sprinted. Blood streamed from the rips in her chainmail. She gritted her teeth against the pain and vaulted onto the monster's neck as the head reached out. Confused, the dragon tried to toss this annoyance off, but Hope clung on with grim determination.

The neck bowed, razor sharp talons rose and hovered menacingly. Hope sprang upward with sword raised. The blade plunged down. The tip hit bone. She twisted the hilt violently and shoved, rolling out of the way. The claw crashed on the pommel of the sword, driving it deeper.

A howl filled the cavern.

Hope ran.

The mouth of the cave filled with light, red and gold, the red dominated. For the first time Hope saw what attacked her.

A demon stood with a wooden staff raised in its hand, scarlet fire emitting from the ironclad tip of the rod. The monster wore the body of a man, the head of a bull. Long, curved horns sprouted from either side of the skull. Short, black fur covered the breast.

The creature forced Brian down the slope. It bellowed in rage, sending bolt after bolt of fire at the human from the staff as it advanced. Brian's golden flames deflected each, both lights shot skyward in a display of fireworks that lit the night.

Without pausing, Hope pulled her short sword and hurled the weapon. The blade connected with a meaty thump as it sank into the demon's back. Her momentum carried her into the monster. Wrapping her legs around the creature tightly, she locked the crook of an arm around the neck in a strangle-hold.

Fire shot into the air as the demon dropped the staff onto the trail. It clutched at Hope's arms, tugging in a desperate attempt to struggle away.

She clenched harder, and the demon's body shuddered. The head sank lower and the creature fell to its knees. With a last, gurgling bellow, the tremors stopped. Shrieks filled her ears.

"Hope, it is all right, you can let go. He is dead."

Hope realized the screaming was hers. Her body, still glued to the demon, trembled violently. In revulsion, she released the creature and scrambled erect, backing in disgust. "What is it?" she gasped.

"A moloch," Brian replied. "By the looks of him, one of their Lore Masters."

Hope toed the demon, and then pushed the monster on its back with a foot. Dead brown eyes stared at the sky. "Where did he come from?"

"After you entered the cave he appeared and crept behind," answered Brian. He gestured to a group of boulders. "He approached from that direction, but when I

59

saw him I pursued."

It was strange to feel gratitude. Dragonkillers always operated alone after their short apprenticeship. For so many years, cunning and speed comprised her sole defense when facing danger. She didn't know how to react to a person's protection, and unsure if it was an enjoyable experience. "You saved my life," Hope said in a quiet voice. "For that I'm grateful."

Brian laughed shyly. "As you did mine. He would have bested me in the end if you had not intervened. Lore Masters are strong with power."

Hope reached down to pick up the staff. Brian grabbed her arm, uttering an oath of hatred. "Do not touch that. The magic flowing through the rod is evil and would destroy you in a heartbeat."

She jerked away quickly. "Why do you suppose he wanted to attack me?"

He frowned, puzzled. "The question is what was he doing around a dragon's lair in the first place?" Brian gestured toward the boulders. "Let us see what lies beyond those rocks."

He yanked out his sword, holding the blade in one hand while he clutched his wand in the other. Together, they stole around the edge of the cave, ready for danger.

"I see nothing," Brian whispered, "but…"

A flapping of wings knocked him over as a black body shot past his head. Before Hope could react, the creature, whatever it was, soared into the night.

"Brian, did you see…?"

"No, but whatever it was, that was not a dragon."

"The dragon," Hope gasped, "I must finish him." She ripped the bloodstained short sword from the moloch, and raced back inside the cave.

Brian stalked behind, searching walls and back trail for any more signs of danger, but stopped dumbfounded as Hope vaulted on the dragon's back, snatched out her long sword, and commenced to hack at the beast's neck.

"Why are you mutilating the corpse?" He watched as chips of iron scales and blood splattered everywhere. "The dragon is dead."

"No it's not," Hope gasped. She stopped to catch her breath, swallowed hard, and started chopping again. "If the head is not removed he will revive." She kept cutting.

Brian surveyed the frantic swinging a moment longer, then, with a sigh, put away his wand and gripped his sword. He strolled to the opposite side of the beast, pushed up the sleeves of his tunic, and began cutting also. Soon he started to sing: "Master's gone away, have no time to play, going to chop this dragon's head, all through the day."

Hope stopped and stared at him, mouth open, breathing hard. "What are you doing?"

Brian glanced up, flushed from the unusual exertion. "Singing. Chopping dragon. I never realized killing monsters was so much fun." He swung again and grunted. Blood splattered his trousers. "Are we allowed to keep the head as a trophy? I may have to send back to my tower for a wagon."

Hope laughed her face lighting in triumph. "No, but after we're done we receive a prize." She lifted her sword. "Master's gone away..."

When they finished Hope gutted the dragon and displayed the gizzard to Brian. "Watch." She cut into the flesh. A few gems dropped out, and those of poor quality.

"Strange," she muttered, rolling the jewels around in her palm. "This is the cache of a young dragon, maybe not fully of age yet. How could he drive a mature dragon out of his den, even an old one?" Her vision centered on the scarlet stones glowing from the recent battle. They were identical to the marks on the mountainside. "Could that moloch of yours have helped him?"

Brian went blank. "It is possible," he admitted, "Why would...?" His face blanched. "We must inform the king."

He stumbled away.

"Wait, why?" Hope hurried after him. "What happened?"

"The monsters only join together if they plan an attack." Brian swallowed hard. "I do not know if it is against the valley, or perhaps a tribe of their kind, but the knowledge must be given to Gregory and the word spread. This means war."

They reached the horses.

"Wait." Hope rushed back to the cave mouth. "I want to see that demon again."

"Hope," Brian called, "Forget the Lore Master. He is dead."

She ignored him.

The body of the moloch lay where it fell. Swarms of night bugs already crawled over the corpse, drawn by the scent of blood. Hope studied the face of the demon in the darkness, zipping through her mind the description of the monsters learned. She wasn't positive, but they resembled a molek, one of the deadliest demons that once stalked her world. On more than one occasion, they fought the free companies to a standstill, in the end, exterminated when the troops merged after vanquishing the remaining demons from the land.

Hope trudged back to the horses deep in thought.

Brian lit one of the torches. As she approached, he lifted the flaming brand high to light the way. In the flickering brilliance, he saw Hope clearly. "You bleed."

Mingled with the gore from the dragon, blood dripped from a ragged gash in her chain mail.

"I've suffered worse," Hope replied, brushing at the tear. The hand came away wet. "The wound looks graver than it is. Most is the blood from the moloch, I think."

Brian grimaced. "Best be taken care of now. Once we start riding we will not stop." He hurried to his saddlebag, withdrew bandages and a pot of salve.

Hope shrugged and removed the chain mail. Agony laced through her chest. *Must have broken a rib,* she thought, gasping as the pain continued.

The undershirt was a bloody mess. She hoisted it up to her breasts, revealing a jagged slash running from hip to ribcage. "Careful," she murmured with a small gasp, as Brian smeared ointment into the cut. "That hurts. Think I cracked something."

Brian nodded, but said nothing, lightly dabbing the smaller slices. Hope lifted her arms and winced as he wrapped bandages around her chest. "Better?"

"Tighter," she ordered. Brian rewrapped the dressing.

Hope inhaled deeply. The throbbing persisted, but not as bad as before. "That's fine."

Brian examined his handy work with satisfaction. "When we return to the castle, the surgeon will do a better job. Let us make haste."

She reached for her mail.

"No need for armor now that the dragon is dead," said Brian. "Nothing else roams the mountains we must worry about." He put the salve away and mounted. "We better hurry."

Throughout the night, they rode in silence. Normally the plight of a valley would not worry Hope, but great expectations for this world still embraced her. The urge to help tore one way, while the desire to speed home dictated the opposite. She was still lost in thoughts when Brian exclaimed, "What…?"

Off in the distance flashes of light brightened the night sky. They halted. "What is it?" Hope watched the flicker with a sense of foreboding building inside.

Brian froze and then said in a hushed voice, "I do not know, but something is amiss at the castle." He snapped his reins and dug his spurs into his horse. "We must lose no time investigating what transpires."

They stopped on a knoll overlooking the fortress.

Above, bolts of red moloch death streaked downward, while from the castle's parapet, balls of white flame soared up, shot from giant crossbows.

"The king is under attack," whispered Brian.

Fire struck one of the shadowy figures, illuminating both rider and mount as they ignited. Bat-like wings flamed, leaving behind a trail of smoke. Both fell downward.

Hope watched the battle, the urge for combat flaring inside. Every fiber of her soul craved to join the fight and help. "Who are they?"

"Molochs riding baitals," Brian replied.

"We must protect the castle." Hope spurred Satan.

"NO."

Brian seized the reins, halting her.

"Why?" Hope blazed. "They are your people, friends, relatives. Are you a coward then?"

His expression of concern turned to exasperation. He vaulted from his saddle, shouting, "I am no coward, but neither am I a fool." He gestured to the battle, voice burning with anger. "The portcullis is dropped. They will not let us in. Would you ride and shake your fist at what flies above?"

He saw the shock as she realized the truth of his words. He added, "We would be as ducks swimming on a pond waiting for the huntsman to shoot his bolts."

Hope scrambled off Satan and stood beside him. "Then what can we do?" From over the castle, bloodthirsty cries of victory reverberated as one of the Lore Master's balls of fire crashed into a catapult. The defenders hurled over the wall, while the fire spread along the walkway like a creeping serpent, engulfing more soldiers within its maw as they tried to extinguish the blaze.

"You, nothing." Brian muttered a curse under his breath. "But perhaps I..." He fumbled at his waist for his wand. "Stand back."

Fists clenched, he spoke words. They appeared over his head in the shape of fierce runes and entered the wood. From the tip of his wand, gold fire erupted and flew toward the assaulting molochs. It fell far short.

He tried again, frustration twisting his face. Once more, his sorcery failed. In desperation, he searched for something to help him. He saw Hope watching and seized her wrist.

Brian jerked her down beside him. An electric shock entered Hope's body. In panic, she tried breaking free as her life force flowed into him.

Brian clutched tighter, his fingernails biting into flesh. His golden flames sailed forth again, this time bursting in between the flying shapes.

Hope's mind spun. She slumped to the earth, the night sky revolving above her. *He will kill me if he doesn't stop. He is killing me.*

Another flash of gold exploded in the heavens; molochs and baitals tumbled. With her last dregs of strength, Hope lifted a foot and kicked Brian in the groin.

He crumbled, screaming.

Hope struggled on the ground to rise, panting, as the man withered. "Serves you right, you bastard," she grunted, pushing herself into a sitting position and staggered upright. Brian uncurled, groaning hoarsely.

He stared up. "Why?"

"Why?" She snatched out her short sword, stepped forward, loathing for this man dripping for his betrayal. "YOU ALMOST KILLED ME." Hope screamed the words in his face.

Brian grimaced, wavering upright, and confronted the fury who stood before him. "I thought..."

"You thought you could take without asking?" she shot back. Her lips curled down in contempt. She said through gritted teeth, voice seething, "Is that the man you are? Seize what is not offered to you?"

"I–I…" He dropped his head, rubbing his face. "I did not think," he stammered at last. "I am sorry." He looked at her imploringly and reached out a hand.

"Do not touch me." Hope fought the urge to lash out, make him feel pain; powerless, out of control like a piece of meat thrown down by the butcher. Instead, the sword slammed away with a snort of disgust. "Let us go and learn what has happened – *warlock.*

Chapter Five

"I will leave in the morning." Brian checked each face in the conference room where the king and nobles sat. The hall, which had rung with argument a few minutes ago, fell silent. He heard no dissent.

Hope watched each face as the barons debated their options in loud and often contradictory views. All reflected fear, indecision, all except Brian's. His was the lone voice demanding action. The nobles insisted on sealing the valley, retreating to their towers against further attack.

Although Hope seethed inside, she had to admire his courage. He was scum, and probably a fool as well, but her kind of fool. He was right. To sit and do nothing was the road to disaster.

Brian, on the other hand, insisted the lords send a party onto the plains, and investigate what was happening among the half-breeds and demons. When none of the nobles volunteered to attempt the trip, he declared he would explore alone. The barons quickly agreed, glade to leave the dangerous trip to him.

Idiot. Then she reconsidered. *Was the sacrifice of one life worth the saving of the many? Was that the reason he'd put her life in jeopardy?* The more she thought about it, the more she realized she would do the same thing.

Hope and Brian hadn't discussed what happened between them as they entered the castle, nor as King Gregory hastily summoned his vassals from the nearer estates. Brian still acted embarrassed by his action, his face marked in sorrow. Each time he glanced at Hope, it deepened.

Hope was livid beyond words, turmoil boiling within. She fought an overwhelming urge to fly at his face, rip at his eyes, each time his gaze fell on her.

"I will leave in the morning, also," Hope announced, rising to the assembly. "Your dragon has been killed as Sir

Brian can verify."

Brian stood again. "The monster has indeed been slain. I helped cut its head off. The beast will bother us no more." He swung to Hope with a bow. "At least, for now, our Mictian is safe thanks to Mistress Hope."

Fury mounted. How dare he speak as if nothing happened? She wanted to swing and call him every vile name that described his character; tell him to go to hell along with the monster. Instead, she said to Gregory, "I wish I could stay and help you with this battle, but I have obligations at home."

The king nodded. "I understand. You have fulfilled your part of the bargain." He addressed his nobles, "We are all in agreement? Brian shall ride to the Southern Plains to investigate what is afoot there, and discover if secret alliances are building."

Praises rang out for Brian. One or two younger sons of the barons allotted their elders dirty looks. Clearly, they wished to go with Brian and been forbidden to do so.

Gregory waited for the meeting to quiet and said, "The rest of us will prepare for battle, and I will send messengers to the Northern valleys requesting a council." When no dissenting comments materialized, he rose and said, "I have spoken."

Hope wandered back to her chamber and prepared for the morning. A light knock sounded on the door and Princess Rehana entered. "May I come in?"

Hope patted the bed and sat, moving her bundle to one side. "Sit."

Tears gathered as Rehana huddled close to Hope. The princess blurted out, "I hate to see you go, all this fighting and talk of war." She sniffed hard, a wan smile spreading over her face. "I was hoping you would remain. I feel safer when you are here."

Hope wrapped an arm around the girl's shoulder. "I wish I could too or at least revisit." An expression of regret passed over Hope's face. She kissed Rehana on the check. "Go now. I must finish packing and leave in the morning. I have a long and dangerous trip ahead of me."

Rehana wept, hugged Hope, and fled to the door. "Hope? I may be out of place, but I sense something has happened between you and my cousin, Brian."

Was it that obvious? Hope glanced down at her pack, pretending to roll clothes. "There is nothing wrong between Brian and me," she said lightly. "I must depart, that's all."

The princess put a fist to her mouth. "You do not have to tell me, but I want you to know, Brian is a good man. Anything he has done was without malice, I assure you. Thoughtless perhaps, but whatever he said or did had good intentions." A timid smile crossed her lips. "I will miss you." Hope heard a sob as Rehana left.

Hope finished packing and climbed into bed, curling into a tight ball.

This should have been the place to bring Apophis, a land of new beginnings, free from the fear of discovery and death hanging over their heads like a sword. This valley accepted half-breeds. Now everything was ruined. Damn the demons for starting a conflict. They'd destroyed everything. She couldn't take her son into a war.

Damn Brian too. Warlock she'd named him, and warlock he was. *Deceitful from the first,* she fumed, *not telling her they traveled to a different world.* Arrogant. Did he think he could single-handedly defeat this whole demon world?

Hope took time to review what monsters prowled the savannah. The *Shaddrad* listed many, and dragon killer training meant studying them all. Did this Brian presume he stood a chance against any of the array he was bound to meet? She laughed bitterly. Maybe he planned to make puppy dog eyes at the dragons and smile, sing his silly songs and cause the demons to swoon. *Ha.*

Hope awoke the next morning still fuming. She slung

her pack over her shoulder and trudged down to the stable.

One of the grooms had Satan saddled. "Has Sir Brian gone?" She would tell the oaf personally what a swine he was before leaving.

The stable hand, a boy of twelve, nodded his head, "Yes, Ma'am, just gone, Mistress Hope." The boy smiled and said in admiration, "He is brave, is he not?"

Hope cursed under her breath. "He is stupid," she replied, mounting Satan.

She rode north.

A simpleton indeed. Even if he did discover an alliance between the demons, what good would it do? He said himself the free companies would not fight. This world had no monster hunters. Better for him to stay in the valley and help prepare to defend the people. Yes, an oaf on an oaf's errand.

A weight like an anvil pressed down on her as the valley pass came in view, rising on the horizon. Had she done something wrong? Was part of this her fault? Did Brian somehow take her eagerness to help the castle during the battle, a signal to allow him to kill her? It wasn't what he'd done that matter so much, it was the way he did it. Presumptuous, too. She added that to his list.

Hope paused at the top of the divide. Behind, green fields of bola spread on either side. What if no conspiracy existed? Perhaps this was a random act between beasts with no consequences. This world could still be a safe haven for herself and Apophis. What if the demons knew of the link between this land and hers? How long before they invaded her country again.

Either way, this was valuable knowledge worth having before returning home.

Hope gazed at the savannah regretting the choice of not waiting an extra day to start her journey. Yellow prairie stretched in an endless panorama as far as she could see. When Brian and she entered this world they traveled southeast, but Hope realized with dismay even a slight deviation from the back path would cause miles of aimless wandering in the wrong direction.

"DOUBLE DAMN." She halted Satan. "You know, boy, I can't remember how to return, do you?"

The stallion responded with a questioning snort.

Hope patted his neck. "My fault, not yours."

It was necessary to hasten back to the castle and beg a guide. How many knew the location of the doorway? It couldn't be common knowledge, otherwise more fools would have wandered in long ago.

No, not the castle, she'd have to locate Brian. He tricked her here. He knew the way back, probably necessary to keep him safe from demons until he finished his quest. Hope chuckled. It wouldn't do at all to have him slaughtered like a herd animal. Besides, it was a chance to elicit useful intelligence.

She sighed, and spun Satan on his heels. With renewed energy, Hope urged the horse into a gallop, seeking the southern road. A weight, which pressed, lifted as the cool morning air flew in her face, carrying the smell of fresh mowed hay.

He can't be that far ahead of me. Hope pushed Satan harder. *I must be crazy. I should wait at the castle until he appears.* A flock of barn fowl, escaped from their coop, scattered on the road as Satan sped past a farmhouse. *Probably kill myself, trying to save him from a demon.*

Ten miles. *He is a fool.*

Fifteen miles. *I am a fool.*

Twenty miles. *We will both die.*

***

Brian whirled at the clatter of hoof beats. "Why are you here?"

Hope fell in beside him. "I don't remember the exact route to the portal, *Warlock,*" she replied, emphasizing his new title with as much contempt as possible. "I'll have to

71

wait until you've concluded your quest to show me the way back."

"Is that the only reason you are here?" His dark gaze bore into hers, searching.

"Of course not." Hope sat upright in her saddle. "I must discover for myself if this threat is real or not, and learn if the demons know of the portal, *Warlock* before I depart to my home world," she snapped, staring straight ahead. "I will ride with you. Two swords are safer than one."

Brian broke into a grin. "I am glad for your company then. It is always wise to have a friend on a journey like this."

Hope swung in her seat, glaring in scorn. "Don't call me friend, Warlock. A companion for our mutual protection, and a guide back to my homeland if we're not destroyed first, nothing more. Understand?"

His smile disappeared. "So be it," he murmured. His shoulders hunched lower and he studied the road with unusual intensity. "Companions it is, for protection. When we are finished, I promise to lead you to the portal between our worlds."

The silence between the two stretched throughout the day as they trekked into the mountains. Hope thought they would locate a pass leading across the bleak landscape, and proceed to the plains beyond. Instead, Brian chose a faint trace weaving itself deeper into the hills. After they passed a trail leading downward, the curiosity inside her rose to an uncontainable level, coupled with the aggravation still churning for Brian.

"Why are we going this way?" she complained. Ragged peaks loomed on all sides. The wind howled, freezing her side. "Are you lost already?" Hope gestured to their right. "Even I know our path lies that way."

Brian pulled his riding cloak tighter around his shoulders. "Before we venture out among the plains I must seek a man, a powerful wizard, who lives in these mountains," he replied, his voice tainted with relief he rated enough for conversation. "If we are to succeed we need his help."

"Help? What help?" she snapped. "Is this world plagued by warlocks whose magic doesn't work right?"

Brian disregarded the remark, and said, uncertain, "This is the rub. I am not sure what aid he has the ability to provide, only that I feel we must talk to him."

Hope scowled, not satisfied with his answer, but he refused to discuss the matter any further until they hit a wide flat clearing. The path ended, surrounded by three vertical walls that protected them from the wind.

"Now we camp," Brian said.

"Here?" Hope pounded her hands together and blew on her fingers. It was dark, freezing cold, and the wizard they sought was nowhere in sight. "You expect to meet someone in this place?" she asked, stunned.

Brian did not answer at once. A pile of kindling stood along one edge of the wall. He mounded wood and proceeded to build a fire. "He will know we are here."

"Stupid," Hope muttered. She huddled close to the blaze and shoved her hands between her legs. She should have brought her winter gloves along with the work pair, she thought bitterly. The night was pitch black. Stars glowed overhead in the clear air, and the light of the fire reflected off the rock.

Brian grinned and nodded, shifting closer to Hope, as if offering the warmth of his body. She frowned, eyes narrowing to mere slits, bestowing a scowl displaying the ire he was likely to receive if this situation didn't improve. She edged away, yanking her cloak even tighter around her shivering frame.

Better to have gone by myself. Could've been on the plains by now, learned what was needed, off on my way, and to hell with a guide.

73

Hope cast a sideways glance at Brian. He squatted by the fire, seemingly content to wait all night for whatever was to occur. Demons or not, if they sat here doing nothing until their tails froze she would kill him herself. It would offer something to do, and the exercise would keep her warm.

A deep cry vibrated in the stillness. Hope jerked her head up. Two yellow eyes glowed out of the darkness, advancing up the path toward their camp through the darkness.

A snow cat padded into view. The animal surveyed the clearing, first resting its gaze on Hope, and then fixing on Brian. The cat hissed. Hope fumbled in desperation for her sword.

Brian's hand shot out, seizing her wrist. With a smirk he said, "Hope, meet Eldridge the wizard, and my teacher."

The snow cat released a yowl and reared on its hind legs. The haunches elongated into legs and feet, while the rest of the body and head shimmered into the shape of a man clothed in a white robe.

Hope watched the transformation in fascination, the freezing temperature forgotten, and didn't realize the change was completed until blue eyes twinkled in amusement from above a snow-white beard.

Eldridge scowled. "*Former* mentor, you mean." He withdrew a wand and approached one of the rock walls. With a flourish, he rapped three times and a wooden door formed. He swung it wide and announced, "Well, do not stand there." He waved Hope forward with a bow. "Enter and warm yourself." He glowered at Brian. "You have brought me a pretty girl to visit, so I suppose you may be granted entrance too."

A spacious room greeted Hope. Soft, warm glows of pearl emanated from the walls, lighting the interior. A fire crackled in a stone fireplace set at one end, while a massive table and bench dominated the center. Shelves set on the walls held jars and baskets overflowing with powders and herbs.

"Sit." The wizard shuffled over to a cupboard and grabbed two trenchers. "You must be hungry." He placed small loaves of black bread in the bottom of each and set them before his guests. "Stew coming up," he announced. He wandered to the fireplace and brought back an iron kettle warming on the hearth, and shoved a ladle into the pot. "Eat."

"Th-thank you," Hope stuttered glancing around. She dipped fragrant stew into the trencher, and soaked up the broth with the bread.

Eldridge sat next to her; he smelled of honeysuckle and wild roses. "Now," he said to Brian, "What do I owe the honor of this visit?" The wizard bestowed a warm smile on Hope. "Have you perhaps brought me a new student who is not as lazy as you are?"

Brian slumped lower on his bench and looked guilty. "We need your help," he mumbled. "We found a dragon and moloch in leagues together, later molochs astride baitals attacked King Gregory's castle."

The wizard tugged on his beard at this news. "Molochs riding baitals is not unusual. They've long been allies, but molochs and dragons?" He put his fingers to his mouth. "They are sworn enemies."

"I know," Brian agreed. He finally gained the courage to stare his former teacher in the face. "This woman and I venture onto the plains to discover what occurs."

"And you wish?" The wizard scrutinized him with intensity, swung his gaze on Hope, and back to Brian.

"That is the problem." Brian raised his hands in frustration. "I am unsure. We might be out there for many days. If conspiracies are afoot, we must gain the confidence of demons that would otherwise kill us on sight." He paused and focused on the trencher before him, "Perhaps a way to disguise ourselves so the demons will not recognize our true intent? Change our appearance to make us resemble the beasts of the plains?"

Hope looked at him. What did he mean, not be recognized? Was he planning to change their outer form in some way? She pictured herself wearing a mustache or the heavy horns of a moloch.

The wizard tapped his wand, thinking, and then twirled the rod end over end in his fingers. "If you had stayed here and continued your studies as I urged," he said to Brian with a stern glare, "you could do this yourself. You would not need to beg my assistance."

Brian's face flushed red. "You know that was not to be," he retorted angrily. "I did not have the talent in me." His dark gaze grew blacker. "To waste anymore of your time was a jest, as I was well told by those who know me well."

"You are wrong," the old man thundered. He slapped his wand on the table, breathing hard. "You possess the ability within you. Acquire the confidence to bring this power out. If you had…" He stopped, shaking his head, frustration at his former student plain as the furrowed wrinkles in his forehead. "Let me think this through," he sighed at last, his shoulders slumping.

Even though she was still mad at Brian, didn't trust him, she felt sorry for him. The expression on his face proved how humiliated he was before Eldridge. What had happened in his past? He *was* confident. Every situation they'd faced, he handled like a bold and fearless warrior. Hope wondered what had happened to him to make magic different.

Eldridge picked up his wand. He spun it again. The rod moved faster in his fingers until it shifted into a blur.

The wand stopped.

"To change your appearance is simple," he said at last, "but that would not serve. The exterior is not the solution, but the inner. Many humans walk the plains unmolested, but some creatures of the outer savannahs sense a person's disposition, if he is good or corrupt. That is what you must transform." The wizard bent forward and whispered, "We will make your thoughts appear evil." He motioned with his wand.

"Rise."

Hope stood.

A sick feeling started in her guts. She was not evil, did not want to be evil, or think evil. Eldridge was preparing to turn them into demons.

"I will not stand for th..." Before the sentence was finished the wand pointed. Overhead, a grey cloud blossomed. Hope tried to duck but some power froze her in place. Black ash rained down like snow, coating her scalp and flesh. It burnt cold.

Brian squinted, his face a study of concentration as the ebony dust covered him also.

The burning stopped. Hope exclaimed, "I feel no different." She held up her hands. They were unchanged.

The wizard Eldridge laughed. "Nothing has altered, but the evil that is in any man," he bowed his head to Hope, "woman, has risen to the top. The good in you is now buried where none may see it."

"Trapping spell?" Brian asked in comprehension.

"Yes, which you studied and should perform on your own," the old man lectured. He sounded exhausted.

"How long will it last?" Hope asked suddenly, the churning in her stomach unabated. The thought of people, even demons, perceiving the evil within her was wrong.

"It will last until a stronger emotion, love, or happiness, washes it away," Eldridge replied. "Remember, however, those who have the power to see within you will detect the wrongness. To those who cannot, you still have to appear vile and corrupt."

The wizard let loose a deep sigh and suppressed a yawn with the back of his hand. "Your horses will be safe

77

outside. I am going to sleep." He waved vaguely to a pallet of hay in the corner of the cave by the fire. "I suggest you do the same."

Two bundles of straw sat by the fireplace, one closer to the blaze than the other. Brian unerringly took the one farther one. He gestured to the other. "I have slept in this cave before and the nights become chilly. That one will be warmer."

Hope was ready to thank him when she remembered she was still angry at his conduct. She muttered "Thanks," and flopped down, facing the wall, and fell asleep.

***

Before they left the next morning, Eldridge held a whispered conversation with Brian, ending with the old wizard shoving a small leather bag into the younger man's hands. Hope would have liked to edge closer and eavesdrop on what they discussed. Before an excuse proposed itself, Eldridge addressed her.

"I sense great things in you, and greater works to come, but beware," he cautioned, wagging his finger, "you will face many hardships along the way, and your patience will be tried sorely. In those instances, trust your heart, for out on the plains things are never what they appear."

They rode out of the mountains.

Hope wondered what Eldridge meant. Of course, she'd accomplished heroic things. She was a dragonkiller, protector of the people against terror. Greater things coming? No doubt, he meant she'd kill more demons. In this world, plenty of opportunity presented itself. Vexed?

She was still irritated with Brian.

After their descent to the plains, Brian swung right and rode parallel to the mountains. Hope assumed they would ride straight onto the yellow savannah in search of demons. They'd left the trail far behind, but the peaks were still within hailing distance.

She wondered if Brian was cautious about attack, and

used the foothills as a potential refuge for escape in case demons or monster struck. Hope was confused, but bit her tongue, until inquisitiveness compelled her to ask, "Where are we going? Do you have *any* idea?" No danger presented itself. She scanned the sky, but detected no threat in that direction either. "I don't see..."

Brian cut her off. "It is best if we ride to a town. One lies two days from here along these hills. There we can pick up news."

She asked, "I saw Eldridge hand you a sack. Better travel ration than the ones we carry?"

"Nothing to eat, I am afraid," Brian chuckled. As Hope grew more talkative, his spirits had brightened considerably. "Things we might use along the way. Gloves made from the inner membrane of a dragon's hide. Extract from the bola plant, if need be, to deliver strength."

"I understand the bola, it will come in handy if we fight or run," she said, surprised, "but gloves? We have gloves of good tough leather, and I know the membrane of a dragon. It can't wear well." They had risen before the sun. Perhaps the old man couldn't think straight first thing in the morning. Why would he give them an item as useless as that?

Brian read the puzzlement. "They are one of his most prized possessions, passed down from one wizard to the next."

"That was sweet of him," she said hesitantly. "Perhaps they will be useful if our work pairs become lost."

Brian studied her for a long moment. "Eldridge hid our character, but not our personalities. As a hand smeared in the mud leaves a print on a rock that which is 'we' is transmitted to inanimate objects." He leaned across his saddle to see if she understood what he meant. "This impression of ourselves, we might want to hide also from prying minds."

Hope nodded. Tales flooded the world of former

sword owners staying with the blade, or personal objects that had constant use, stolen to work magic against the possessor. She made a mental note: After this was over, she wished no trace of herself left behind in this world. Her actions were her own, and she had no desire for others to influence her actions.

On the morning of the second day, the outlines of a walled town rose. Hope expected to see a primitive camp, perhaps rude huts with a wooden palisade, not buildings containing towering spires, arrow slits for archers, and catapults mounted on the parapets. "Demons have cities?" she exclaimed in surprise.

"Of course," Brian answered. "Was this not so in your world?"

"No." Hope stood in her stirrups to have a better view. "They were solitary animals, sometimes gathering into roving clans or packs, but no towns. It seems, human."

"Of course, this is more of a half-breed town," he continued, "some humans and demons included, of course, but a true demon city is the same."

"Sounds more like a menagerie to me," She huffed. "The next thing you'll show me are towns where herd animals and predators live together in peace and harmony."

This world was a dream, or a nightmare. Whenever this land felt comfortable, something emerged to rearrange everything she thought was true. It was like waking up in bed, walking out to the herb garden, and discovering she knew none of the plants.

"You are in for a surprise then," Brian said. A faint smile flickered on his lips. The expression on her face was worth the whole trip. "For once, I will teach the great Hope Nearwood, Dragonkiller, a lesson about demons."

She gave Brian a sideways look. "That'll be the day." Hope remained expressionless, but inside, delight of gathering new knowledge about her profession consumed her. She *was* learning about half-breeds and demons, and she wasn't even bothered she learned from *him*.

The guards flanking the main gates watched carefully as they entered the town, but said nothing. They progressed along the main street and tried staying as inconspicuous as possible. Hope watched a human woman buying vegetables from a half-breed moloch, while a man containing dragon blood patiently waited his turn to pay. This might be any human settlement on Hope's world. She said in shock, "Is this how the demons live here on the plains? They act, *normal*."

"From the outside I suppose you would think so, at least they do not battle." Brian's gaze met hers. "Do not confuse coexistence for merit. Within these walls, the different races interact together with politeness, but trust in small respects. Foreigners are always suspected."

He shook a finger at her, making a point. "An innocent remark spoken to one of the same lineage can be taken wrong by a member of a different species. For someone who does not dwell here and know their customs that furnishes a good way to develop a knife sticking out of your back."

"Still…" Hope protested, observing a human male saunter by, "are most evil?"

"It depends. To those they judge friends, if they are the same clan, probably not. To those they perceive are enemies or easy meat for the plucking," Brian shrugged, "who can tell how they will react."

They stopped in front of a tavern, a green bush hanging over the door indicating it was open for business. The inside was crowded. No one looked their way as they entered and sat. The tavern keeper hurried over, wiping his grimy hands on a cloth as soiled as his apron. "What may I serve you?"

"Flagon of wine," growled Brian.

"Money?" The man waited.

Brian reached into his purse and scattered hexagonal

bronze coins on the table. The tavern keeper picked up two and hurried off. He reappeared a second later and slammed a pewter jug down and two wooden cups.

Brian fished around in his moneybag again, this time producing a wedge of silver. He left it lying in plain sight. "What news of the outer plains? We proceed that way. Raids? Wars? Who battles against whom?"

The man fingered the coin and pursed his fat lips. "You are lucky. No fighting that I know of. *Too* quiet, if you must know." He tapped his chin, thinking. "A moloch traveled through here a week ago, recruiting for his chieftain, that way," he waved his hand toward the southeast, "I think. Thought it was odd at the time, they usually enlist their own kind for fighting, hinted about riches everyone would receive." He chuckled. "They always say that, though."

Hope eyes lit up. "Is he still here?"

The tavern keeper shook his head. "No, stayed one night and left. Said his ruler ordered the word spread." He regarded Brian and Hope shrewdly. "Why, you want to join a moloch army?"

The man was growing too nosy for Hope's taste. She pretended to shudder and poured some wine. "Of course not."

Brian flipped the silver over. "Here. If you remember anything else, inform us."

They sipped their wine while casting glances at the patrons crowding the bar and tables. "We quest southeast then." Hope whispered, "Molochs recruiting different species? That's what we seek."

"Maybe," Brian agreed. "If we learn nothing better, that is the way we shall go." He scanned the room. The tavern keeper was whispering to a group of half-breeds. When he saw Brian watching, he stopped with a slow wink to his customers and strode to the other end of the bar.

One of the group rose, a half-breed moloch, and

swaggered over to their table. Close to seven feet high, his horns were short but still deadly. He towered over their heads. "We hear you go out onto the high plains," he sneered to Brian in a deep grunt. "Safe enough for you maybe, human, but a young woman should not go." He bent down and smirked at Hope. His breath smelled like sour wine. "I have plenty moloch," he touched his groin. "You're better staying with us where you can be protected." He reached a hand out.

Brian's belt knife flashed. The blade slammed between the demon's long fingers. "This is my woman, beast," he rumbled, with a hiss. "Move away or you lose that hand." His voice dripped malice. He shot his stool back and crouched into a fighting stance, weight balanced on the balls of his feet. "You are taller than me. Maybe I should cut off a part of your body lower at first."

The half-breed glanced at the knife, and then at Brian. "Your loss," he said to Hope, and strolled to his companions without a backward glance.

Hope's short sword was half-drawn, ready to take on the half-breed if he didn't back off. As the moloch moved away, she slipped the blade into the sheath. A wave of appreciation surged for Brian's quick action. His next words shocked her.

"Do not worry, Hope, I will not allow anyone to hurt you in this place." He swiftly assessed the mood of the rest of the patrons. "We had better leave. It is not wise to dally here anymore."

Brian protecting her? Hope's gratitude withered, replaced by anger. How dare he think she needed a man to rescue her from these poor excuses for demons? She had undertaken this quest to defend *him*.

"Next time let me fight my own battles," she hissed to Brian. "When I desire your help, I'll ask." Hope stood. "Let's go, we have discovered everything possible." She drained her glass in one swift gulp and stalked out the door.

His woman, indeed.

Chapter Six

"If this moloch chieftain is recruiting all races it means trouble, especially if the dragons ally themselves with him." Brian slumped in his seat, and with a grunt of frustration, peered in a wide circle.

"As I recall," Hope searched also, "Eldridge said they are enemies. Perhaps not many will follow him."

The tension in Brian's body increased as they scouted farther into the savannah. Hope tried to dispel some of his worry and stayed upbeat. "Maybe this is nothing more than a clan fight, or a moloch with delusions of greatness, and the dragons wish no part of him."

"Even one or two enlisted would cause a disaster." Brian was not jollied. "If men unite with him it will be worse. They can infiltrate the valleys without our knowledge. Which town could stand against the combined strength of demon, dragon, and man?"

Hope was well aware of what that meant. The battles in her world would pale in comparison to the war tearing this land apart. She racked her brain for a solution. Somehow, she must find a way to rescue this world – for its people, Apophis, herself, and yes, even Brian. Nothing proposed itself.

The smell of rotting flesh in the hot sun wafted their way. The knee-high savannah grass to the right shook. Hope clutched her sword tighter and wished they'd thought to bring bows from the castle.

Brian stopped. His eyes narrowed as he sniffed. "Carrion eaters," he said at last.

"Will they bother us?" It killed her inside to admit that the plains frightened her. The valleys evoked the familiar feelings of safety, but long ago predators in her world had vanished from the savannahs, eaten by the demons. Humans, in turn, had destroyed the monsters. The endless expanses transformed into a vacuum which man repopulated at leisure.

"I hope not."

"You hope?" She scowled at him. "Don't you know?"

He took his time answering. "I can only speculate. If it were demons they would have attacked by now." He fished out an empty parchment wrapper he carried from their travel ration, crumpled it, and tossed the ball at the waving grass. Answering squeals greeted the intrusion and grey animals with long whiskers poked their muzzles out before returning to their meal.

Brian gestured to the creatures. "You see? Vermin." They guided their horses to the left and continued on their way. "You must understand," he said, "the brave or foolish from the valleys venture out onto the plains. I am far from brave. I may be foolish," he grinned, "but not addled enough to travel out here often. These lands are as strange to me as they are to you."

"Still you rode across searching for my world," Hope wondered. "Wasn't that brave?"

"That was necessity," he replied.

He'd faced the plains to find her, sacrificed his own safety to venture out, trying to discover if his valley was under threat, yet called it necessity. She labeled him warlock in a fit of anger, but maybe judged too soon. This man displayed more than it seemed. Hope found herself admiring his strength.

Brian gasped. "Hope, look what approaches."

At first, she thought two logs traveled across the rolling prairie toward their position. Crawling logs.

The pair stood.

Not logs as she first surmised, but brown lizards, their high-domed heads denoting intelligence. As the creatures closed in on Hope and Brian, they presented a better view of their appearance, soft skin, black with red stars along their bodies, clawed hands and feet, with fleshy tails.

"Cherufe."

Brian leaned close. "You have seen their like before?"

"I know of their kind," Hope said, watching the pair approach. "They are long gone from my world, exterminated in the wars that destroyed all demons. I have read accounts of their appearance and how they fought."

Brian halted. "Do you think they will attack? I confess I have never seen their kind in these plains. If they are here now some force drew them to this land, or they were exiled from theirs."

"Perhaps so." Hope cradled the pommel of her weapon, thinking back to her studies. "I was told they favor warm climates. In great numbers, they cause earthquakes and volcanoes to erupt by digging into the earth. In some cases, they brought down town walls or whole mountains in this manner. Otherwise," Hope shrugged and withdrew her sword, "they are carrion eaters, preferring to feast off the kill of stronger predators. Unless more than two lurk in the grass, I do not think we're in danger."

"I will accept your word for it." Brian's expression relaxed. "You are the Dragonkiller."

The way he said 'dragonkiller', made Hope's lips rise at the corners. She added in an amused voice, "Right, but that's *dragon* killer, not cherufe killer. I hope they are the same as in my world."

As the demons drew into earshot, Hope shouted, "HOLD. Approach no closer unless you wish to die." She placed the sword across her lap in open view. Satan shifted nervously.

The two lizard men glanced at each other. Hope heard nothing spoken between them.

The tallest of the pair answered in a hissing lisp, "Be not afraid. We will not attack. Do you travel to the summoning?"

It was Hope's turn to look at Brian, but a quick nod indicated improvisation was in order. "We obey no summons," she said in contempt, "but we seek he who calls."

The two conferred in their silent language. "We search for him also. Temporary alliance while we travel? Four are stronger than two."

This time Hope needed no confirmation. "So be it," she agreed, trying to act as arrogant as possible. "You will lead. We will follow, but beware." she held the sword up, letting the blade catch the sun to blind the pair. "No treachery. We are armed, and our rations are scarce. Betray us and you are as so much meat to our larder."

The spokesman nodded. "My name is Izar. This is my brother, Kis. We plan no deceptions. We will go ahead." Both cherufe dropped to all fours and scurried off to the southeast.

Brian rode next to Hope until their knees touched. "I fear it is worse than I thought." His face was a mask of worry. "Demons are coming from the southern regions also. If they are journeying that far…" He left the sentence hanging.

Hope whispered back, "At least we have guides. Perhaps we'll acquire information from these creatures. We must be careful though. One wrong action and we will expose ourselves." She wondered how long they could maintain this charade. This pair didn't act too smart, but their wordless communication made her feel uneasy. What were they really saying they wished to keep hidden?

As it grew dark, they halted and made camp by a small grove of stunted trees. All day Hope kept vigil on their two traveling companions. Apprehension intensified each time they bumped together, conferred silently, especially when coupled with glances in their direction. Nevertheless, no change in behavior developed. Still, an unmistakable chill spread.

She kindled a fire. The cherufe huddled close and settled by the heat as near as possible. When Brian began a circuit of their camp, casting his gold fire setting a protective barrier, they picked up their heads and watched with intent interest and fear.

"You use white magic?" hissed Izar. His eyes glowed red in the firelight. "You are a wizard then?"

"No worker of good am I," Brian snapped back, "but a warlock," he shot a glance at Hope, "I have been called. Remember that creature. I use any magic I choose, good or evil. In this case it is better to weave what demons fear most." He gestured into the darkness where roars and screams echoed through the night.

Izar nodded and settled down. "I had not thought of that."

"How long have you traveled, creatures?" Hope sneered, trying to project all the disdain imaginable for these two into her voice. She snagged a brick of travel rations from her bundle, cracked it in half, and handed a portion to Brian.

"A messenger visited our clan a moon ago," Kis replied. His eyes flashed crimson and he glowered at Hope. "We were promised much meat. The rest of our kin did not believe, but we did, so my brothers and I came."

"Your brothers?" Hope was alert, a hand automatically creeping for her weapon. "I see but one more of you."

"We started as four," Izar said in his hissing voice. "Two weeks out we were attacked at night and lost one sibling. Three days later, a dragon swooped from the sky and we lost another."

"The plains are a dangerous place," Brian agreed, "yet still you journeyed on?"

"Food is scarce in our country," said Izar. He watched Hope chew her rations. "We are many." His eyes closed to mere slits as he studied her, mouth dripping saliva, fangs bared. "We crave meat." His tongue flickered.

Hope jerked out the sword and waved it into Izar's face. "I don't like the way you're looking at me, demon. If

89

you want meat, I'll cut off your leg and shove the toes down your throat."

The cherufe emitted a squeal and scurried backward a few feet. When Hope made no effort to carry out the threat and stowed her weapon, he crawled back to the fire. "You are too fresh," he hissed. "We like our meat rotted."

"You think you will acquire this at the gathering?" Brian growled.

"If this summoning proves true, we will pass word to our clan. They shall inform the tribes of our kind, and the whole nation will feast."

Izar shifted and Hope slid her hand over the sword. The cherufe settled down. "When did you learn of the summoning?" Izar asked.

Brian rubbed his chin. "A few days ago. We heard a rumor of a rumor and thought to discover the truth. What else were you told?" he snarled, directing the questioning back to the cherufe. "We do not want to chase all over the plains for a tale that is nothing."

The shrewd faces watched Brian carefully. "You ask many questions, human. Why would anyone chase gossip?"

Hope face clouded up. "How dare you?" She slammed the rations down and sprang upward in fake rage, gripping her weapon as if determined to strike. She towered over the startled cherufe.

"Please, do not kill us." The two lizard demons huddled close to each other in fear.

"Were you not listening, creature?" She hissed, happy to see the act accepted so well. "If there is something to possess, we want it. What matters if we pursue a rumor half way across the world? We take as we go. Although," she studied Izar, "I know a place where your tanned hide would fetch a good price, and the distance we need covered would diminish. We still have Kis to ask questions if need be."

Izar cowered in terror, wordless communication flashed between the brothers. "You mistook me, human. I only speculated on the reason for your long journey."

"Keep your speculations to yourself next time, beast."

His lips lifted in an attempt of a smile. "It is plain you do well," he answered meekly. "As for what we heard, all that desire riches are gathering in the Red Hills and seek a moloch with four arms." Izar stopped, confused. "Molochs do not have four arms, do they?"

"Not that I know of," grunted Brian.

Hope yawned. "I will take first lookout with Izar," she said loudly, as if the pronouncement brooked no argument. She retrieved a blanket from her pack and spread it out. "We will keep each other awake. Later Brian and Kis may guard." *And we can watch both of you bastards.*

They settled down. Hope sat on one side of the fire with Izar curled opposite the blaze in a tight ball.

The crackling of the logs shot sparks flying into the air, hypnotizing Hope into a trance accompanied by deep yawns. She had to admit, the day had been long, too many things to worry about and not enough time to think. The flickering light from the fire swelled as her chin sank down. She blinked hard, struggling not to fall sleep. When she looked up the cherufe stood by her side.

"What are you doing?" Her short sword lay across her lap. Hope swung the blade wildly, sat straight, and leveled the tip at the demon's head.

Izar froze. "I throw more wood on the fire," he replied with a weak flick of his tongue. A clawed hand reached out, picked up a branch, and placed the stick on the fire. The blaze did not need the extra fuel.

Three hours later when Brian assumed the watch, Hope uttered one word in his ear, "Beware."

* * *

In the morning, the terrain roughened, cut with gullies and ravines. Tall buttes sprinkled the area, and the Red Hills rose into view. Small bands of demons sprang up, all heading in the same direction.

As they drew closer, Hope scrutinized each group. All were small, four or five individuals each, and comprised creatures of the same species. She noted with interest two types that were conspicuously absent, humans and dragons.

"I don't think it is wise to use white magic among this group," Hope whispered as they passed a band of demons. Ten eyes and long fangs marked their progress. "You are able to fool these cherufe, but these new beasts display more intelligence." She fought the urge to swing around and assure herself nothing was sneaking up behind to attack.

Brian swung in his saddle and scowled at another band of creatures as they ambled past. "You are right," he replied, settling himself in his saddle, back straight. "I do not know black magic, but I have learned something that is neither light nor dark. I will use that if need be." He touched the butt of his sword, "This is what I will rely on most."

The earth beneath their feet glowed with a faint scarlet covering, as if a giant blister burst, spewing blood over the bare dirt. The low hills separated and they tailed the rest of the demons through a divide.

The path emptied into a basin where hundreds of creatures milled about. In the center, a brooding figure rested on a rough-cut throne of granite. Those closest listened with intense interest as he bellowed out words. The demon rose from his throne.

A pure black moloch with four arms.

"He is the one we seek," Hope said in a low voice dripping with determination.

"How do we get closer?" Brian replied.

The cherufe merged into the crowd, slithering between the legs of the listeners for a better view of the speaker. Hope threw her cloak over her shoulder, assumed a haughty expression, and ignored the protests of the crowd urging Satan forward, trampling clawed feet and tails without regard. When they'd pushed to the front, she and Brian dismounted.

"My name is Ose. I have summoned you here to enroll in my army," the moloch bellowed. He clutched a Lore Master's staff in one hand over his head. The rest of his arms gestured wildly. "For once the people of these plains shall unite together and take what is rightfully theirs."

The demon measured the crowd, his gaze settling on Brian and Hope with delight. "My army shall march to the north, south, the east and the *west*. Over all the lands of this *world*. Who shall join me?" He paused, hands on hips, waiting for the crowd to respond.

A coal black demon stood. Long donkey ears twitched, and sharp yellow teeth showed in a snarl as he said, "You promise us meat and riches. The towns of the plains and the holding of the valley are small, many poor. Where do you propose to locate these riches?"

Around Hope, low growls of agreement ignited.

Ose held his arms up. "You are right, but some contain hidden riches if we are bold enough to take it. The least defended will fall first, providing us food. With each conquest we will become stronger, until the wealthy places fall to us also."

The black demon wavered. He tugged on his beard and nodded, squatting and conferring with one of his own in whispers.

Ose continued in a lower, more confidential tone, "I also know of a different land secret to me, far away, through the hills on the Northern Plains, where riches beyond belief exist, waiting for us to pluck what we want."

Hope heard muffled growls of assent. The moloch lifted his staff higher and the hum swelled into a roar. The demon nodded in satisfaction.

The creature gestured behind him.

"I have erected a stone of loyalty." A large black rock

stood waiting, the size of a table. "Those who wish to unite with me must touch its surface to become one of my army." A few of the nearest demons immediately sprang up and hurried forward, slapping their claws on the top.

Ose said in a menacing voice, "If you refuse, flee to your clans and tribes. Warn them of my coming, for surly I will conquer this land with or without you. That is your choice, be a soldier or a slave."

The crowd broke up. Many shuffled to the rock placing hand or paw on the rough top under the scrutiny of four moloch Lore Masters. Those timid, mostly half-breeds, hurried away in fright, glances over their shoulders showed they feared for their lives. Enough of both remained to make a long line.

As the throng circling the throne dispersed, more took their places. All pressed forward to hear the words of Ose.

Hope and Brian backed out of the mob. "I have heard enough," said Brian in a dark voice. "He plans to lay waste to the whole world if possible. It is best if we leave and warn my valley that war is imminent." He took the reins of his horse and led it to the entrance of the vale.

"Wait." Hope tried to think. "We still don't know enough. What of the alliance between the molochs and the dragons? I see none here."

Brian gave her a cynical look. "Does it matter? Dragons or not, we still know battle is forthcoming, that is for sure. Look at all the different demons who swear allegiance to this monster, half-breeds, too." He gestured to the stone of loyalty where the creatures who listened to Ose placed their hands.

"What matters which monsters volunteer?" Hope whispered back with contempt. "It is the dragons you must fear."

"Are you insane?" he blurted out. "He reaches out to different species. That is unheard of in this world. They never cooperate in this manner. Even if he recruits a few from each clan, think what a…" Brian stopped talking and put a hand on her shoulder. "Beware, someone approaches."

The queue, which lined up at the stone of loyalty, emptied. Izar was whispering urgently to the molochs who watched the beasts swear their oaths. Two of the demons glared at Hope and Brian. They left the stone, stalking their way.

"Are you two enlisting?" the biggest growled. "If so, swear now. If not, leave. We have word you may be scouts from the valleys dispatched to infiltrate our ranks. We do not want human spies in our camp."

The shorter Lore Master attempted to circle behind, trying to divide their attention.

Hope glanced at the swearing stone. The two cherufe vanished into the crowd. Her teeth grated in silent rage visualizing what mayhem confronted Izar when she caught him.

The Lore Master grunted. "Well, what is your decision?"

With a sneer, Hope stepped toward the moloch before her, relying on Brian to oppose the smaller demon if necessary.

She drew her sword. "Does Ose have so many captains he can afford to have one split up the middle?" she asked. It was vital to play this right. Not enough arrogance and the moloch would label them fair game to kill. Too much, and she and Brian would encounter a fight to the death. The balance of the demons watched, debating if they should help the Lore Masters to display their new loyalty to Ose.

With a wave of a hand, Hope shouted in dismissal, "Be gone. You would better spend your time tracking down those who spread false rumors about us. When we complete our discussion we'll inform you of our decision."

The moloch glowered. He pointed to her sword with a

95

broad smirk on his face. "So, the cow has a horn," he answered.

"Why, you..."

The other moloch growled and leveled his staff at Hope. Brian stepped in front of the stave, his short sword drawn and ready. Scorn for the Lore Master's weapon etched in the stance of his body as he directed his blade at the Lore Master's belly.

More demons gathered. Shouts sprang up, urging each side to start fighting. Above the bedlam, a loud voice rang out, deeper than the rest.

"HOLD."

Ose glared at his men from his stone throne. "Leave the humans alone," he bellowed. "Both of you attend to your station. You have work to do."

"You are summoned." Brian clenched his short sword tight in his fist. He waved the blade toward the rock. A line of demons waited for swearing in.

They sized each other up one last time. "This is not over, human," snarled the moloch. His companion issued a rumble deep in his throat. Shaking their horns in anger, they stomped away.

Hope slammed her sword back into the sheath with a snort of triumph. *That was close,* she admitted to herself, *came near to cutting that bastard in two and setting off a riot.* The idea was to collect information, not kill if possible.

Out of the corner of her eye, Hope had caught Brian's act of bravery. She didn't trust him completely, but was glad if they encountered danger his protection existed if needed. She silently forgave him for the incident back at the tavern. How could anyone stay mad at a person willing to lay down his life for you?

From somewhere, an emotion swelled within her heart. She pushed it aside.

Hope snapped out of her reverie. This wasn't getting

them anywhere. "We can't leave yet," she said to Brian. She took deep, calming breaths. "Ose said he knew of another place to attack. Was he speaking of the portal?" Her greatest fear was coming true. "I think it's better if you go. There are still things I must learn."

"I see you are troubled." Brian threw a quick glance at the molochs by the stone of loyalty. They were busy watching the demons swear in. "It matters not. If he speaks of the bridge between our worlds, warriors can stop him in your land after you spread a warning."

Stop Ose? She laughed at the demons he assembled with scorn, but who in her world would halt this monster? The free companies disbanded years ago. Yes, one on one, demon hunters like herself could kill many, but were there enough to stop an army? She never investigated how many killers remained, but knew their ranks dwindled over the years as the number of demons still surviving shrank to nothing.

No. No one stood between him and the valleys once the moloch invaded.

The fact remained, she did not know if Ose spoke of the portal connecting their worlds, or not.

Hope made a decision.

Their journey uncovered too many questions. However, Hope was certain of two things. Somehow, there must be a way to stop this demon. If so, she could save this land, create a place for her and Apophis to live. If not, she must discover what he knew of the portal and close it before it became too late.

Brian was impatient. He waited for her to stop balking so they could leave.

"I'm staying."

Chapter Seven

Brian buried his anger with a visible effort of will. "You cannot remain here," he grated out between clenched teeth. The molochs watched closely from their rock. He held her by the arm. "You will be killed."

Hope set her jaw and shook him off. "I told you to go, what more do you want from me?" she snapped back.

Curious onlookers strained to hear their argument. Brian reached out again, thought better of it and dropped his hand to his side. "I cannot let you stay by yourself." His body slumped in defeat. "If you will not leave, neither will I. For the time being, we will both remain. Perhaps you are right, and we need more information."

The anger Hope felt vanished. She snatched Satan's reins leading him farther out of the vale, away from the prying ears that listened, while waving Brian along.

When assured no one eavesdropped, she said, "You have a duty to warn your valley. That's why you undertook this mission the first place, remember? I'll be okay."

Brian cleared his throat. "True, but I also have an obligation to you. I used guile to trick you into this land, and promised to guide you back. Besides, my people are already preparing, regardless of what news I fetch." He watched the swirling mob of demons and half-breeds. "This army will not march for many days. There is yet time to glean more knowledge." He started to say something else, cut off abruptly, his eyes wishful.

He walked his horse around to block them from view. Fumbling in his saddlebag, Brian withdrew the pouch Eldridge furnished him. He groped inside. "If we are to stay we must touch the stone. Here," he fished out a rolled bundle, no bigger than a finger, "slip this on your right hand."

Beneath the parchment cover, she discovered a small glove, almost transparent. Glancing about to guarantee no one watched she wedged her fingers in. The material blended against the skin as if part of her hand. "What...?

"Eldridge's dragon glove," said Brian, slipping one onto his own hand. "This way we can appear to swear allegiance without really doing so." They led their mounts back into the vale. The molochs guarding the stone issued loud growls of hatred as they approached. Both split their attention between Hope and Brian as they scrutinized the demons pledging homage to Ose.

"You didn't have to do this."

Brian smirked. "I do not want you returning to your world spreading rumors of what oafs live here." He made a slight gesture with his chin. "These two Lore Masters have created a bad enough impression already, I think."

Hope burst out laughing. "This world is fine," she answered. "You..." she tilted her head with mock sternness, "...I could live with. But you're right. The molochs will receive a bad report."

The queue of demons waiting at the stone emptied, leaving the space vacant. Brian cleared his throat and flashed an encouraging smile. He whispered, "Let us proceed, but be careful."

The molochs they argued with earlier watched carefully as Hope and Brian approached leading their horses. Two additional demons, more mist than flesh, floated behind their heads. Long tentacles drifted from the gaseous body with sickly yellow sparks shooting up and down. Hope couldn't decide if they lived or not. Nowhere did she recall a mention of these creatures.

Brian neared the stone, slapped his hand on the surface, and hurried on. Hope summoned up her courage, stared at the molochs in the most indolent fashion possible, and slammed her fist on the rock.

"Hold."

Hope whirled. Ose stalked toward the swearing stone. "I am glad you decided to demonstrate your loyalty to me," he rumbled. "You and your companion, I wish to speak with you both."

Her heart sank. The prospect of remaining inconspicuous among the creatures of the army was lost. Now, for some reason they'd sparked Ose's interest. With a budding sense of nervousness, Hope composed herself and faced the moloch.

Satan reared, pawing the air. She held his reins and calmed the agitated stallion. Brian rushed back and shouted, "Lord, we have taken your oath, what else do you need of us?" He walked his horse between the moloch and Hope, and stood, waiting.

Ose retreated from the sharp hooves of Satan. He surveyed the animal with amusement and chuckled, "Your mount should have taken that oath also. If you are as fierce in battle as he, I am well served."

"You will find us worthy *allies*," Brian emphasized the word, "and our horses obey where we lead."

Ose folded his arms. "Come, let us walk." He strolled back to the middle of the vale. Hope noticed he stayed out of Satan's way.

The moloch climbed onto his rocky seat with a grunt and stared at Hope and Brian. "I see you are the only ones of your race who answered my call," he rumbled. He folded all four arms around his amble middle. "Why is that?"

The knot squeezing inside Hope relaxed. He was not singling them out. *At least for now.* She waited on Brian, unsure what a proper response would be.

"The men of the valleys are, of course out of the question," Brian replied carefully. "The humans who roam the savannahs," he waved his hand in a wide circle, encompassing the plains, "are known for distrusting your kind." Brian waited to see what reaction he would get. The moloch scowled.

"It is true, they feel superior to the demons of the plains," Ose rumbled.

Brian nodded in agreement. "They may cohabitate with different breeds, but the trust is never there." He expelled a barking laugh. "Most of the time they do not hold confidence with their fellow humans."

"How about you?" asked the moloch, "Why do you swear allegiance?"

This time Brian doubled over in mirth, Hope found his laughter infectious. "You promised riches." he said at last. "Who cares if moloch or human supplies them? As for trust," he shrugged, "he who delivers money into my pocket is the one I put my faith in."

Ose scratched his beard and nodded. "Tomorrow we march into battle against the town Goron. I am interested to see how your kind fares. It may be I do not need humans at all, but if I do, you two will make good ambassadors." With that, he waved a hand in dismissal.

Hope and Brian hurried away. Once out of earshot, Hope said, "For a moment I thought we were unmasked."

"Me too," replied Brian. "I am glad he did not quiz me longer. I was running out of lies."

Hope judged he'd been doing a good job, and glad the speaking fell to him. Political intrigue was not her strong point, she conceded with a slight upturn of lips. She was more kill-and-let's-be-done with it kind of person.

Ose erected huge cooking fires and fed any demons who decided to stay. "Let us eat and camp for the night," suggested Brian. "I had thought this moloch would wait longer before marching to war, but it seems I was wrong. I hope he has estimated his strength correctly. However, we had better rest for tomorrow."

They located a secluded spot in the hills with plenty of grass. Unsaddling the horses, they spread out their rolls, and went to draw rations.

Small groups occupied the hollows around their camp. The babble of soft voices sifted through the mounds. Hope bent over their fire and ate slowly, examining each bite before chewing. She'd been careful selecting the cooks who prepared the rations. Some had roasting carcasses behind their serving tables with human arms and legs still attached to the spits. "What do you know of this Goron?" she asked.

Brian leaned over and stirred up the fire. "A mixture of half-breeds and demons, I believe," he said, thinking. "I have never been there, but I am told they control the trade routes on this part of the lower plains. They extract tribute from caravans trekking through to the mountain valleys on this side of the range. Small place."

"The town possesses wealth then," Hope speculated, gazing into the fire.

"Maybe, but we will never know until it is taken. Regardless, it is well defended." Brian bobbed his head up, his dark eyes masking the worry in his voice. "Unless Ose has powerful weapons or more troops hidden, this will not be an easy victory."

"Let's hope he is a good general," Hope agreed. She listened to the bellows ringing out from the feasting army around their fires. "I don't want to be hurled as chaff against the wind. If so, we'll perish."

Brian's vision shifted from the fire to her. "That is not to be the case. We run," he answered firmly. "I will not sacrifice my life for this moloch, nor will I see you either. We can obtain news in a different way." A half smile flickered across his lips, "Unless you insist on dying, of course. In that case, I have no choice but to stay and perish with you."

Hope gawked at him in disbelief and broke into a laugh. "I think I'll let you off the hook and we shall both live. I wouldn't want to deprive Mictian of their most famous noble."

In the morning, the army marched to the city. Ose dressed in battle gear, a sword clutched in his left hand, two stuffed in scabbards, while he held his Lore Master's staff in his right.

The warlord received no more troops, but he brought with him weapons Hope never saw before.

Trailing behind, sweating slaves hauled huge war engines on wooden sleds. When they reached the town wall, Ose commanded the machines positioned well out of arrow range and set up.

The town defenders lined the parapet of the city, hurling taunts at the army, challenging the demons to attack.

"Well, it is the humans." The moloch captain from the swearing stone strode along the line behind Hope and Brian. "Make sure you are in the front ranks," he sneered. "That is an order. Ose wishes to see how brave you are."

Peeking out between his legs were Izar and Kis. The cherufe cast malicious glances at Hope, their red tongues flickering.

"Those two," Hope challenged. "Will they fight in the front ranks, or have you adopted pets?"

"You need not worry about these," the captain snarled. "Ose has plans. They travel back to their homeland to persuade more of their kind." He touched his staff. "Now line up, I am watching you."

"I bet you'll do it from the back row," Hope said.

"Why you…" The moloch reached for his staff.

The two cherufe scattered from sight. Hope laughed and waved the Lore Master off with contempt, nudging Satan forward until an empty expanse stood between her and the town. The defenders howled and shot arrows that fell short.

Hope paid the bolts no mind, concentrating on the activity behind where Ose's secret weapons prepared for the attack.

Tall wooden poles rose to the sky with slings attached, and heavy rocks at the bottom. In the belly of the machines wheels stood. Four husky molochs entered the wheels and began walking, winding down the arm and raising the boulders.

When the arms rested in the dirt, soldiers locked the shafts off and round stones rolled into the slings. After everything was ready, Ose nodded in satisfaction. "Now they will see the power of my army," he shouted to his troops.

The moloch raised a hand and checked to guarantee everyone watched. "FIRE."

The triggers of the war machines released. The rocks at the end of the poles dropped.

The arms swung in a long arc and the slings whipped outward, releasing the boulders. Each hit its mark, booming like a thunderclap.

The walls shattered.

The molochs manning the war machines scrambled to reload. Ose urged his crews to greater speed. Each time the defensive barrier of the city crumbled, until the only thing remaining was a low mound of stone. More boulders struck buildings, carving avenues where none existed before.

Ose took a position before his army, sword and staff raised over his head.

"CHARGE."

Satan leaped ahead, and Hope drew her sword. The stallion jumped over piles of debris at the wall as Hope chopped down at defenders pouring from the gaps to protect their homes.

"Beware."

Archers took up positions behind the crumbled buildings nearest the walls. One stepped out with a shaft notched. Hope slumped as the arrow zipped over her head. Brian crashed into the bowman and flew out of his seat. Hope jumped off Satan and threw herself forward, swinging at a demon with a human head and arms running on four legs. Her sword clipped one of the forelegs and the creature crumbled into a heap with a howl. Hope tripped over the demon, sawed air trying to regain her balance, and sprawled to the pavement.

Brian grabbed Hope by the arm and jerked her erect. "Are you all right?"

Hope shot him a grateful look and shook him off. "Yes," she gasped, the urge for battle surging through her. "They retreat back into town." She flourished her sword, eyes gleaming. "Let's give chase."

She sprinted ahead and disappeared into a side street. From hidden positions on roofs and windows of buildings, archers peppered the invaders. Ose's troops fell, more spread out with growls.

Two bolts sped close to Hope's head before she sought cover behind the remains of a wall. Brian zipped past, running. He paused, searching for her hiding place.

"Brian, to your right!" Four molochs darted around the side of a building, heads lowered, their wicked horns gleaming. They spied Brian and charged.

Hope scrambled out of concealment to help.

The molochs had no swords, but with their sharp horns needed none. They swung their weapons up and down, attempting to slash Brian to ribbons. Two discovered Hope and changed direction, aiming at her belly, bellowing in rage.

Instead of retreating, Hope bounced in close, slicing at a furry neck with her blade, while crashing her left elbow into a face. She pivoted as the creatures stopped in confusion, swinging the sword, waiting for the chance to attack.

Brian struck with looping bolo chops. Hope braced herself and hacked.

The four molochs sprawled on the pavement, dead.

The struggle raged deeper into town. Hope raced on with sword high, for the moment unmolested. Brain shouted, "Hope, wait," and tried catching up. "There is no need to keep fighting. Let us wait until the battle concludes."

Hope still faded into the maze of streets.

She stumbled into a courtyard. Seven of the townspeople surrounded one soldier. Three more, wisps of smoke flashing red from limbs that protruded beneath their underbellies, hovered above the lone figure. Fire shot down in bolts around the soldier, blasting holes in the pavement.

Hope heard the cursing of the warrior, the clashing of steel against steel as the creature fought for its life. Without thinking, she yanked out her short sword, and waded into the fight.

Jaws snapped and a sword flashed at her head. Squatting low, the blade passed over; her short sword jabbed upward and drove through a demon's guts. With the long sword, she swept whatever legs were near as she jumped away.

One of the mist demons drifted toward her. Fire shot from its body. Hope threw up her sword, the blade absorbing the bulk of the energy. The rest seared into her arm up to the shoulder. She screamed and dodged as additional bolts struck, heaving up gouts of flame and stones from the street.

Overhead a blue light flashed, exploding the mist. A glimpse displayed Brian standing there, wand out, sapphire lightening rocketing in all directions.

Screams of death filled the air. She swung back to the battle; the rest of the townspeople sprawled in grotesque positions. The blue mists had vanished. One figure remained.

Ose.

Smoke curled from his ebony skin, his four arms held bloody swords. At his feet rested the remains of his Lore Master staff. Two of the blades vanished into scabbards and he jammed his hands on his hips.

"It was my lucky day when you enlisted with me."

Hope jumped as Ose spoke. His voice rasped too loud

in the sudden stillness of the courtyard. She cast about wildly, searching for more demons to kill.

The warlord gestured with his swords. "I still hear the joys of fighting." He kicked the broken staff and stalked away.

At the sight of Ose disappearing, Hope's battle rage vanished, replaced by nausea. Damn, what was she thinking? She stood staring numbly at the dead bodies in the courtyard, innocents, defending their homes. If she did nothing the threat would have finished. She had murdered. Stupid. Stupid. So stupid.

Wrapped up in her own thoughts, she did not realize Brian stood beside her until his hand squeezed her shoulder. Hope stiffened, wondering if she was about to be yelled at. His face was a frozen mask.

"We must seek our horses before they are lost or stolen," he stated, his voice noncommittal. "The battle is almost over. They will not need our help."

"Brian…"

The din of fighting faded. They stumbled through the wreckage, stepping around the dead when they could. Hope tried to think of something to say, explain, when Brian said, "It was the battle rage in you. I know. As I have difficulty controlling my magic, you too have trouble containing your emotions when aroused. We each suffer in our own way." He added in a soft voice, "Do not worry, there will be other times."

He knows. Is this the real reason I kill dragons? Not for revenge, but for the release of all constrains? There is no Apophis, no Diane. I'm not Mistress Nearwood, First Family. I can let myself go, be free. I don't have to worry about anyone else; my true passions emerge?

"Sometimes the fury of my life boils up inside me," Hope admitted. No further explanations offered themselves. Instead, she lifted the long sword and examined it.

The once shiny blade used since monastery days, her

father's sword, blackened to ruin. Panic registered. She thought of what he would say as she ran fingers from the point to the hilt. Deep gouges burned by the demon fire pitted the edges, the tip itself melted into a ball.

"It is ruined."

"We will buy you another," Brian assured her.

"This was my father's," Hope murmured, "and his father's before him." She remembered how proudly the sword hung above the mantle. She'd snatched it down before leaving for training, vowing to kill the last of the demons stalking their world.

The smell of smoke drifted through the air as they picked their way out of the town. When they reached the remains of the outer wall, looting had begun. Out on the plain, in front of ruins of the city wall, Ose erected a throne, a golden one this time, pilfered from the ruler's palace. Booty piled around him in heaps.

Satan waited where Hope left him, Brian's mount blocked from escaping by a brick wall. The stallion stood as if guarding the horse. Hope noticed his hooves were bloody. As she approached, he whinnied and tossed his mane. She patted him on the neck and whispered in his ear, "Good boy."

Squads of Ose's soldiers tramped by, placing more loot on the massive piles. One group hustled a long line of children, half-breeds, humans, and demons, chained at the feet. The acid smell of smoke and death clung to their bodies.

As the guards passed, Brian called out, "What are you going to do with those?" He tried to keep his voice indifferent, as if asking a casual question.

The moloch guard shouted back, "If anyone hungers, meat for the pot. Maybe play toys. Ose will decide."

Those children not already crying gripped their neighbors in terror and whimpered. One boy gazed at Hope pitifully, tears drawing lines down his dirty face. She listened to the wailing, steeling herself against the impulse to rush out and free as many as possible.

"Can't we save those children somehow?" she whispered. Hope furiously racked her brain, devising and dismissing idea after idea. Nothing in her training prepared her for this. Her lips tightened in mounting frustration at the inability to discover a solution. "I don't know how."

Ose sat in judgment as the soldiers dragged the children before him. The moloch waved his arms in dismissal, gesturing toward the kitchens. A guard snapped his whip and hustled the group into the camp.

Brian's jaws locked in rage. "I have no idea either," he grated, "but I will think of something."

During the day, more children stumbled by in chains, along with men and women. Hope watched in helpless fury as some of the defenders, begging for mercy, had their guts ripped out on the spot to the laughter of the demons. By the end of the day, the rape of the city was complete. Hope had long ago run out of tears. Her only comfort was Brian's arm wrapped tightly around her, holding her close, while she watched him think.

Ose commanded barn fires built to supplement the light from the burning buildings. He called his army together.

"We now divide the booty," he declared with a wicked smile.

A cheer erupted from his troops. One of his captains read from a scroll, calling out names or groups. Each stepped forward and received jewels, gold, and sometimes bags of expensive spices or herbs.

Ose spied Hope and Brian standing at the edge of the fires. "Approach," he bellowed, waving all four hands, "for defending your general, my heroes deserve a special reward."

They shoved through the crowd to the envy of those who thought they deserved special attention from Ose also.

109

"Choose," the moloch gestured to the piles of riches scattered in the dirt and hunched forward to watch what they selected, "anything you desire."

Brian studied the plunder and shook his head. "I see nothing I care for, however I spied children taken captive. What is to become of those?"

Ose pursed his lips as if he had not given the prisoners much thought. "Roasted for supper. Some of my men enjoy their flesh. The rest," he sat back and raised his shoulders, "sold for slaves. Why, do you want one?"

Hope glanced at Brian, wondering if the cunning he utilized so easily had leaped to some solution. What was he up to? She hadn't devised a plan for the children's rescue. Had he? She examined his face. It had assumed a crafty expression.

"I had a thought," Brian rubbed his chin, "would they not provide a better use if delivered to a human valley and left there?"

Ose's red eyes opened wide in shock. "Of what good would that do?"

Brian continued smoothly, "The humans contain soft hearts. They will not send children away. This displays your generosity, and perhaps wins favor with those who otherwise would strive against you." He gave a slow wink. "In case you lay siege to a valley, the extra mouths eat up precious food stocks, bringing starvation. It might make the difference between a long battle and a short one."

The moloch leaned back on this throne. "I had not thought of that," he muttered, regarding Brian in a new light as he rubbed his beard. He broke out in a broad grin and reared up, roaring, "You are right." He held two arms skyward stamping the ground with a new Lore Master staff. "Let it be so."

Brian did it. Hope's spirit lifted, feeling a surge of admiration for this man who stood next to her. Perhaps she'd been wrong to label him warlock. *Or,* she thought

110

with a wry smile, *maybe his devious mind was working to their advantage.*

"How about you?" Ose said to Hope. He waved at the pile of treasure. "What will you select?"

Hope startled. The children were safe, that was what mattered. The trinkets displayed held no interest, and even if they did, she was too tired to investigate the spoils. The energy expended during the battle drained her lust for killing, she thought bleakly, remembering the innocents she slaughtered. All she wanted was rest. Her arm throbbed from the burns. Her stomach growled from hunger.

"I–er..." *Let's finish this quickly.* She sighed. *He expects me to select something.* In resigned compliance, she wandered out among the piles.

A long wooden case caught her attention. A feeling of urgency drew her to the box. She handed Satan's reins to Brian and wandered over, lifting the top.

Radiant light flashed from inside. She gasped and turned away blinking until the brilliance dimmed. A silver blade sat nestled in velvet. The light that nearly blinded her emanated from a clear crystal acting as the pommel. Without thinking, she reached out and lifted the sword up.

A thrill ran along her arm, eradicating the pain and filling her soul. Hope made a few experimental swings. The sword acted like an extension of her body, perfectly balanced.

"You have chosen Vajra, have you?" Ose's voice held awe and fear as he stared at the weapon. "Or it has sought you. I thought to destroy that evil, but did not know how," he admitted. "The blade is yours if you dare wield the power that resides within." By the expression on his face, Hope guessed he was happy to get rid of the weapon.

"Th-thank you," Hope murmured, gazing at the sword. A low babble rippled through the assembly, and she realized hundreds of demons riveted on the blade. She stumbled out of the circle and hurried to Brian.

"Look." Hope held the sword out. "What do you make of this? Ose was afraid. Is there some danger we should know?"

"Vajra. I have heard of a weapon named that," he rumbled. Brian examined the length of the blade without touching the edge. "In the ancient language it means, 'God's Sword'. Tales speak of a powerful lord who carried this weapon before either man or demon walked this world. Wielding it, he slew many of his enemies before he was transformed into a celestial being and traveled to another realm."

"The blade drew me to it," Hope murmured. She tried deciphering the runes etched into the metal. She gave up. It was hopeless. "What do you think this sword was doing in that city?"

Brian shook his head. "Who can tell, now? Perhaps it passed in trade, and none knew what they possessed. Maybe, they realized what they held, but were afraid to use it as Ose was." His expression turned grim. "Will you keep it? That blade may be dangerous."

Hope pulled out the old sword and compared the two, side by side. Sorrow laced through her. Even the most skilled metalworker she knew would throw up his hands in frustration trying to restore the damaged weapon. "I have no choice, do I?" She slipped the new sword into her scabbard. "I will have to take that chance. There must be a reason the blade chose me."

Was this what Eldridge meant? Events didn't always appear to be what they were on the plains? Was this chance or some design of fate that brought her to this blade? She determined to investigate more closely when she had the chance.

Brian touched her old sword. "What will you do with this?"

Do? It hurt to think about tossing her father's sword away as if the weapon had no value. The blade held years of memories she didn't want to abandon, to do so was like denouncing a part of herself.

"Wait here."

Hope hurried away.

She ran until the light disappeared from the burning city, and the noise of the army vanished. After the night was silent, she stopped, panting, and fell to her knees.

It killed Hope to leave the sword, but she was determined no one else would ever possess the weapon. The blade had been hers for eight years and her father's for thirty. It saved their lives more than once, and killed seven, no, eight dragons.

She pulled her short sword and dug a pit, deeper than the length of her arms. When she was in trouble of falling in, she kissed the sword reverently, placed the blade at the bottom, and filled the pit quickly before she could change her mind. Using the direction of the demon army as a guide, she placed a large stone on top to mark the spot.

One day I will return, Hope promised the blade. Again, the sword would hang over her mantel in a place of honor.

Trying to restrain tears, she walked back to Brian. "It is done."

He draped an arm around her without saying a word. When the trembling in her body stopped, he said, "Let us pray this new sword serves you as well."

Hope smiled back. "I'm sure..."

A roar reverberated through the night. A burst of fire filled the sky. The beating of a thousand drums assaulted their ears.

Out of the darkness flew a dragon.

Chapter Eight

The winged monster swooped down before Ose. "Apep, you participate in the battle after the fight, huh?" sneered the moloch. He slid his legs out and crossed his ankles, regarding the latecomer with displeasure.

The dragon waddled close to Ose. "I do your bidding," the dragon whispered back. His wings flapped. A blast of wind knocked over those nearest, causing a howl of rage.

"Control yourself, you dim-witted fool!" roared Ose. "I do not want you killing warriors who fought valiantly for me today."

Apep regarded the soldiers who scrambled back to their feet with a mixture of contempt and humor. "So sorry, My Liege," he murmured. He folded his wings tightly to his body. "It will not happen again." The scattered piles of loot caught his attention and the long neck snaked out. He sniffed a bag of gems that had ripped and spilled on the earth.

"You think you have earned yourself a reward for your tardiness and stupidity?" Ose scoffed in surprise. He leaned back on this throne and bellowed with laughter. "Unless you are delivering good news, think again, my scaly friend."

The massive head swung in Ose's direction, the plate-sized eyes burning red. Small flickers of flame shot out of his nostrils in quick bursts.

"The council demands more than my declaration of your greatness, my Lord. It is not my fault," he whispered to Ose. "I told you they needed persuading. My people have never trusted your kind, but I have made progress. Yes, good progress."

Ose's lips formed a silent 'O'. "You have done more than bragged about your prowess then, to the council. What are their demands?"

"They wish to observe and speak to some of your soldiers," the dragon replied. He lifted his head and swung it at the moloch captains who lined up behind Ose. "Not one of your lackeys either. They want common warriors, unconnected with your breed, who will furnish a fair description of your exploits."

Hope nudged Brian and whispered. "They're speaking of the alliance. Ose is using this snake to persuade the dragon nation to ally with him."

Brian replied with a nod, his concentration riveted on the pair.

"...and why do they need that?" Ose replied. He stroked his shaggy beard, perplexed. "What purpose could it serve to hear tales from untrained soldiers?"

Apep refolded his wings, creating a tent around the clearing, and sank to all fours next to the throne, his head even with Ose. "They wish to view what manner of warrior rallies to your banner, hear from their lips the reason for enlisting, and why dragons should do the same."

"They are unreasonable," grumbled the moloch. He waged a finger at the dragon. "Too long have we played these games. You told me..."

"We must do it their way, Master," replied Apep. He spoke in a lower tone. "We are so close now. I have already enticed some of the younger sons to my side who wish to take the place of their elders and..."

"Yes, and it has cost me warriors and baitals I can ill afford to lose at this stage of my plans," countered Ose with a sour smirk. "Also one of your own, your kin, I believe. What good has it done me?"

Hope tugged on Brian's sleeve. "They're talking about the attack on the castle."

He nodded without replying and edged closer, trying to hear what the two said.

"Would you ruin all our plans by not yielding to their

115

requests?"

This is the opportunity we've waited for. While we're in his good graces, maybe...

She stepped forward. "Ose, I apologize for overhearing your conversation, but if I may speak, my companion and I volunteer." she shouted. "We are the only two humans in your army, and no one dare call us lackeys."

The moloch sat in cold calculation, regarding Hope while contemplating the offer in his mind. With a nod, he jeered at Apep, "Are these two acceptable to you and your council? Or does the dragon nation wish me to march my whole army before them for review?"

The dragon stretched out his neck and inspected Hope and Brian. A grunt laced with sulphur blew over them. "Yes, they are mere humans, but they will do." His muzzle shifted back greedily to the bag of jewels. He sniffed.

"Go ahead," the moloch snorted in disgust with a flick of his hands. "We will acquire many more as my empire expands. Make sure the council is aware of that."

A red tongue flicked out and the bag disappeared.

Ose's fingers tapped on the side of his throne as he brought his attention back to Hope and Brian. "You two will leave in the morning with Apep," he declared. The moloch added with a sly wink, "I trust you will present our cause in a good light."

***

That night as they prepared for sleep, Hope asked Brian, "What is this council of dragons?" She frowned. "In my world dragons are loners, they never gather, except when nature calls to mate. Even then, once they've coupled, each separate and never seek a partner again until the season approaches to reproduce."

"I have heard of this council, but rumors only," admitted Brian as he lay down next to her by the fire. He rolled on his side and supported his head with one hand. "With demons and monsters, though, it is always hard to separate the truth from what is fabricated." He settled back and put his hands behind his head. "It is well you spoke up, even without consulting me. Perhaps we can sabotage this alliance before it commences."

Hope rolled on her stomach, pillowing herself with her arms. "That was my idea." She gave him an archly smirk. "If nothing else, we'll discover if the dragons plan to enlist with Ose and warn the valleys of the combined danger."

***

"Your beasts move too slowly," snapped Apep. He flew a hundred yards and hunkered down in the tall grass, waiting for Hope and Brian to catch up. When they reached his location, he complained, "The council is not use to delay. They are *im-por-tant.*" He hissed the words out with loathing. "Yes, very important. We should have reported to the queens by now." He whipped his tail in aggravation.

Hope's displeasure showed all over her face, making it plain his complaints were unwelcome. "We have not set out on this journey to kill our horses. If you're in a hurry, we'll mount *your* scrawny back and you can fly us there. If not, we'll arrive when we arrive."

"They move fast enough when I chase them in the wild," grumbled the dragon. He flapped his wings, blew dust in their faces, and set off into the distance, tossing an evil glare behind him.

Hope watched him go and swoop down on a beast foolish enough to graze in his path. A roar issued along with a shaft of fire, as the dragon tore the hapless animal apart and devoured the entire morsel in two swift gulps.

"Before today, I've never held a conversation with a dragon, and now I know why," she griped. "Do they all complain like old fisherman's wives?"

Brian broke into guffaws. "I am not in the habit of talking with them myself." He gave her a shrewd look. "Since he is inclined though, it is a good chance to pry information from him, if not concerning Ose's plans, at least about his council of dragons."

They caught up to Apep again. Hope called out, "Who is this assembly we must impress that you're so eager to deliver us before? I didn't know your kind travels in flocks." They passed the dragon and kept riding.

Apep waddled after the pair. "These are the elders of each clan. If you take that attitude with these highborn ones Ose will not be pleased. I have spent many months trying to convince my leaders to embrace our side, not to insult them to their faces."

Hope ignored his comment. Apep hurried to keep up. "Is there one among this group who must be addressed with more deference?" She tried to hide her smile behind a hand at the dragon's awkward gait when not flying. "You have a king or headsman?"

"Stupid human," hissed Apep. "The leaders of dragon clans are always female. Shasha is the oldest." He twisted his head to stare at Hope with scorn. "If you wish to think of the exalted one as *queen*," he sneered, "you may do so, however each leader decides for their own tribe what is best."

"Will Ose attempt to conquer the dragons if they don't support him?" Hope asked. "What are his plans for your people? Allies, servants?"

The monster bounded, twisting his head over his shoulder, puzzled. "You do not understand my people, do you? Addlebrained, also, I see. I wonder why Ose agreed to let you represent him. He must be as..." He stopped and stretched his neck up, glaring down. He hissed, "No one conquers dragons." He spread his wings with a huff and zoomed off into the distance.

"I guess not," Hope said with a laugh to his receding back. "I still know enough to slice you open when the time presents itself."

"I will help you if that happens," agreed Brian. "This

118

one has a low opinion of us, and apparently Ose as well. It will be fun."

Hope couldn't refrain from the memory of working together in the cavern after the moloch attack. She pushed her chin down to her chest and started singing in Brian's deep baritone, "Gonna chop on Apep's head all through the day."

An answering sputter exploded from Brian as he choked and held up one hand, red-faced.

"Enough," he gasped at last. "If your singing does not kill me, this blasted heat will." He glared at the sun and wiped sweat from his face. "Once we have learned what the dragons will do I must alert Mictian," he said. "Whether we succeed in sabotaging this alliance or not, whatever information we gather must be told."

Hope nodded. She wondered about the children. The morning after the battle, groups marched away in different directions. "Do you know what valleys Ose will send the captives to?" she asked. "Perhaps Mictian?"

Her words brought a smile to Brian's face. "Still worried about the prisoners? Do not be. Whatever valley they go to will protect women and children. Mictian is the closest, but it is on the opposite side of the mountains and difficult to reach from here. I have a feeling, though, that some refugees will settle in my valley eventually."

Apep decided to ignore them with distaste except for occasional rasps of condemnation for humans. After one barb where the dragon speculated whether humans should be roasted or eaten raw, Hope asked Brian, "Do you think Ose will attack the valleys of the north soon?"

"If Ose plans an invasion, he will choose the weakest and easiest to reach first," he replied gravely. "Mictian defends itself well, as he has already discovered. Let us hope he tries persuasion first. This moloch knows it is easier to win humans over with friendship then fighting."

"What will happen to the exiles from the wars?" Hope

wondered aloud. "Especially the children." She gazed at the plains, the far distant peaks, and thoughts of her son jabbed her heart. "I know you have mixtures in your valley already, but still, these new ones are the spawns of the demons and half-breeds of the plains. Will they be well received?"

Brian swore, indignant. "In this world we do not judge a child by its parents, but by what he or she does and achieves, even the adults if they behave." Hope heard shock in his voice as he spoke to her. "They were all young, not tainted by any evil they have seen in the town. Families will accept them, raise the children, and if they act well, will have no problems."

For the next two days, Apep continued to whine, complain, and insult Hope, Brian, and their mounts, about the unhurried progress.

"Dull-witted beasts and humans," he snorted. "I will be happy when Ose eliminates your species from the valleys." He buffeted his wings in amusement to see the horses panic. "With luck the beasts that call themselves people on the plains will be chattels, too. They are all worthless, except dragons." He flapped hard and landed in front of Satan. "My kind shall rule."

"What happened to Ose?" Hope asked, grinning. "You have forgotten the molochs."

"Oh, of course, the molochs, too," amended Apep hastily. "Have I not named him Lord?"

Hope grew so tired of his criticisms that she ripped up prairie grass and kept it handy to stuff in her ears when the dragon approach.

The one undeniable fact remained, however, Apep proved invaluable at night. Brian stopped casting his magic around their campfire. No beasts or demons approached when the dragon was near.

On the morning of the third day, they encountered a small city. Apep landed beside them in a clatter of noise.

The disturbed people ran to the edge of town, watching the three with intense interest.

"You will remain here for the night," the dragon ordered in his angry lisp. "I go ahead and prepare the council for your meeting." His long neck pointed toward the smoking cliffs rising in the near distance. "I suggest you plan what you will say to the elders and get a good night's rest. You will need it tomorrow."

Hope inspected the startled villagers. "I'm surprised they stay so close to dragon's lairs," she said. "Don't they feel like beasts at a feast?"

"This is the village of Aniste. It is considered neutral territory," answered Apep with a flick of his tail. "Instead of being the meal, they supply the council with food animals. For this they are permitted to remain untouched." He blew a shaft of fire in the air. "They are safer than most. Who would attack a village protected by dragons?"

"We will wait for you tomorrow on the edge of the town," replied Brian. "Let us pray your preparations are adequate."

"I go now." Apep spread his wing, hissed in their faces as a sign of farewell, and glided toward the far hills.

They rode into town.

Hope tried to ignore the curious people who watched them enter the city until she noticed most were half-breeds, dragon and human. Hope stared until the frowns she received made her feel embarrassed. "Do you see an inn?" she asked Brian, to refrain from gawking at the natives.

"No, but I smell wood smoke," he declared. He stood in his stirrups, sniffed the air, and pointed. "There, and I can taste the scent of good food cooking, too. That will be our home for the night."

They left their horses at a small stable in the back and strolled inside. "Food and chambers for the night," Brian told the innkeeper as they sat at a table.

"Food we have in plenty," acknowledged the man. As

he wiped his hands on his apron, Hope saw faint scales running up his arms. "Sleeping chambers, we have one. A single bed if you desire."

Brian glanced at Hope. His lips widened in enjoyment waiting for a reaction.

Hope trembled inwardly at the force of his dark eyes. The intense gaze awoke a primal urge buried inside so long and all but forgotten. To hide her discomfort, she frowned and said, "If the bed is large enough."

The innkeeper chuckled. "Plenty big for the two of you."

"You have bathing facilities?" Hope asked. Tightness engulfed her chest. If she must share a bed with Brian, she didn't want to stink.

He nodded. "Bath is outside, in the back, next to the stable." He looked from Hope to Brian and stuck a greasy hand out. "Payment?"

Brian rummaged in his purse and produced one of his opals, a red one this time. "Here," he flipped the jewel into the waiting palm, "this should cover everything, even our breakfast for the morning."

The innkeeper ogled the gem and rubbed it with his fingers. "Indeed it will, sir, indeed it will." The opal disappeared into his pocket. "Food coming right up."

After they ate, they entered their chamber. A large feather bed filled the room. Hope fell back on the mattress to gauge how much distance she would have between her and Brian. *No more than a hand's breath.* The tightening in her chest arose, usually felt when stalking a dragon. Hope reminded herself sharply she was not dispatching a monster. A good night's sleep was all she needed. She didn't know what she wanted.

Brian surveyed the bed, a small smile flickering on his face as he watched Hope confusion.

"If you wish, I will sleep in the stables with the horses," he said. "It is of no great matter to me."

Hope pushed away her agitation. "We have spent how many days on the trail together alone? I think I'll be safe enough. If not," she touched the handle of her short sword with a wink. She dragged her pack across the floor and tossed it on the bed, withdrawing a piece of cloth she used for washing. "I am going to see what kind of bathing arrangements this pigsty has." She stepped close to Brian and sniffed, wrinkling her nose. She stared him in the eye. "You'd better come along and hope they supply soap."

The 'bath' consisted of two wooden stalls, separated by planks, with fiber curtains. Three half-breed boys stood ready with buckets of lukewarm water, which they kept hauling from a kettle, to dump over the top. Hope found soap, sort of, a tray of scented sand tucked on a shelf. She scrubbed herself raw, removing layers of accumulated dirt she'd acquired for weeks.

Between the slats of the partition, Hope could observe Brian as he washed. She was not body-conscience. Nudity of neither men nor women ever disturbed her. It was a way of life where servants helped groom the upper classes, and the lower wore breechcloths or nothing at all, while working on hot days.

This was the first time Brian completely undressed, and the sight of his deep chest with short curly hairs, and thick muscular shoulders, sent an electric shock through her body.

After almost drowning in the shower, they dried themselves quickly, hurried back to their room, and climbed into bed.

At least the sheets are clean. Hope snuggled into the mattress and stretched. She heard Brian release a grunt of approval as he made himself comfortable. In the dark, she sensed him beside her, wriggling his hard body to find a better position.

Mixed emotions battled within. He was kind, considerate, and thought of the people around him. He was also devious. He had none of the phobias the men of her world harbored about half-breeds or the women who bore them. Yet, in times of stress, he'd behaved as if she were a mere vessel to empty at his will, almost killing her in the process.

She smelled the faint scent of leather and sweat the sand hadn't completely washed away, heard the deep breathing, felt the warmth of his body. Hope wondered if a hand would reach out.

When no touch came, she said, "Brian?"

His gentle snores greeted her.

Hope smirked and went to sleep.

***

Apep impatiently clapped his wings the next morning as they moved to the edge of the town.

"What took you so long?" he rasped, flicking his tail. "The council waits. This is no way to win their favor."

"We would impress your leaders less if we present ourselves tousled-haired and half asleep," yawned Hope. The bed was comfortable and Brian found it necessary to shake her awake twice. With a contemptuous waved of a hand for his constant whining, she dismissed his newest complaint. "Lead on worm, we're here now."

The dragon shoved out his long neck and hissed. "Follow me then, *humans*." He leaped into the air.

Rage filled Hope as they rode after Apep. She kept it under control. She would fix him later. First they had to deal with the council.

Cracks developed under their feet. Tough grass gave way to burnt earth, dust and cinders rose around the horses' hooves as they minced toward high cliffs. Apep waited at a gap between the hills. He glanced at the fissure and said, "I will go first and announce you. Remember, the moloch depends on your testimony so present yourself well."

Brian said to Hope, "I wonder what the penalty is if we do not do well?"

124

Hope didn't answer. Instead, she loosened her sword, stalking behind Apep through the gap.

Twelve mounds fashioned a loose circle around a dusky pit. Long necks poked from cave mouths, weaving back and forth. Tongues flickered, tasting the vibrations of Hope and Brian long before they crossed into plain view.

Apep squatted in the middle of the depression. His head swayed in sympathy with the dragon queens.

"These are the warriors Ose sends you," the dragon exclaimed. "*Humans.* Even humans now rush by their own volition to promote his banner." He swung his massive head toward Hope and Brian. "Examine these warriors as you wish, discuss the moloch's power. They will speak the truth." He bowed his head and backed out of the circle. Before he left, his voice dropped into a whisper for Hope and Brian only to hear, "The largest cave is that of Shasha. Mark it well." He ducked his head low one more time to the queens and left.

Brian raised his voice. "As Apep said, we are warriors of Ose. What do you wish to ask us?"

One scaled head bent to him, red eyes glared. "You are human. Why do humans wish to unite with Ose when he vows to make war on the valleys?"

"We covet power and the scent of power," Brian shouted back for all to hear. "Ose grants wealth, or destruction. We chose wealth." He injected all the arrogance possible in the next sentence, "If you crave to preserve your riches, fear him, for he will take all you possess."

Hope heard babbled whispers among the elders. One said, "We are dragons and fear no one, certainly not a moloch, even if he has an army behind him."

Another head snaked down, this one centered on Hope. "These are not ordinary humans. This one has the smell of power."

The first dragon answered, "I sense only the odor of

125

magic." She sniffed Brian. "Good or bad, that will not harm us."

"Not him, the female." The serpentine neck twisted, angry eyes searching along Hope's body. "She holds a sword of power. The blade has killed many of those that lived before."

Warmth radiated up Hope's thigh. She touched the hilt of the blade and felt the crystal of the sword emitting faint warmth.

She braced herself, unsure if the dragons were preparing to strike or were curious about the blade. When no attack occurred, she took the opportunity to analyze their faces, observing their expressions.

Eleven sets of eyes riveted on her. Hope searched for the twelfth. They had withdrawn back into its cave. Shasha hid herself from the potential danger of the weapon. All that showed was a red gleam and occasional flash of dragon breath.

Hope repeated to herself one of the monk's favorite sayings. *Boldness leaves with age. The old monster is the wisest and slyest. Beware the old.*

"Is this the power that unlocked the gate between worlds?" A third elder sniffed cautiously.

They know. Hope tried to think of something to say. How to extract the information needed?

She shook her head. "No that is for Ose. He alone commands the door."

"You lie, human," the dragon hissed back. "For centuries our young have wandered through. The knowledge of where the portal is was lost, but passage remained free until the earth itself is closed. Lately the council has sensed a change in the sky. We felt a rumbling underground that was not the usual quaking of the earth, but something different. The door may have reopened. Again I ask, have you unlocked the doorway between worlds?"

They do not know where it is, but how is that possible?

"If your dragonets have beheld the portal and roamed between, one of your people must know its position. Why not check for yourself? I think you're the one who lies," Hope challenged.

Shasha's head emerged from the cave. She whispered, "Many wandered in, few leave. Children are forgetful. They are more akin to wild animals than dragons. None remembered the journey well enough to relate it to adults."

An answering rattle of assent echoed off the cliffs from the balance of the dragons.

Shasha continued, "Long ago, our ancestors forbid the young from entering the hills where the passage lies, but still some fell under its power and were lost to us. In time, the gods who live in the earth shook the mountains and closed the doorway. Its location was forgotten, and the portal dissolved for a time."

"Do dragons fear every rumbling of the earth?" *They don't know its location, or that it's accessible. Is this why they negotiate with Ose, to discover the truth?*

The heat within the enclosed space was unbearable. Sweat trickled down Hope's side, running along her chainmail shirt.

Shasha's head weaved in an intricate pattern, the nostrils shooting out short blasts of sulphur-infused flame. "Dragons fear nothing, but if the passage is exposed, we do not wish to lose our children. Apep talks of the moloch marching an army through. We do not care, but our young must be preserved against this threat."

Shasha and the rest clattered their scales, ominous growls issuing from their throats. "We wish to be guaranteed that none of our offspring will venture through the passage. Apep makes hints, but promises nothing. We are not even sure Ose knows the location."

The temperature within the circle had reached

127

physically unbearable levels. Hope whispered to Brian, "We have to leave, this heat is killing me." Perspiration darkened her clothes. The bare soil shimmered with scorching air rising.

Brian nudged Hope and offered a barely perceptible nod. "If Apep will not talk of the doorway, neither are we allowed to," he shouted, "but note this, Ose does not bargain. He demands loyalty and friendship from those beneath him. He will conquer both worlds. Be a subject people and perhaps he will grant your wish, in time, or not."

Three of the elders vented bellows of disgust and withdrew their heads. Brian continued: "As a vassal you rule your own hunting grounds. As slaves, you will not. The choice is yours."

Silence fell in the circle.

Shasha surveyed the remaining elders. "You have offered us much to think about, humans. We are creatures of passion, and must wait a time before we make clear decisions. Retire to the village. Tomorrow we will speak again." The remaining heads gathered and Hope and Brian found themselves alone.

"Thank the gods," Hope gasped as they hurried out into the cooler air. "If we had stayed in that oven one more minute I would have fried."

Apep wait on the far side of the cliffs. "I listened," he said. "You did not speak well. I do not think Ose will be pleased when I report what you said."

"They must know," Hope said. "All must realize Ose's greatness." She paused, thinking. "What is this doorway between worlds they speak of? Ose told us nothing, nor did you mention we need speak of a portal we are unaware of." She waved a finger in his face, pretending outrage. "Perhaps it is you who have not done well. You should have prepared us better." *If you know his plans, how do we extract them from you?*

"Ose will not say if he possesses exact knowledge of the doorway," Apep admitted. "He hints, and so must I. In that regard you acted well." Apep's long neck swung toward the cliffs. Fire swept the sky as the elders debated. "If you are asked again, repeat only the moloch holds that information and it is his and his alone." He stretched his wings. "I fly to Ose to report what has occurred so far."

"You are not waiting to hear what the council decides?" Brian asked.

"I will return, if not tomorrow then the next. Once you receive their reply, go back to the army. I will meet you on the trail." He leaped into the air and soared off.

They mounted their horses.

Brian watched him go until he vanished. "We shall leave," he said at last, "Mictian must be warned."

Hope shook her head. "We can't, not yet. There's too much we still don't know."

Brian's eyes bore into hers. "We have learned enough. Ose plans to conquer this world. He is trying to recruit the dragons. Whether he holds the secret of the passage makes no difference, nor does it if the dragons obey him." His jaws were set in determination.

"You're right," Hope said. A twisting in her stomach threatened to engulf her body. Duty called. With mental anguish, realization dawned. His support was not only anticipated, but carved. Without realizing it, this man had become an extension of herself, a part never missed until it vanished.

Hope gulped and said, "You go and warn your people, but I will remain."

Shock filled Brian's face. "Why? You must go with me."

"I have to discover what Ose knows about the doorway," she said, urgently. "Is he repeating a rumor he heard, or has he navigated the passage himself? If he plans to lead an army through, my people are in a much danger as yours."

What of my son?

Agitation filled Brian's voice, his expression grim. "What will you tell Apep when you face him? When he sees me missing he will suspect something is wrong."

Hope was wondering the same thing. "I'll think of an excuse," she said. She smiled at him, laying a hand on his arm. "Now go, everything will be all right."

Brian slumped. He gazed at Hope bleakly with indecision and worry, the cords on his neck bunched as he struggled to decide what to do. "I will go," he replied at last, "but after I have warned Mictian, I will find you. I cannot leave and allow you to deal with these demons by yourself. I..." He started to say something else, shook his head, and instead, reached out and gripped her hand tightly with both of his.

Hope replied with a hard squeeze of her own and fought back the desire to pull him close. Brian released her slowly, and without a backward glance, tugged on his reins and rode away.

Hope's heart sank as she watched him go. Was she being too stubborn? Time remained to catch up. He was right. She could leave and then warn her people of possible danger.

No. To shout an alarm of danger without positive information was worse than useless, they would call her a liar. If she brought townspeople to the passage to prove the story true, she would be believed, but at what cost? War between her world and this one? The cries of "Kill the demons," rang in Hope mind. She must stop Ose if he really planned invasion. If not, discover a way to destroy the passage.

Hope rode back to town. The room was still unoccupied, and took it for another night. For the first time in her life, she felt alone. On missions abroad to kill dragons, she never experienced a sense of loss before.

Maybe it was because she would be home in a few days. Brian and she trekked together for weeks now, constant companions, facing danger. She missed him.

Don't be silly, he's a client, she told herself. *As soon as I confirm what this moloch knows, I'll be gone. Probably never see Brian again unless I settle in Mictian valley, and if the bridge between our worlds is terminated...*

With more determination than she felt Hope forced Brian out of her mind and fell asleep.

***

Screams outside her window woke her before the sun. A glance in the street at the village and surrounding area told why.

Shasha approached. The dragon queen bellowed fire across the sky announcing her approach. The townspeople ran in panic, dragging their biggest and best herd animals forward as she landed on the hard packed earth.

The dragon bent low and swallowed an animal whole. "Enough," she declared as one more bleating creature was offered. "I seek the female human, where is she?" Shasha blew a stream of fire into the air to emphasize the demand.

The townspeople erupted in a babble of confusion.

Hope threw clothes on and hurriedly buckled her sword belt, leaped on Satan, and raced to the edge of town. "I am here. Have you brought an answer from the council?"

The gigantic head swung until Shasha's face was scant feet away from Hope, the smell of brimstone filling the air, her sinuous body coiled in menace. The dragon queen grumbled, "The answer is, no answer."

"What?"

Fire leaked out either side of the dragon's nostrils. Satan cantered backward as a scorching blast of air engulfed the space they had rested.

Hope patted the horse's neck and eased him forward again, muttering words of encouragement to the frightened

131

animal. "Is that the word I shall fetch to Ose, then?" Her voice dripped with humor. "The dragons can't make up their minds?"

The sound of levity was not lost on the dragon queen.

"Of course not," Shasha snapped back. "The council did not reach any decision, but wish to send an observer they trust," she retorted. "It was agreed to dispatch my newest son. He is young, and has only seen fifteen years, but wise, and he is one of the few who have passed between lands and returned."

"He has seen this new world?"

The dragon's head bobbed up and down, sweeping the sky for her offspring. "Yes, we thought him dead for months, until he stumbled back into the rookery, confused. We coaxed enough from him to realize where he had been. His name is Bane, he will arrive soon."

Hope froze. Bane. The sound forgotten for so long. The name the attacking adolescent dragon kept screaming. The dragon who... The memory of lying on the earth, bloody, in pain and shock flooded back.

Hope's voice quivered. She said, "Does he remember what he did in that world, the people he met?"

Shasha checked the air again. "I sense him approaching now." She said to Hope. "No, when we discovered him he was in shock. For many weeks he did not speak at all, but cowered, crying his name over again, not realizing he was home, safe with his own kind once more." Her voice mellowed at the thought of that time. "He was still a dragonet, and they retain little. Afterwards he could recall but few impressions of a world bereft of his own kind."

He doesn't even remember? Hope clenched her teeth, staring straight ahead in concealed rage. How? She would never forget, nor forgive. Never.

A black dot expanded in the sky, spread wings, and made a soaring landing beside the old dragon. Two necks twisted together in an embraced and untwined. The young male studied Hope with curiosity, while his dame announced with pride, "This is my son, Bane."

Chapter Nine

Hope's first urge was to leap on the beast, draw her sword, and drive the blade into his heart. Her hand crept to the hilt, fingers closing around the grip, knuckles white. She would cut off his head and *eat* his heart. *Rapist. Monster.*

The blade was half drawn. Beneath the hand, the gem glowed hot, responding to her anger.

Hope stopped. *Not yet.* Her mind whirled, devising heinous ways of greater magnitude to seek revenge. *Stab his heart, cut off his limbs and wings. Yes. The heart would regrow first. He would live, but be helpless as she had been.* She would tell him what he'd done, what pain he caused.

Hope slid the sword back into its sheath. *I won't kill him now. No, a quick death was too good for this animal. Better to confront him out on the plains, alone, where I can slice him up slow.*

"He is the one who'll accompany me?" Her voice was frozen.

Shasha nodded. "Yes." The long neck swung in a wide circle, hunting in all directions. "Where is your companion? He is missing."

Hope had worked on this lie and practiced all night until she believed the story herself. "He speeds to the nearer valleys of humans to recruit more soldiers for Ose's cause. He will rejoin me at the army."

Shasha inclined her head as if that sounded reasonable. She said to Bane, "Remember, watch and listen. The council waits for your report." With a flap, she was gone.

That's right, Mamma, fly away. Leave me with this one. Hope sized up the young male and said, "We have a long journey ahead of us. We must depart also." She jerked on Satan's reins and ambled off into the yellow plains.

Bane waddled beside her, for a long minute neither spoke. Hope braced herself for the dragon to acknowledge her presence somehow. *He lied, he must remember me,* she kept repeating to herself. She shot him sideways glances, waiting.

When he remained mute, she said, "Your mother tells me you have crossed into this other world? She said you recall nothing? I don't believe it. How could you not?" *Let's see how you squirm out of this, you snake.*

His reply was slow in coming. "I remember cold. Cold and wind," Bane said in a low whisper. His eyes opened wide, his claws curling and uncurling like Hope remembered them the day he attacked her. "I was lost, hungry, scared, and the smell of the death of my kind engulfed me." A shudder ran down his spine. "All around was hate for any of my race." His voice whispered even lower; his head sank to grass level. "I cried out my mother's name, my name. I felt confusion. I ran, flew, and ran again."

"You recall nothing of the people you saw or the things you did?" She watched his eyes closely, sure he was hiding the memory of their meeting. How could he violate a child and forget about the encounter?

"Only dim thoughts, more like dreams than reality." Bane's long tongue flicked out and tasted the vibrations in the air. "Pain and fear filled me. I lost all sense of time, where I went, what I did. Cold surrounded me when I entered that awful world. When I was there, it was a nightmare, best forgotten." His body shivered.

Hope stopped and stared at him fully. His eyes were large and stared into space, puzzled. *I don't believe it. He doesn't remember.*

"You dragons must be savage little brutes when you're young," she muttered, "to behave with no regrets for your acts afterward."

Bane's tone softened. "The one sound I think I

135

remember is a voice crying with me in my pain. This I recall. I was not alone. The voice saved my life. Without it I would have died there."

Hope tried to close her mind to the memory of that moment. *I wasn't crying for you, you bastard, I was crying for myself.* "I'm sure that made you feel better, whatever you did in that world." *Blind him, also. He'll remember my voice then, it'll be the last thing he'll hear.*

She nudged Satan into a walk, trying to gauge how far to go from town before putting her plans into reality.

"I sense you disapprove of my journey and lack of thought in that world," Bane said, looking at Hope gravely. "We all do things in our youth that are wrong, and we forget. Children are foolish in that manner. Is that not true with humans also?"

She remembered her father saying not to ride into the mountains alone. How dangerous it was. She had nodded solemnly and after he left for town, saddled Satan, a colt then, and ridden away. The thrill of discovery and the taste of the forbidden driving both farther than they'd ever gone alone before.

How right Father was.

She straightened in the saddle, wetness streaking the sides of her cheeks. In order to hide her emotions, she bent and stroked Satan's neck. "Perhaps."

What did it matter if he doesn't realize what he did? He's an animal, a monster. Get him out on the plains and have revenge.

The town faded behind them.

Vacant prairie stretched to the horizon.

Hope's hand inched to her sword. "Bane, this is the perfect place to…"

A red fireball crashed between Satan and the dragon, more struck behind. One of the blazing orbs hit Bane on the tail, elating a howl of pain and fear from the startled monster. In reflex, he swung his head. Fire shot into the sky.

"Baitals," Hope screamed. Five black shadows zoomed above as she dug her heels into Satan's ribs. "MOLOCHS RIDING BAIITALS. The horse leaped and broke into a gallop.

More balls of fire slammed into the earth. Hope yanked left on the reins, and then right, starting an evasive action she hoped would throw the demons off her trail.

Dragon fire shot over her head. Hope twisted in time to see two of the molochs burst into flame along with their mounts as Bane swooped down on the pair.

He set off after the surviving three, flapping hard to catch the baitals. The demons checked their headlong flight and soared straight into the sky, looping to fall behind the dragon.

Bane reared in mid-flight, breaking with his wings and curling in the air. Dragon blaze met Lore Master fire in a shower of sparks that left Hope dazed. When her sight cleared, Bane was landing beside her, black streaks scoring his wings and body.

"Are you all right?" he asked.

"Yes." The smoking, charred remains of molochs and baitals scattered in heaps all around. The yellow grass burnt in a wide circle, leaving Hope and Satan standing in a black clearing.

One of the baitals, wings shattered, attempted a hopping escape. Hope sprang off Satan, her long sword clutched at her side, and strode after the fleeing creature. The gem of the hilt pulsed madly as she caught up to the monster. Rage built inside as she towered over the bloody animal.

The demon stared back, growled, showing sharp fangs and blood-red eyes glistening with evil. As if on its own accord, the sword jerked her hand up and chopped down.

She slipped the blade slowly from the crumbled body, fingers frozen to the hilt in shock. That was not her act. No, a strange force, not her own, had guided that killing stroke.

Hope held the weapon up. *The sword is possessed. I cannot trust it.* Faint runes shown in the smoking blood, seeming to wiggle in delight as she gazed at the long lines. Hastily she cleaned the blade on an unburnt patch of grass.

Bane waddled up beside her. "Why were we attacked?" she asked.

The dragon searched the sky, his eyes smoldering. Satisfied no further assault was imminent, he replied, "Ose is not the only moloch vying for power in this land, nor the sole demon. Perhaps there is some infighting we are not aware of." He checked the air again, "or a random meeting. Who can know?"

Lore Masters astride baitals in the middle of nowhere? Hope didn't think so. Someone wanted Bane or she dead. Maybe both. She scrubbed at her face, made a grimace as black soot fell off her scalp, and remounted Satan. The stallion reared, his body trembling in fear. Instinctively, she calmed the horse with a pat, whispering soothing words into his ear. A low rumble shook the air. Bane was watching. The vibrations he made were a mark of approval. Hope looked apprehensively to see what damage he had sustained.

The scorch marks along his tough scaled body rapidly dissipated. Within a matter of minutes, they faded away. "I thought magic didn't affect dragons?" Hope said.

"The darkness bothers us some," Bane examined his skin. "But as you see, the results are negligible." He snorted, unconcerned. "It is the difference between white and black magic, "The light will not draw a mark, because dragons, by nature, are of the good."

"We had best keep moving," she said in disgust. Smoke from the fires bellowed to the sky. She waved a finger upward, pointing, "If more demons are in the area that will act like a signal for our location." She nudged Satan into a gallop. The horse jumped, glad to distance himself from the flames.

Bane kept up in a half-flapping, half-waddle gait. "You need not worry," he advised. "Dragons have far-sight. I see no one else in the area."

Hope slowed Satan to a walk. "Are you sure?"

"Yes," Bane said, "and if by some chance we are bothered again, I am here to shield you. The attack took me by surprise this time. I will be on my guard for the next one."

Guilt rang in his voice. His eyes glowed scarlet at the thought that base creatures as molochs and baitals had marked him, even slightly.

Hope frowned and cursed under her breath. "I need no defending by a creature such as you." Emotions clashed within. He had acted bravely and saved her life, volunteered protection, but…"You are different from the other dragons I have met. Apep would not offer to safeguard a human. Why do you?"

"I have been changed." Hope noticed his head never stopped scanning the sky, but the red was gone from his eyes. "*That. Place.* Made me different. As for Apep," the dragon snorted with a short burst of flame, "he may well be the one who dispatched those molochs. He is a sly one. He leaves his scales in too many places."

Hope chuckled despite the seething hatred for Bane. "I like that expression. I must remember it."

"Really?" Bane said delighted Hope was more relaxed around him now. "It is an old dragon saying. It means someone that conspires."

Much to her horror she felt herself drawn to Bane. *Enjoying* his company. Hope released a sigh.

***

When they broke camp the next morning, Apep landed. The older dragon glared at Bane and then rasped to Hope, "What was the verdict of the council, and what is he," Apep shot Bane a malicious glance, "doing here?"

139

Before Hope answered, Bane stuck his head straight out and hissed, "The council has ordered *me* to accompany Hope to Ose's camp. I am to observe and report."

The bigger dragon loomed above him. "What nonsense is this? Cannot they make up their minds?" He stepped menacingly forward.

Bane elevated his head, kept his ground, and stared at Apep. "It is not for *you* to decide what the council will do or not do." His stance displayed malice. Small puffs of smoke shot from his nostrils in quick spurts.

For the first time, Hope noticed the skin under Bane's throat swell and turn red. This phenomenon was totally unexplained. None of her instructors mentioned it. She wondered what the bloating implied.

Apep fixed on the color, and backed off, grumbling. He said to Hope, "Ose is on the advance to a human valley. I will show you the way." His head swung in a circle. "Where is Brian?"

"Gone to recruit more of our kind," Hope replied quickly, "but now that Ose is marching, I don't know if he'll locate us."

A deep growl reverberated in Apep's throat. "It does not matter. If he wishes to find Ose, let him search the sky for smoke from the burning valley, or listen to the wind and hear the shrieks of the dying." His nose pointed to the northeast. "We travel that way." He beat his wings and lifted into the air, landing a quarter of a mile away waiting for Hope and Bane to overtake him.

Bane watched him go with contempt. From his throat, a deep, gurgling roar issued forth. Apep looked back, the same snarl echoing from his mouth.

Hope blinked at the exchange between the two dragons. The growl in Bane's voice startled her, bellowing out like the warning moan of a predator on the hunt. What was that all about? She dismissed it from her mind for the moment and hurried after Apep. She needed to know if the

140

valley he talked about was Mictian. If so, she would have to warn the people.

She reached the dragon. "Which valley is Ose attacking?" she gasped.

"Does it matter?" snapped the dragon. "All human valleys are the same, all are our enemies." He left again.

Hope estimated the direction in which he flew. If she remembered correctly the brief glimpse she'd had of the map in King Gregory's main hall, then their path would take them past Mictian, farther north toward the tip of the mountains the valleys nestled in. She still recalled many human settlements marked on this side of the range, but at least Brian's home was safe for now. No divides existed enabling Ose to invade the Southern regions easily.

Bane overtook Hope with a flap of his wings. His tail flicked in displeasure, while a deep gurgle of hatred rumbled in his chest.

"I sense ill will between you and Apep," she said, unsure if she should rile him again.

Bane blew a long stream of fire. "When he was younger, and had attained his full strength, Apep challenged my mother for control of our clan, a thing unheard of. Males may not be the elder of a dragon clan." The thought made him hiss. "The fool was defeated, of course. No one can dethrone Shasha." He said the last proudly and lifted his tail. "Bad blood has grown between him and I ever since."

"I'm sure Shasha will rule for many years yet," Hope temporized. She breathed a sigh of relief. The last thing wanted was these two battling right now.

Still annoyed, Bane continued, "When Apep was defeated, the whole clan laughed at him for his folly. In his rage, Apep renounced all ties with us. Since then he has snuck from dragon clan to dragon clan, spreading rumors and lies, trying to subvert my mother's voice in the council. From the time he united with Ose, it has grown worse. He tries to divide the tribes using fear of invasion by the moloch as an excuse."

"Apep is devious, all right," Hope agreed, watching the dragon as they moved toward him. "If he's also using Ose for his own ends, it wouldn't surprise me."

Bane lowered his voice. "This is one of the reasons the council decided to send someone back with you. We must learn if Ose wishes us for true allies, or Apep has devised some scheme for his own ends."

"He holds the fruits of alliance out with one claw, and the stick of slavery hanging over one's head if you refuse," Hope answered. "Neither one of which he possesses at the moment."

Bane's eyes sparkled and he bowed his head in agreement. "You are wise. You think like a dragon."

Three days travel brought the trio to the foot of the mountains. No more outbreaks of hostilities exploded between the two dragons. Apep stayed away from Hope and Bane as much as possible. He only addressed the two during the day to grumble at the slow pace they made. At night, Bane went so far as to make a protective circle of his head and tail around Hope, Satan, and their fire, as if defending the two against possible attack from the older dragon.

Smoke rising in the distance indicated the location of Ose long before the valley materialized. The moloch sprawled on his throne drawn along the path by a wagon, his Lore Master's staff cradled in his arms across his black stomach, the army crawling up the slopes. The clashing of battle reverberated from the heights, while the earth shook from the explosions of Lore Master's fire.

Chained to the rear of the wagon, two molochs tried their best to keep up. Dragged and bleeding, their horns severed at their skulls, they issued bleating noises begging Ose to put them to death. One of the prisoners was the captain Hope argued with the first day she and Brian enlisted with Ose's troops.

Ose bellowed orders to his army, Apep beside him, whispering urgently in his ear as they bumped along.

"Where is Brian?" Ose demanded at once as Hope rode up beside him. "I am told he has deserted and fled to the valleys."

"Not desertion," Hope declared. She shot Apep a look of hate. "He visits humans across the plains to recruit new soldiers for you. This one," she gestured to the dragon, "was told that. What he whispers now I do not know." She changed the subject. "We did not think it necessary for both of us to escort the emissary from the dragons here, nor would your campaign of conquest start so fast." She waved to Bane. "This is Bane, son of Shasha, elder of the dragon council." Hope realized she was introducing the monster who'd attacked her to the demon that wished to conquer this world. *I hope I'm doing right.*

"Why are these dragged along by your wagon?" Bane asked the moloch, pointblank. The two demons cowered on their bleeding knees, waiting for Ose's favor.

The disgraced captains glanced fearfully at Bane, but shifted to Apep with greater terror.

"They thought to conspire against me," Ose replied with a neglectful waved of his hands. "These two are the leaders. They refused to talk of who else plots for my downfall." He gave the dehorned ex-captains a malignant glare. "This is their punishment before they die."

The dragon studied the two, unconcerned by their fate. "Your wrath for those who oppose you will be reported to the council," Bane replied with a bow of his head.

Ose dipped his horns slightly also. "I am honored to meet you," he replied. "We will talk about this and the balance of our concerns later." He waved all four arms at the summit of the pass. "As you can see, my army fights now, however the battle is almost finished. Stay with me and you can observe how my soldiers crush all before

143

them." He gestured to Hope with his staff. "If you have any questions in the meantime, the human female will answer."

The towers guarding the entrance to the pass lay shattered. Crushed bodies of the defenders sprawled like broken dolls in the dirt. Troops poured through the gap into the valley below. The wagon Ose drove in bounced upward until it reached the top and they had a view of the troops assaulting the castle.

Large sections of the landscape blazed, crops ripe for the harvesting on fire. The sky was black with baitals, their moloch riders hurling balls of flame on anything that stirred. Over the castle, the assault was intense. The towers smoked, huge chunks of the parapets had vanished, while the keep blazed with red creeping down the sides.

Around the outer wall, Ose's army swarmed like ants. As they watched, part of the barrier crumbled.

"You see," Ose shouted to Bane and Hope. "Nothing stands up to my might. *Nothing.*" The troops rushed the fissures that sprang up all over the wall. The moloch nodded in satisfaction.

Hope winced, thinking of the death the inhabitants of the castle would suffer at the hands of the invading demons. *I hope these people had sense enough to evacuate the women and children before the fighting started. Please let the children be gone.*

A malevolent laugh issued from Apep. His whispered words to Bane, "They thought they were safe because a dragon promised to live in their valley, one of the lesser clans they made an alliance with. He never reached this vale, and now one of my own has his lair."

Bane displayed no reaction. Instead, he said to Ose, "You have indeed assembled a great force." He watched as the baitals landed to help in the looting. "Who will be your next victim?"

Ose cackled and swung his arms in a wide circle encompassing the sky. "Everyone who does not bow to me," he exclaimed. The moloch hinted broadly, "In this world and others also."

He does know. Hope glanced at Bane. The dragon scrutinized Ose as if reading her thoughts.

After the battle, the moloch ordered a victory fire built. Barrels of wine and ale, looted from the valley, stood waiting for the demons. Ose presided over the dividing of the booty, lounging on his throne still atop the wagon.

Amidst the shouting of the victors and the cries of the victims he announced, "We will continue along the mountain chain, attacking towns and valleys in our path. You have all seen our power. Nothing stands in our way." Ravenous eyes gleamed back in the firelight. "Soon all the Southern Plains will bow their necks to us."

A roaring cheer of approval spread. Among the loudest was Apep. He huddled close to Ose, head reared, forked tongue flickering in excitement. When the moloch raised his arms, the dragon blew a shaft of fire into the sky and howled with glee. As the flames died away, he swung his head, the last wisps of fire playing over the two moloch prisoners secured to the wagon.

"What have you done?" shouted Ose, rising from his throne and waving his staff in rage. "Stupid dragon, cannot you control your fire? You have killed them before I questioned those two." Fire of his own shot from his staff, threating to destroy those closest to him, Hope retreated, placing Bane's tail between her and Ose for protection.

Apep cringed, abashed, his head slumping between his forelegs like a scolded dog. "Your Majesty, I am sorry," he whined. "In my excitement for your great victory today, and more to ensue, my joy exceeded my sense." He kept his head bowed in supplication.

Ose glared at him, breathing hard. With slow deliberation, he sat in a huff. "I will overlook this mistake of yours for now, however..." his staff shook at the dragon, making a ripping motion, "...if it happens again you head will hang on this wagon as a warning to those who foster mistakes instead of obedience. Understand me?"

"Yes, Sire. Thank you, Sire," moaned Apep, groveling closer in gratitude. "I am your faithful servant forever."

Hope and Bane watched from the outer edges of the throng. "That was no accident," Hope whispered to Bane out of the corner of her mouth. "Look at his expression."

Apep had resumed his position next to Ose with his head high. The dragon crowed with malicious glee as guards dragged the remains of the two charred molochs away.

* * *

During the next days and weeks, Ose fulfilled his promise of bloodshed and conquest. Hope was used to seeing the devastation left from the aftermath of dragon attacks, but the carnage she witnessed now caused a physical churning in her stomach she couldn't contain. Body parts littered the trail of the army, left by the marauding demons who tortured their victims on the march. The screams of the dying echoed in dreams.

Time lost meaning. Long afterward, all Hope remembered were burnt arms and legs protruding from the trampled mud, and whole towns smoldering in ash. The stoning of half-breeds and their mothers was bad, but even at the height of the demon wars, when free companies and monsters struggled across the plains for domination of the world, brutality on this scale was unknown in her land. At night, the nameless faces of the dead haunted her dreams. For some reason the phrase, 'Bloody Earth' kept echoing through her head.

Hope created excuses not to participate in these battles, explaining to Ose that Bane demanded she stay close and explain what was happening. "And of course, the magnificence of your battle strategy," she fawned, all the while hoping the moloch would not insist they stroll the battlefields with him and gloat over the devastation.

As time wore on, however, Ose cast scowls in her direction. Apep was a constant whisperer in his ear. The disapproval of the moloch's comments reached a point Hope feared for her life, only Bane's presence kept Ose from hauling her physically into battle. At one point, he suggested throwing Hope into the front lines to recount a battle first handed.

As the conquests continued to mount, Apep became Ose's chief source of communication between the moloch's ever-growing empire. Every day or two, the dragon took flight, bringing messages to the captains of the territories he left behind. Hope watched as the power of Apep increased, and her insides twisted harder.

Bane was a mute witness to this destruction, neither making comments, nor showing emotion, approval, or dissent. Nevertheless, his shrewd eyes picked up every detail of the savagery, and especially the influence Apep had over Ose.

He did say to Hope once after observing the torture of a prisoner for the amusement of Ose and his captains, "This would not be the behavior of dragons. We kill for food, yes, out of anger or fear, but never for the pure joy of murder."

Hope shuddered as the half-breed ahuizotl had his ribs cut off his spine and his lungs pulled out like wings. Ose and his cronies guffawed in joy. "Only the most base of creatures, humans or demon, would commit these crimes." She turned away to hide the tears.

On two separate occasions, Bane tried to engage Ose in conversation about the portal. The moloch was evasive. "Yes, I know of a new land. I will conquer it in time," he declared, "but that belongs to the future."

Bane was frank in his reply without revealing the true nature of his query. "My people wish to know where this land is to verify its existence."

The moloch brushed him off with, "Your people shall be informed about my plans when they unite with me."

147

The second time Bane brought the subject up, Ose was blunt. "I must have a yea or nay first. Afterwards I will decide." He glared at Hope. "No more humans have rallied to my cause, and as my victories swell, it appears I do not need the help of dragons either."

By the time Ose and his army reached the tip of the mountains, Hope could stomach no more of the slaughter, and events boiled to a head. After one brutal fight, Ose summoned his soldiers and gestured to the west. "In five days, we sack our richest prize yet, the town of Endsland. I have sent emissaries to ask for their surrender and they refused. They trade with valley and town, north and south, and their wealth is beyond measure." He paused while the babble of his men rose to a roar, and then extended his hands for silence. "Have I not done as I promised?"

An answering shout came back, *"Yes."*

"You shall have more. This is only the beginning." Ose nodded in approval at the roars of blood lust, and glanced quickly at Bane and Hope. "All those who will not kneel to me shall feel my wrath, and he that lags shall be lost."

He beckoned to Hope. "Our companion Bane will not need you anymore to recount my exploits. He has seen for himself, and can interpret what I do on his own. When we attack the town you fight in the front with the rest of my men." He waved her away in dismissal.

Hope tried to act indifferent to the threat. She bowed. "Of course, mighty Ose, as you declare," but hurried out of the circle of demons. She'd witnessed enough. No reason remained to stay with the army. Brian never returned. She'd given him up for lost, perhaps he deserted their cause. From the numerous hints Ose dropped, she was sure he knew of the portal to her world, or at least, the general location.

Her most important reason though, was the town. She must warn the people of the impending attack. She crept into her campsite and sat hunched by the fire, thinking.

Hope didn't give a damn about the city itself. That would fall, but the women and children who lived there could still escape. The mountains loomed. Fleeing to their safety was simple. The inhabitants would hide in the canyons until Ose stormed by. Maybe they would flee to the valleys of the north.

Bane wandered into the campsite and stretched out close to the fire. During the previous days the dragon grew increasingly quiet, his attitude meditative.

Bane. What to do? She toyed with her blade. At first, she planned to kill him, take revenge. A subtle difference in thoughts about him created doubt, but if murder was the answer, the time was now.

Hope hesitated. "Have you decided what you will tell your council?"

Bane raised his head until he looked directly in her face. "I will inform the leaders what I have seen since we traveled with this army," he replied.

"Don't you have an opinion, though?" She knew Shasha would ask him. What he replied would mean his life.

"I have not decided." His raised his neck and surveyed the camp. The screams of torture rang from somewhere in the darkness. "Soon I will know."

That was not an answer; Bane was trying to evade the question. If he urged repudiation, she needed to learn now. If alliance... "You must have some idea what you will say."

His massive head swung back and forth, his forked tongue tasting the air. "These are evil creatures."

Hope made her choice. She put her hatred aside. He would live. "I am leaving," she said in a low voice. "I wish you well, whatever you determine." She grabbed her bedroll and started packing.

"Yes? Where to?"

She trusted him, but not that much. "I don't know," she answered, concentrating on bundling up gear, "away from here."

Bane's eyes widened. "I will not tell," he whispered.

Hope finished packing and saddled Satan. After securing her roll, she said to Bane, "Good luck, I will miss you."

The dragon bowed his head in a sign of farewell.

The camp was quiet, the soldiers settling down for the night, resting for their next day's march.

Hope rode off into the night.

Chapter Ten

"You must let me in." Hope finally dismounted after an hour's wait, and stalked to the portcullis, waving a fist at the sentry in frustration.

"I tell you, an army of demons approaches," the guard called down from the wall. "We have orders not to allow anyone in. Now, be on your way."

Hope released a deep oath. "That's what I'm trying to tell you," she shouted, pounding on the iron bars. "I have escaped from that army. They're two days march behind me, maybe less. You must evacuate the city, otherwise you will all die."

The sentry, a moloch, glanced at the twenty-foot thick walls, and high towers mounted with giant crossbows. He smirked. "We have been attacked before from the plains and our city still endures." He waved a hand in dismissal and flourished his sword, jabbing it at her. "Now, be gone, cow. I have wasted enough time. If not, I will come down and paddle your rump."

Hope yanked out her sword and beckoned with the free hand. "If that's the only way I'll persuade you to raise this gate, fine, you bovine idiot. Be prepared to leave a steer."

The rest of the guards erupted in loud guffaws, describing in detail to the sentry what Hope would do with his private parts afterwards. He sputtered in rage and stomped away. A few moments later, the gate slowly rose high enough for the guard to stroll out.

I must not kill him, Hope cautioned herself as the moloch swaggered in front of her, *enough to get his attention and make him listen to me.*

The guard was twice Hope's size, well-muscled, with a shaggy beard and long sharp horns. He stopped and posed, maybe to frighten, or for the benefit of his comrades, who watched from the top of the wall urging him on with crude jokes.

Hope called out, "Are you waiting for someone to paint a picture of you, demon, or have you achieved some sense and decided to let me enter?"

The moloch cursed. "I shall split you like a rotten piece of fruit, human." He lowered his head, raised his massive long sword, and charged.

The attack would have worked, if Hope stood still and waited for the goring. As the blade swung down meaning to chop her in half, and the horns jabbed at her abdomen, she leaped to one side. To increase his humiliation, Hope bent low and stuck a foot out.

The moloch hit the outstretched leg and tripped. His momentum kept him stumbling until his face struck the hard packed dirt, tossing up a cloud of dust. He leaped erect, sputtering, to the jeers of his fellow guards who lined the entrance of the city for a better view.

Hope beckoned him forward. "Here, bully-bully. Come to mamma and play."

The guard bellowed in rage and ran at her with a dancing assault, swinging his sword at her legs. Hope swung back, not at the moloch, but at his blade. The two met, metal hit metal with the clang of a hundred gongs ringing at once, and his weapon cleaved in half.

The moloch stared at his blade, incomprehension written on his face. He looked up at Hope in confusion.

Hope stepped back and tilted the point of her sword at his groin. "Moo."

"HALT."

The officer of the guard, a human, pushed his way through his men, striding to Hope and the sentry. He placed himself between the two and demanded, "What is the meaning of this?"

Before the confounded moloch replied, Hope answered, "I traveled with the demon army and escaped to ride here with a warning. You must evacuate at once." She gestured to the walls. "Even this will not stop their attack. I have seen the war machines they use destroy cities and valleys. No one in this town today will survive."

The officer wiped his hand over his face. "I talked to their emissaries and have received reports of the demon forces, but we have no first-hand knowledge." The way he said this reflected the weariness of long nights of worry. "You have seen this army in action?"

"Yes." She put her sword away. "I marched with Ose and saw what he did," Hope replied earnestly. "I'll supply whatever information you ask, but I implore you now, send your women and children to the hills if you want your families to live."

His expression remained impassive, but behind his gaze dwelled a trapped animal. He sighed, "Accompany me, we will talk." He said to the befuddled guard, "You should have reported this arrival to me at once. Put yourself on report and resume your station. Next time use your head." He glanced at the broken blade the creature held in his hand. "How can you guard this gate with half a weapon, and your appearance?" he snorted. "Were you born in a pigsty? I would say you have been rolling in the mud, too. Find yourself a new weapon and change your clothes. You are a disgrace."

The officer swung on a heel, shaking his head and called over his shoulder, "You will excuse my men, with this talk of war they are all nervous and not at their best." He led Hope within the town.

A small guardroom adjoined the inside of the wall. He entered and sat behind a desk, waving to a seat opposite his. "Sit. Now, tell me what you have seen and know, woman. You say the army is two days away?"

Hope leaned forward. "Yes. I left his camp five days ago. On my second day out, cipacti chased me and I was forced to swing to the north. On the third day, one of his

153

captains, a dragon named Apep, searched for me and I hid in a cave."

"There are dragons with the army?" The man's eyes filled with dread.

"At least one," Hope replied. "When I turned back this way, I had to evade Ose's forward scouts. He may be closer than two days march, he can't be farther."

The officer probed her eyes, searching for truth, but beneath his gaze, Hope saw gloom and hopelessness. He drummed his fingers on the desk. "We thought this was an army of molochs. What additional clans have joined?"

Hope willed herself to remember the monsters and horrors observed while on the march.

"He has legions of demons from all over the plains with him now, even cherufe from the south to undermine your walls and feast on the dying, stone throwers that hurl hundred pound rocks, and squads of molochs Lore Masters riding baitals to drop their death on you."

The bitter words rocked him to silence. He stood, paced the floor, his face clouding over. Finally, he stopped and exclaimed, "I have heard of those siege machines, but believed they were rumors of rumors. You swear this is true? You have seen this in person?" He cocked his head as if he already knew the answer.

Hope rose also. "Yes, and more." She issued her dire warning. "I have seen what happens to the prisoners afterward. Men and demon impaled on stakes, lit on fire and used as torches to brighten his camp. Humans roasted alive to feed his army, their blood poured in goblets to drink."

The officer blanched, Hope felt her stomach churn, remembering the screams. "Let you and your men stay. Fight if they desire, but please send your women and children into the mountains where they'll be safe."

"You have convinced me." The officer stopped pacing and surveyed her ragged appearance for the first time. "Do you ride tonight, or stay? It grows late and the plains are not safe even in the best of times." He gestured to an adjoining door. "I have a cot if you want to rest."

She smiled back at him in gratitude. "I have been riding and hiding nonstop. I would be grateful for a night's sleep without dodging demons or cowering every time a bird sings," she breathed.

"I understand how you feel," the officer agreed.

She remembered Satan waiting outside the wall. The black stallion has sustained massive amounts of punishment from the hard journey. Dried sweat covered the animal; salt marks streaked his coat white. "My horse? I need to purchase food, water, and stable him for the night somewhere. He's in worse shape than I am."

"Of course. I will have one of my men take care of him for you," the man promised. "He will be ready when you wake."

A surge of dizziness swept through her. Hope gripped the edge of the desk to keep from falling. "Thank you again," she said. "I think I'll use that cot now."

The officer opened the door to the room and she saw the bed waiting. She fell forward kicking off boots and tossing aside sword belt.

Sleep came slowly. Her overwrought mind kept picturing Bane as she'd left him, Bane's face was replaced by Apophis. She kept whispering "I forgive you," until the two faces merged into one. She wasn't sure who was forgiving who.

***

The rattle of wagons and crying children awoke Hope the next morning. As she rushed outside, the same officer stood on the street watching the procession hurry by. He greeted Hope with a sour nod.

"Some of our families have already left," he informed her as an overburdened cart rolled past. "The rest who wish to leave are fleeing now."

"Thank the gods," Hope breathed as she strapped on her sword.

He smirked. "After you fell asleep last night, I sent scouts out. You were correct. Ose's army will fall upon us today." He gestured inside the shack. "Dried rations are on my desk if you are hungry," he apologized. "I have all the cooks manning the walls."

Hope nodded and grabbed a handful of the hard-packed bars and hurried back outside. Along the main road, running through town, a long line of wagons rolled toward a gate in the rear wall, driven by women and older children. Horses with teetering loads clomped along the edge, all evacuating in the same direction.

"Any man who possesses a sword is staying," explained the officer, directing more soldiers to the wall. "We will not abandon our homes."

"It is a shame you have decided to stay," Hope muttered gravely, watching the people go, "but I understand how you feel. I wish you well." Along the inside of the wall bedlam reigned. Men, half-breeds, and demons hurried, hauling more bolts for the giant crossbows. Women who refused to leave dragged firewood used to heat sand for pouring on assaulting enemies.

"Where is my horse?" She expected Satan saddled and waiting.

The man chuckled. "You are almost as anxious to see him as he is to see you." He put his fingers to his mouth and whistled. A few minutes later, a soldier led Satan out of a stable across the street and brought the stallion to her.

"Washed, dried, curried and fed," the officer recited. His chuckled when he saw Hope's expression. "We had him reshod too."

Satan whinnied, tossing his mane in greeting. The dull black coat was shiny ebony, his tail swished like a puppy.

"Something in the air, Captain," one of the guards

called down to the officer, "is flying our way."

The man and Hope looked up. In the sky, a black dot approached, and then two more appeared.

Hope clutched the officer's arm. "Scouting parties of Molochs on baitals. Ose approaches. Soon his army draws near."

The man shielded his eyes against the morning's glare, straining to detect the enemy. "I see more to the east," he answered, his voice blank. "If you plan to escape, do so now. We close the rear gates."

A terrified shout issued from the wall and the officer hurried off.

They're all doomed. Hope vaulted onto Satan. *Soon this burns into a pile of rubble.* Without a backward glance, she fell in behind the last of the wagons. *At least these few might live.* As Hope passed through the rear gate, she heard the portcullis drop and the drawbridge slam closed.

The hills beckoned a few miles away. Some of the first wagons to flee were disappearing into their ravines and folds. On the side of the trail, she spied a toddler, a half-breed girl no more than three, picking flowers.

Hope stopped and checked along the line for her family. Nothing. She dismounted.

"Honey, where is your mommy?"

The girl looked up, smiling. "I don't know. I left to play."

Hope scooped the baby up in one arm and supported the child on her hip. "This isn't the time or place to play, honey. Let's find your family and you can play with them." She lifted the child onto her saddle. "Hold tight," Hope cautioned as she scooted behind the toddler. "Ready?"

The little girl beamed back. "Fun."

Hope caught up with the procession and rode along the line searching. On the side of the trail, a wagon pulled aside, a human woman frantically scurried back stopping the refugees. She saw Hope approaching on Satan and released a cry of joy.

"LONA." She ran up and Hope passed the baby down to eager arms.

"I take it she belongs to you," Hope laughed.

The frantic mother repaid Hope with a grateful smile. "She was sitting on the back of the wagon." The woman pointed to a cart where a human boy and moloch girl sat watching. "I turned around and she was gone."

Hope blinked. Were those her children too?

"I see you are wondering," the woman added glibly. "My first man died, his first woman died. So..." She shrugged. "He is a soldier." She gestured to the town. "He is staying to fight."

"Mommy? Horse ride?" The girl reached out to Satan.

"No. Wagon ride," the woman said firmly, hoisting the girl onto a hip and glancing at the caravan of wagons bouncing away. She smiled at Hope again. "I had better hurry. Thank you."

A small smile flickered on Hope's lips. *How different this world is. My son and I would fit right in. I wonder if this is what life would have been without the free companies, or killers like me.*

The tail end of the procession rolled toward the hills. Cries of battle rose from the town. The attack on Farland had begun.

Figures from the main body of the army broke off and raced Hope's way, marauders bent on capturing the fleeing wagons before they hid themselves. She glanced from one to the other. The women and children would not escape in time, the soldiers moved too fast.

Somehow, the demons must halt.

No one stood to oppose them.

Hope sighed and pulled her sword.

She didn't need to die. She would not die, she told herself. *Slow them up, allow the wagons to escape, and run like the wind.* Hope kept repeating that, trying to believe it.

She spurred Satan into a full gallop toward the demons.

The foremost soldiers were all molochs. Satan trampled into the mob as Hope swung her sword. Long horns flashed back, while the tip of a blade sliced Hope in the calf. She winced, screamed, and chopped. Bone and horn splintered.

Satan reared, iron-shod hooves lashing out. The molochs backed off. Then Hope was through the pack. She hit a second wave of demons tailing the first, slithering and yelling curses.

Hope was screaming, Satan also. The hilt of the blade glowed with power as she swung again.

A voice rang in her head: *It is a good day to die. We chop like this, and like this. The blood of our enemies soaks the earth, and the bards sing our song.*

The molochs doubled back to attack, surrounding Hope. A quick glance confirmed the wagons had vanished. A grim smile played on her lips. The women and children were safe, concealed in the mountains. That was all that mattered. Horns, swords, and fangs confronted her, creating a solid ring that brooked no escape.

Yes, it was a good day to die.

Satan slashed with his rear legs. Hope catapulted forward. She hit the earth rolling and sprang up swinging as horns jabbed at her middle. Something soft and rubbery leaped on her back. She slumped forward and the cherufe clinging flew into the face of a moloch. For the moment, Satan and she stood in an empty space staring down their enemies.

Two of the mist demons floated above, their tentacles poised, and ready to strike with bolts of energy. The circle of beasts tightened again. Hope braced for their final assault.

A golden beam flashed overhead and the mist demons vaporized in a white explosion. More yellow rays surrounded her, striking the monsters and exposing a small alley of escape. Hope swung her blade, chopping off the horns of a charging moloch. She leaped over the smoldering remains of a creature burnt by the shafts of light as it fell to the ground.

"It's about time," Hope grunted as Brian stormed up. His wand was out, hand weaving too fast for the eye to see, flashes of power emitting in every direction. Hope dodged a stream of vitriol shot from the mouth of a lizard demon and chopped back, cleaving the snout.

The remaining marauders retreated with hisses and snarls. Brian swung his wand like a bullwhip, snapping its power among the demons. They yelped and fled.

"For many days I have searched for you," Brian gasped as he rode close. "Rumor from those fleeing to the north told of Ose's army marching this way." He wiped sweat from his face, keeping track of the retreating soldiers. "I heard the noise of battle, saw the wagons fleeing, and hastened to investigate, thinking I might help," he continued, flashing a grin. "I found you instead."

Relief surged through Hope as she gazed at those eyes. She tumbled into their depths, a sense of giddiness engulfing her. She staggered, caught herself, and struggled upright again. "It appears your timing was right," she breathed. The unsteadiness hit again and she discovered herself sitting. Brian hovered over her with his arm for support.

"Hold still," he ordered as she tried to rise. He brushed dried gore from her face, and wiped her forehead with a damp cloth. "Here, drink this." The nipple of a wine pouch slipped between her lips. He squeezed gently and the sour liquid splashed into her mouth. Hope gulped, sputtered, and drank more.

"Enough," she gasped coughing, and pushed the wine away. "What happened?"

"You fainted." Brian touched her leg, and then a shoulder, drawing away a wet hand. "You have lost a lot of blood."

Hope glanced down. Her tunic was soaked red, a long rip showed through the chainmail, an oozing wound gapped underneath.

The cries of battle from the city were fading. Black smoke covered the walls and towers, curled into the sky, showing the fate of the town and its defenders.

"If you have clean cloth, shove it into the hole." Hope nodded to the rips in the mail. "If not, don't worry about it, I won't die. But we can't remain. Ose will be dispatching soldiers." She grasped Brian's arm and hauled herself erect. "We must leave."

Brian held her steady until he assured himself she would not collapse. Hope gulped and nodded. He hurried to his saddlebags and returned with dressings. Cursing at the clumsiness of his hands, he wadded the bandages up and wedged the mess beneath her mail. "That will have to do for now." He appraised his work dubiously.

"Where's Satan?"

A nicker echoed. She swung at the noise. The stallion stood among a pile of broken bodies. With mincing steps, he walked between the corpses in their direction. Blood dripped down his side from the gore of a moloch.

Hope gasped and wavered to the stallion, her guts knotting up inside. *Must get a hold of myself. He lives.*

She examined the slash. The horse was not mortally injured, a deep flesh wound, nothing more. Satan would survive, but she doubted he was fit to ride unless she wanted to kill him in the process. "It will be okay, boy." She patted his flank and looked at Brian numbly.

Brian scratched his chin. "I studied some healing magic, but I am unsure…"

"Do it."

His face went blank. "Wait." He raced to his saddlebag and retrieved a pouch. "Take this." He dropped a pellet into Hope's hand. He shook a few more out and fed

161

them to Satan.

"These are from Eldridge. The bola extract he handed us," Brian reminded her when she gave him a questioning look. "The drug will strengthen your body."

Hope shrugged and tried to swallow the pill, gagged as it lodged in the back of her throat, and snatched Brian's wine pouch. A long drink washed the pellet down and sent her coughing again. Brian pounded her back. "Better?"

"Much." Hope sensed the drug taking effect at once. Exuberance soared, perception expanded, pain drifted away as renewed vitality surged into her body.

"How long will this last?" The drug produced a sense of euphoria and power never experienced before.

"Hours," Brian replied. "Now let us attempt the horse." He approached Satan with his wand out.

A dim blue flame flickered from the tip. The light touched the wound and died. The flesh shimmered but remained unchanged. Brian cursed under his breath. Beads of sweat gathered on his forehead.

"I am unsure how…?"

Hope seized his arm in a vicelike grip. "Take," she commanded. When Brian appeared irresolute, she gazed deep into his eyes. "Now."

He blinked and nodded. Gritting his teeth, he tried again.

Hope felt the newfound energy flow into Brian as he drew upon her strength. Again, he approached the stallion with his wand, this time confident. His flame burnt brighter, shining like a sapphire as the light played over the gash in the stallion. The wound puckered, closed, and vanished into a shiny scar.

The draining of strength stopped. Hope released his arm. Brian smiled and swung his wand on her. "It is done."

The drug was taking its full measure on Hope and the horse. She said confidently, "Let us ride."

Brian clutched his wand and stepped closer. "We

should…"

Hope shook her head and pointed to the burning city. "We have spent enough time already. Ose's soldiers will report I am here, you also. Soon he will send pursuit. We must depart. I will survive until we find a safe place to camp."

She leaped on Satan's back, wishing the fighting was finished, but knew it had just begun. The horse pranced in response.

They traced the curve of the mountains heading west. Hope felt able to ride forever. They flowed across the earth like a fast rushing stream. The touch of the powerful animal clutched between Hope's thighs transformed her into a conquering goddess.

Hours later, she became aware of an ache in her side. Annoyed, she checked the bandage. It was soaked in blood. She ignored the wound, concentrating on the sense of power she still retained.

Brian read her face, saw the agony, and stopped his horse. Hope ignored the implied suggestion to rest and kept riding.

She realized Satan was slowing. Beneath her, his ribs heaved, lungs laboring for air. The pain shooting through her body heightened, coupled by new throbbings that increased by the moment. Her stomach seethed, threating to rebel.

Brian continued to scrutinize her, aware she proceeded by stubbornness alone. Each time, she waved a palm at him, urging Satan to forge onward.

Finally, Brian uttered a deep oath and pulled his mount up short, blocking her path. "We camp for the night," he ordered gruffly. "It grows too dark for the horses to see. We cannot chance a broken leg."

Hope flinched and held her side, anger flaring. "If we walk them slow and still…"

"Enough." Brian rode close, for once his rage

surpassing hers. "My horse is jaded and I will not push him any farther. If you do not care about yourself, fine, but think of your mount. You are killing him."

Shivers wracked Satan's body, froth dripped from his mouth. Guilt rushed through Hope's chest. The stallion galloped nonstop for a week with one brief night's rest. Brian was correct. If she compelled him to keep running, the horse would drop.

"As you wish," Hope sighed. Fury vanished as another jab of pain washed over her. "You're right, it is late." Brian guided them into the seclusion of a grotto nestled in the hills where trees and cliffs masked their resting place from view.

"We will camp here," he declared at last as they entered a clearing with a spring and pool. "Time to rest."

"Sure." Hope couldn't stop yawning. The nausea was gone, but her body felt like raw meat. Her eyes kept trying to close.

Brian helped her from the saddle. She slumped, legs buckling, and he placed an arm around her waist. A fallen tree lay by the stream. "Here, sit," he said gently. "I will build a fire."

Brian scavenged wood and started a small blaze, and then spread out his bedroll for her to sleep on.

Stifling yawns that refused to stop, Hope muttered, "I will stand first watch."

Brian sat close and held her tight. "You must sleep." His eyes expanded as she gazed at him. "That bola is wearing off. Your body has burnt energy that was not yours to grant. The pain you felt will resume. The best thing now is slumber."

"Nonsense," Hope whispered as her head slumped against his shoulder, "I'm fine." His eyes were so big, and dark. She was flying, bouncing up and down among the stars. Her body floated in a place where the people were familiar but didn't recognize any faces. What were their names?

Hope was still trying to learn why Apophis lived in that place when she woke with a start.

She was naked.

Chapter Eleven

Hope bolted upright clutching the blanket around her chest. Brian was tending the fire, roasting a small animal on a spit. "Well, I see you are awake," he remarked as he rotated the stick. "Feeling better?" He sniffed the meat cooking. "Are you up to eating something?"

"Where are my clothes?" Hope demanded. "What have you done to me?"

"Your clothes," Brian answered with an amused grin, "are washed and drying." He gestured to a rock by the spring. "That is, whatever was salvageable."

Her undergarments and ripped tunic stretched out still wet, with most of the bloodstains gone, in a sunny spot on a boulder. The trousers were missing.

"As to what I did to you," he continued, "I bandaged you up right. Look for yourself." Brian removed the meat from the fire and laid it on green leaves to cool.

Hope felt her shoulder. A thick swash of cloth covered it from ribs to neck, wrapped tight. She lifted the blanket and peeked under. More bandages enfolded her leg from ankle to thigh.

Her first reaction as usual was anger. "You had no right to strip me naked."

Brian shrugged, his attitude plainly saying he thought she was being silly. "I could not ask. You fell asleep on me. You were like a sack of grain waiting for delivery to market. So," he examined the sky and rubbed his chin, "I removed your clothes and bandaged you."

Hope realized the anger was unjustified, but still. She was not modest, Brian had seen her naked before. That wasn't the problem. Nevertheless, the thought of his hands moving over her body where they didn't belong without her permission created an eerie feeling of violation. What did he touch? Had he done anything while she was unconscious? Hope blushed in spite of herself.

Brian read her thoughts. He laughed outright. "Was I to let you bleed to death? You have nothing I have not seen before."

"And will not again," she snapped back. "Fetch me my clothes."

Brian stiffened and his lips drooped. He stood, strode over to the rock, and picked up her tunic and underwear. "Here." He held both out in a soggy heap. "They are still damp, but if you want to wear wet garments, put them on. Your trousers are over there in the pool, still soaking. I am trying to remove the blood from the pants legs without much success."

He was going to make her stand up, stark naked, and walk to him. *Okay,* she thought grimly, *if you didn't get an eyeful before he would receive one now.* Hope pushed herself upright, teetered, and sat again sharply. Her head spun and insides grumbled. Bile rose in her throat. She gritted her teeth and rasped, "Will you bring me my clothes, over here. Please?"

Brian was already up and moving when she slumped. He knelt with one hand supporting her. "If I did not think you had witch blood and the ability to counter-act my spell, I would place a kindness charm on you," he muttered without expression. He dropped the clothes on the blanket.

In spite of herself she laughed.

He picked himself up and stared at Hope thoughtfully. "I am going to gather more wood for the fire. If you need assistance, yell." He stalked off, back straight, and did not look around.

When he strolled back with a handful of kindling, Hope was dressed, new trousers from her pack secured around her waist, and sitting by the fire. She blew on a haunch of meat and nibbled carefully. A few bites of the roast settled her stomach, and once she mastered the vertigo, walking was no problem. She still felt weak, but fitter than when awakening. Hope grinned at Brian as he approached.

Relief flashed across his face. He dropped the wood by the fire and squatted. "Better humor, now?" he said, ripping off a hunk of meat. "You are eating. Do you believe you are capable of riding in a few hours?"

"I think so," Hope said, "but I don't know about him." She waved over her shoulder at Satan.

Although Brian's magic healed his wounds, the stallion showed the same effects from the bola as Hope, but magnified. His head hung between his knees, and his legs trembled. Satan cast a sad glance at the two sitting at the fire and whinnied pathetically.

"It is worse for horses, than humans," agreed Brian. "They cannot vomit if necessary." He strolled over to Satan and stroked his back. With a sigh, he remarked to Hope, "If needed we can ride double on my horse, although mine feels the strain almost as much as yours."

Hope bit ravenously at the half-raw meat that passed for breakfast and wiped greasy fingers on her tunic. "Ose won't move his army for a week or more," she thought aloud. "They're busy fighting over the spoils of the battle, feasting on the flesh of their victims, and drinking." A stray fly landed on her food and she brushed it away absently while studying the fire. "We will be safe enough here if we stay out of sight, and let the horses recuperate for one more day."

Brian stretched out and touched her injured shoulder lightly. "Should we try my healing magic on you while we wait?" he asked. He held his hand up in a pledge. "I promise I will not look at anything I am not allowed to."

Hope hid her mouth with a hand and giggled. "I'm sorry about that," she said at last. "Sometimes I-I don't know, jump to conclusions."

Brian nodded understandingly. "We all do. That is human nature." He touched his wand. "Well, do we attempt magic?"

The strength she'd lent was bola strength, not hers. Without the drug, and in her weakened condition, the effort might be worse than the cure it provided. Her greatest concern, however, was what would happen to Brian's self-esteem if he did not succeed on his own.

"Why are you unable to perform this magic by yourself?" she asked slowly. "Is it you have not studied healing enough?"

Brian shifted and bit at the meat. He chewed thoughtfully before answering. "I have practiced the healing arts as much as any other white magic," he said, "but it was never my best subject." He shook his head. "Sometimes when I am unsure, or confronted by a momentous task, I doubt. My own disbelief is my downfall."

Hope felt sorry for him. One of the first things the monks taught was self-discipline. Trust yourself and your ability. Doubt was the little killer that weakened all things. This was doubly hard in the early days of the monastery, where she had to fight the disbelief of the monks and other novices, proving a woman could kill dragons. It took years to train herself with the help of the monks, hurrying back after a killing to review. Only her burning hatred and memory of her father kept her going. She still had moments of uncertainty, but they always insisted the ultimate test was within her own mind.

"I'm too weak to lend you my strength," Hope said, "and you are tired too, more weary, I think, then you let on. You should not attempt the magic if you believe you can't. Failure breeds failure." She laid a hand on his arm. "I am a quick healer, both Satan and me. Allowed rest, by tomorrow we will both recover."

They spent the balance of the day laying around and relaxing. The spring provided water for drinking and bathing. Even though Hope was unable to submerge

169

herself, she still managed a sponge bath, while ordering Brian, "Scrub well, you smell like a dead herd animal."

Brian was bare to the waist. Without trying to stare, Hope admired his body. The sight of his broad shoulders, handsome face, and deep chest caused a tingling between her legs. She thought back. It had been years since she'd slept with a man. Her position in the valley compelled a clean reputation. Working on the farm, fighting dragons, and managing the business, left little time for play, and, of course, the family secret. She realized with surprise the only person she'd been with for ages was Rehana.

Hope rubbed the padding on her shoulder and leg. Twinges of pain laced through her body. She frowned and sighed. Always something, getting too old, too beat up.

"Hey, daydreaming?" Water splashed in her direction. Brian honed his belt knife to razor sharpness and scrapped off the start of a scraggly beard. He felt his cheeks, climbed out of the pool, wringing water from his dark hair.

"Thinking," Hope replied. "You said you wished to be a farmer one day? When will that be?"

He released a hearty laugh and sat beside her, hugging his knees. "I told you, many years. That is something else I have yet to master. I want to, though." He sighed. "I need to wed the right woman first." His voice became wishful. "In order to be complete, a man needs a wife and children to build a future, a purpose to work for. Life is not worth living without people to treasure and love."

"I have often thought that too," Hope agreed wishfully. "In my world the valleys grow cold during the winter, snow falls, and winds blow from the mountains. I have my sister to talk to, the farmhands," did she dare tell him about Apophis? She shied away from that, "but I become so lonely. It would be nice to sit by the fire, hold someone, or have someone hold me."

"Exactly," Brian said, nodding in agreement. "One day."

The next morning they left for the long trek back to Mictian. After three days, they rounded the tip of the mountains and rode slowly east along the Northern Plains.

They passed a faint trail, the entrance to a valley. Hope was adamant. They must warn the people.

"They have been warned," Brian said indifferently. "As soon as I informed King Gregory of what transpired, he dispatched riders to contact each kingdom, a conclave was called. All agreed to protect their territories to the best of their abilities." He shrugged. "What else need we do?"

"Do?" Hope said, aghast. "Band together, that's what. I've seen Ose crush valley and town, none united to fight him." Hope didn't believe this stupidity. "One valley alone will never defend against the army he musters." She spun in the saddle to face him. "You should know that, you saw what he did to those cities in the south."

"It is true." The path to the gap lay behind. Brian kept riding. "Nothing will persuade the nobles, however. The valleys are independent. Each has always guarded their territory and condones no outside interference. We must try alone."

Hope never gave it much thought, but the free companies were the uniting force in her world. The reason the demons suffered defeated in the end. No free companies existed in this world.

"At least warn those people Ose is on the way," Hope pleaded. She gestured back at the pass. "If he doesn't send his whole army, at least part will descend onto these plains. I heard him."

Brian's face froze to stone. "It would do no good in that valley if I rode in," he mumbled. "I know the prince there of old. He would scoff at anything I told him, and accuse me of being an old woman speaking tales."

"This will be a repeat of the south then." Hope scrubbed at her face. *Why am I staying? They will all die. Nothing I do will stop it.*

***

They reached Mictian. As they passed the towers flanking the entrance, a tense sentry called out, "What news from the south, Sir Brian?"

"Ose still marches," he replied. "His army approaches, but it will be weeks before he challenges us here in the north. Nevertheless, stand vigilant. It is impossible to predict the exact time."

"Brian, look."

On the edge of town, a small village blossomed, this one hastily thrown together with tents and shacks. The smoke from dozens of outside cooking fires curled upward.

"Yes, I know," Brian answered her unspoken question. "They are refugees from the Southern valleys." He gestured to the mountains. "They escaped along small trails, fleeing Ose after he invaded their homes."

Hope tried to estimate their numbers and quit. "How many are there?"

"A few hundred right now, but more trickle in daily," Brian replied. "How many valleys did Ose attack?"

Hope remembered back. She realized the moloch had stayed away from the valleys. "Two. No, three."

"I surmised as much." Brian smiled in agreement. "A valley is harder to assault than a town on the plains, many guarded by dragons. These..." he waved to the shacks "...are from vales not protected."

Hope nodded in sudden understanding. "He seeks the easy conquests and doesn't want to antagonize the dragons."

"Exactly." Brian chuckled. "It appears he takes my advice to flood the valleys with refugees seriously. Once their food stocks dwindle he will return and attack."

They passed cartloads of families fleeing to the castle from the farther fields of the kingdom, and entered the courtyard where a frenzy of activity circulated.

King Gregory himself rushed out to greet Brian and

Hope as they dismounted. His eyes were puffy, the flesh on his face sagged. To Hope he had aged ten years during the weeks she'd been absence.

"You bring word?" he asked. Hope heard a tremor in his voice.

Servants crowded around. Brian numbered the listening ears surrounding them and said in a low voice, "Yes, Sire. Let us go somewhere quieter to talk. Hope is better able to explain what is happening than I."

The king hustled the pair past his main hall to a smaller room. He waved a guard over. "Let no one enter without announcing them first."

A large table dominated the center of the room. They took seats and Gregory said to Brian and Hope, "Now tell me all."

Hope described the destruction of the towns and valleys, the horrors of the torture, and the pledge of Ose to repeat his program of conquest on the rest of the world. She ended with a plea, hoping reason would prevail, and King Gregory, of all people, had the understanding to unite the humans. "If the valleys of the north are to survive, they must unify and raise an army. Only that way will Ose be defeated."

King Gregory bit his lower lip. "I hear the urgency in your words, and comprehend what you advocate, but how…?"

Gregory was over his limit. Hope had pushed him into territory he'd never dealt with before. This world never had anything or anyone to appeal to, no monks, no free companies, who saw the land as a whole. Just valleys and cities, demons, half-breeds, and humans.

A sense of defeat washed through the room. Hope's shoulders slumped. She should be on Satan right now, speeding to her own realm, spreading the warning of danger approaching.

A soft knock at the door interrupted their meeting.

The sentry stuck his head in. "The Princess Maralene wishes to see you, Sire."

"Daddy?" The little girl scooted under the arm of the guard, her brown eyes wide. "Mamma told me to tell you Baron Weber is waiting in the main hall."

The king drew back in surprise. "She sends you?"

A small smile spread across her lips. "All else feared to disturb you."

Gregory's mouth drooped. He rubbed his face and muttered, "Have my rages attained that level?" He rose to his feet, hardly able to contain the sorrow he felt. "I think we are done for now," he said to Brian and Hope. To his daughter he added gently, "Tell your mother I will be right there."

Maralene curtsied and scampered away. Gregory remarked to Hope and Brian, "I have been worried much of late. I guess it shows."

"As you should be," murmured Brian.

"If you will excuse me," King Gregory said, "I must see what the baron wants. I have called all the nobles of the valley together to debate a means of surviving this threat we face."

After he left Hope sat in silence. What would become of Marlene, and of Rehana? And the rest? Ripped apart for the amusement of Ose, or roasted alive to feed his troops?

No.

They needed to mobilize an army. If the valleys refused to supply one, who would?

The answer was obvious. Hope wondered why she hadn't thought of it before. "Brian, what about the demons of the Northern Plains?" she asked, excited. "Would they fight against Ose?"

"The cities?" He raised his eyebrows in surprise. "I doubt it. They are like the valleys. Each town or tribe protects themselves." He settled back and stared out the window toward the plains beyond the mountains. "That is what makes Ose different from the conquerors who arrayed themselves before. He has managed to rally different demons and clans to his cause."

"Oh." She thought again. At their first meeting with Ose, whole nations didn't appear, it was individuals. In that way, his army was the same as the free companies of her world. A few here, a few there, merging for a common purpose.

This land had no free companies. She was the daughter of the last great captain. She would create one.

Hope leaned forward. "We have an old saying in my world, 'The enemy of my enemy is my friend'. Ose will slaughter the towns as well as the humans of the valleys. If we gather a few demons, humans and half-breeds, and bring all three together for a common cause, we'll raise our own army."

"It might work," Brian mused as he thought over Hope's suggestion. "Who would lead this force? I know of no one whom both the towns and valleys trust."

"You and I," Hope said, eagerly. "Remember that half-breed serving girl? I bet she would enlist. Whoever is mixed blood in the valley, or towns would volunteer, if for no other reason than the fear of being ruled by molochs." It would work. She would make it work.

"Ridiculous," Brian snorted in surprise. "No one knows us. Why would anyone flock to our banner?"

"Nonsense. You said yourself you knew the prince of that valley we passed. You probably know the rest as well, or they you," Hope replied with a wave of dismissal. "As for the towns, Mictian trades with the closer cities, right?"

"Some," Brian admitted, "but…"

"You see, how hard will it be?" Hope already pictured the company in her mind's eye, her and Brian astride their horses, swords drawn with banners fluttering, leading a charge that swept the demons from the plains.

"We'll travel from town to town, valley to valley,"

175

Hope continued rapidly, "collecting a few here, a few there, half-breeds, demon, humans. Anyone wishing to stay free under their own rule. We'll spread the word of the horrors we've seen, tell the people of the death they face if they elect to stand alone. We'll build an army the same way Ose did and confront him when he enters the Northern Plains."

Hope was breathing hard, watching Brian to see his reaction.

Brian appeared doubtful, but replied, "I am no leader of men, neither are you." He studied her for a long time. "You keep others out. To accomplish this we must inspire our followers, not only with deeds, but with compassion as well. *I* will follow where you lead. We must insure others do the same."

He stood. "It is worth a try. Let us tell King Gregory your plan. At least heralds can proceed to each valley and announce what we propose."

King Gregory argued in his main hall surrounded by his lords. Most from the nearer holdings, drawn by the news of Brian and Hope's appearance, but newcomers hastened in by the minute. Those farthest from the castle refused to attend, dispatching subordinates instead. The lords claimed if an attack commenced on the valley they would not have time to flee to their castles and defend their lands.

Silence spread throughout the group as Hope and Brian hurried to the raised platform where Gregory sat. "Sire, we have an idea," Brian exclaimed. "Perhaps not a good one, but a thought nevertheless."

A buzz rang out in the hall when Brian finished. The king declared, "It is a good plan. I will spread the word of what emerged here today." His voice tinged with regret and faint wistfulness as he added, "I cannot go, I must stay and protect this valley, but I urge the others here to provide what men and supplies you need."

Baron Wolf shouted, "I do not believe this will work,

but I have a few breeds to furnish. If nothing else, we will slow this Ose down and provide more time to prepare."

Baron Weber rumbled, "I have no one to spare, but I have picked crops aplenty meant to be traded. With the valleys closed to shipments, they will rot." He said to Brian, "My harvests are yours if you wish. You will need food, and I have wagons you may use also. It is not much, true, but a beginning."

More nobles spoke up, donating what they could afford. A few even offered surplus weapons, mostly rusty swords and spears, a few bows. By the time the gathering ended that night, the lords pledged seventy-three bodies and enough supplies for a small army.

Hope found herself sitting at a table with a scribe, struggling to remember which noble offered what, and when he would deliver on his promise. After saying to the clerk, "That fat baron with the red mustache pledged five half-breeds," and the man replied, "Which fat baron, Mistress Hope? They all have mustaches," she knew raising a fighting force was not as simple as first thought.

Nowhere in memory had Hope ever organized something this complex. She was in trouble. In desperation, she searched for Brian, relief embracing her when he approached. "There you are! I need you to ask Baron Weber if horses come with those wagons. He never said…"

"I am not staying," he said, before she could continue. "I leave tonight, but will hasten back tomorrow or the next. It will take a few days to assemble all and convey word to the farthest holds."

"What?" Hope shot from the bench, infuriated. "You can't run off and leave me with all of this. We have to prepare the troops and verify what the lords pledged is delivered. Most of these people I've never seen. How will I know when everything is collected?"

Brian replied in a quiet voice meant to soothe, "Your plan, your responsibility. You are the captain of this free

177

company now. Get used to taking command."

"But…"

Brian placed his finger to her lips. "Not another word. The faster I leave, the faster I return to help you." When he saw the panic rising in her face, he said, "You will do fine." He spun quickly and walked away.

Hope glared at his retreating back. *Well, thank you, Sir Warlock. I thought we'd be in this together. This is what I receive for allowing someone to grow close.*

Hope slipped into bed that night with tremors running up her body. Names of people she wasn't sure of, and sums of donation for the war, most of which had been lowered, danced in her head. The cold knot that started in her back now reached all the way to her throat.

The chamber door swung wide, a shaft of light cut across the room, and disappeared. Rehana snuggled up to her. "Mistress Hope…?"

Hope reached out and stroked Rehana's hip. "I'm not feeling gamesome tonight, sweet one," she cut the other girl off. "Sorry."

"I have not come for that," the princess replied in a whisper. "Rather, to comfort you if you care to talk." Rehana lay on her back. "I saw how worried you were today, and Brian has left. You must be fretting terribly, I would."

A faint smile crossed Hope's lips in the dark. She rolled on her side and draped one arm over Rehana's waist. "Stay then, I welcome the company."

"You are the bravest person I know," breathed the princess into Hope's ear.

"The stupidest, you mean," replied Hope, petting the girl's cheek. "My idea, yes, but I thought Brian would stay to help. I don't know what to do."

"You will figure it out," Rehana said with conviction. "The defense of the Northern Plains was not there for my father to see, or Brian. You found a way." She nuzzled a cheek against Hope's neck. "If I knew of some way to help, but the numbers..." the princess laughed "...they are beyond me."

Hope didn't care a damn about the numbers, those would work out somehow. She already saw what they needed more of, additional soldiers. What gathered now were mostly half-breeds, young boys and girls.

"If you run across five hundred men-at-arms with nothing to do, send them my way," she chuckled. "Now, good night, chatterbox, you've made me feel better, but I have to wake early. I have a busy day tomorrow."

***

"Bring those wagons over here. NOW."

Supplies were pouring in from the farther estates. With a few more additional pledges, Hope accumulated one hundred volunteers to accompany her, ten half-breed women, sixty half-breed men, and thirty humans. Hope was trying to assemble the troops, check the wagons, supplies, and see what weapons they possessed, all at the same time.

Damn Brian, where was he?

"You, you, you, and yes, you too, start tossing those bags of grain into the carts. The rest of you, *line up.*" Four half-breeds leaped to do her bidding. The rest milled about and formed a ragged semi-circle.

Hope started the morning dressed. As the day wore on, she'd stripped off, first her tunic, then chainmail. As the sun reached its zenith, she directed the rest of the army in a sweat-soaked undershirt, much to the delight of the younger men, and embarrassment of the king. Hope didn't care. Her brown mane hung limp, and her shirt clung, unbuttoned down to the waist. If it had been her decision, she would have dressed in the nude by now. Only the fact that these people seemed more modest than in her own world kept her from doing so.

Damn this heat. Damn Brian.

She swatted a mass of swarming gnats out of the way.

"How many of you brought weapons?" Most raised rusty swords, a few lifted bows. The archers she waved forward. "Do you know how to use that?" she asked one of the half-breeds.

Long fangs bared in a toothy grin. "I hunt."

"Good." Hope counted five arrows in his quiver. "Where are the rest of your bolts?"

The breed shrugged and smirked. "Heads and shafts we have in plenty, Mistress. There are no feathers to be had for fletching."

"What?"

"There is nary a fowl left in the valley," he replied, staring down at his hoofed feet. "All have been plucked for the defense of the castle and estates."

Hope jaws clenched so hard she thought her teeth must break. "Collect as many bolts as you see," she ordered tightly, "fletched or not. If I can't beg feathers from the king, we'll use grass or leaves."

Plenty of food with no army to feed, arrows without feathers, what else could go wrong? Where *is Brian?*

She heard her name called. Marlene and Rehana stood on a balcony of the castle waving. Hope painted a smile on her face and waved back.

She'd decided the only way to survive was to pretend this were nothing more than working on the farm. Hectic days occurred spring, summer, and fall. Preparing a wagon train and delivering vegetables to three separate valleys before the produce rotted was no easy task, yet she'd accomplished it a hundred times back on the farm. True, weeks were spent to prepare for the trek, help of seasoned foremen, but the basics were the same. Hope prayed Ose postponed his attack long enough to organize everything correctly, feeling her stomach contort again.

Stay calm. Take it one step at a time.

The king's steward strolled up, trying hard not to stare at her clinging shirt. "Uh, His Majesty…"

"Hey, up here."

The man blushed red. "His Majesty requests your presence in the main hall, Mistress Hope," he said in a rush.

"Feathers."

"Excuse me?" Puzzlement crossed his face.

"I need feathers for arrows," she answered. She stared him in the eyes. "Or I'll take bolts with feathers already fixed to their ends, whichever is easiest to acquire in a hurry. See to it, while I speak to Gregory."

Hope spun on her heels and marched away, back straight, before the startled man replied. A small smile flickered on her lips. *Well, it's worth a try, anyway.*

The king sat in full council with his lords. This time he demanded, and received, the barons from the farthest reaches of his kingdom. Hope felt her suggestion to send a squad of heavily armed soldiers with his herald had something to do with it. As she entered the hall, muttering faded away.

Gregory came right to the point. "Hope, we have news. Part of Ose's army has crossed into the Northern Plains. You must leave soon if you plan to stop him, or not go at all."

Her worse fears had happened. "We're still gathering supplies. I need more men and weapons," she said slowly, "if any can be spared." Maybe she could squeeze out one more day to organize. She must appoint officers, and build a command structure. She studied the faces of the packed nobles. It didn't look good. *Why wouldn't these people provide more than token help?* "I still await the arrival of Sir Brian," she muttered.

"He, you should not wait on," Baron Wolf growled. "When the fool shows his face we will send him after you."

Hope saw it was hopeless. "I leave on the morrow," she said.

The squirming in her stomach swelled, engulfing her chest. She pushed it away firmly. *That's it, I'm on my own,* she told herself. *This is the same as fighting a dragon, no worse. I'll survive. We'll shake down on the way.*

"We'll visit the nearer towns and valleys, marching as we go," she promised. "Perhaps they will provide more reinforcements."

Hope didn't consider herself a religious person. Yes, she attended the temple when she was home, tithed to the priests, as expected, but that was the extent of her beliefs. She wasn't even sure which god to evoke for help, or what to say. She muttered under her breath, "Make it so," and left it at that.

She waited for something to happen. Maybe Brian would appear, or the barons volunteer more men.

Nothing.

Hope raged inside at the hopelessness of it all as she left the hall, and started glumly reviewing the last minute details for the march tomorrow. Even the report from the half-breed archers didn't brighten her. "Mistress Hope, the steward has delivered three score bolts to us and two bags of feathers. What should we do with them?"

Hope refrained from discussing what to do with the steward's feathers. Instead, she replied, "Huh? Oh." She thought how best to use this new wealth. "Divide the arrows equally between the bowmen, and find a few of our people with nimble fingers, pots of glue, and remake our naked bolts into arrows. Tomorrow when we set off they will ride in the wagons and finish whatever is left."

"Rider approaching," a sentry called from the top of the castle wall. "Horsemen behind him and wagons also."

Hope brightened. More reinforcements. The wagons she didn't need, but riders? Maybe she would have a small cavalry.

A moment later Hope heard the prancing of hoofs and the clattering of wheels crossing the drawbridge. A dusty man, wearing a ragged beard, rode up to her. He dismounted. "Well, Hope, I see you have everything under control."

"Brian." The queasy feeling in Hope's chest changed to exuberance. A smile erupted on her face. She threw herself forward and embraced him, and then stopped short, anger replacing joy. "It's about time you showed up. How dare you desert me like that?" Her fury swelled, face sweaty and red, as all the worries spilled out. "For five days I've had to deal with this by myself. I've had to contend with aggravation, balky lords, half completed promises…" She banged him on the chest with her fists for each item to emphasize her frustration.

Brian grabbed her wrists, laughing. "I see you have dealt with each one." He surveyed the loaded wagons and people preparing for the next day's march. He held her hands gently and gazed into her eyes. "You know I would never upset you willingly, but I did not want to raise your hopes until I returned." He gestured to the warriors lined up behind him. "I raided my own estate for supplies, weapons and men. Twenty archers on horseback with bows, and the catapults from the top of my tower, complete with crews. I stripped everything I owned."

Hope tried to still the pounding in her chest. *He had done that for her?* Her throat tightened at what Brian brought, what he'd sacrificed. It was not much more than they had before, but the thought of Brian leaving his hold defenseless rendered her speechless.

"What will happen if Ose attacks the valley and your estate?" she asked, breathless.

"Does it matter?" Brian replied. "I would not be able to stop him with twenty times this number. They are better off with you, us, fighting on the plains."

She watched his dark eyes when he'd said 'us', and a happy wave filled her. She moved her attention to the rest of his supplies. "What's in the other wagons?" she breathed.

"Bundles of arrows, larger bolts for the catapults,"

Brian said, pointing to tightly wrapped sacks as he listed the contents. "I discovered unused armor in our barn and I had my men construct shields." He surveyed the troops milling around in the courtyard and his lips moved wordlessly. "We might have enough for everyone." He chuckled. "I had everyone pounding away, even my steward." He grinned at the memory.

Hope laughed along with him. The apprehension vanished. Guilt replaced the feeling of exhilaration. *How could I ever think Brian deserted me?* "When this is finished I'm sure you will be in need of a new steward."

"Perhaps I can enlist you," Brian agreed. "Oh, and I brought this also." He strolled over to a wagon, threw back the cover, and lifted a leather sack. "I rode into the mountains and sought Eldridge again. He gave us a gift." He poured small pills into his hand. "More extract of bola. He said he had been working on a new batch since we left, thought we might need the extra help." Brian dropped the sack into the wagon. "What do you think?"

Hope closed her eyes. The enormity of what they attempted focused in her mind. She felt no fear.

She opened her eyes again. Brian beamed at her. In the background, the shouts of the army preparing to leave filled her ears. Looking straight ahead, she murmured, "I think it's possible. Given luck, and the courage of these brave men, we can make this work."

Chapter Twelve

"We trade with this town." Brian wiped dust off his face with his sleeve. "For demons they are not too bad."

"Are they all full-bloods, or half-breeds?" Hope asked. She noted the progress of the wagons behind her, and debated whether to ride back and check the soldiers. They didn't resembled an army on the march, more like refugees, but a week of training trimmed some of the rougher edges. Nevertheless, the band of newly recruited warriors offered a poor excuse for a free company.

"Most are full-blooded," replied Brian. "The Tzitme clan, a few half-breeds."

The town expanded as they approached until finally Hope called a halt. "We'd best not advance any closer with our men," she said to Brian. "They'll think we have hostile motives. The two of us will go ahead alone."

"Make it three," advised Brian. "I have one who may give credence to our cause." He waved over one of the women, a half-breed Hope noticed before because she was always ready to help where needed. Hope even saw the girl leave her food unfinished and leap to the aid of their forward scouts after patrolling.

Hope meant to ask Brian about her, she lived in his holding, but something always interrupted. The girl looked normal until one got close, noticed the clawed hands instead of fingers, too narrow waist, and talon feet instead of toes.

"Who is she?"

"Her name is Myra," Brian answered, "one quarter tzitme, three parts human, distantly related to the ruler of this town on her mother's side. They found their way to my tower a few years back and I accepted both into my household. Myra is extremely loyal. I hope her presence makes our plea more believable to the people of this town."

Myra hurried forward, skirted around Satan with a timid glance at Hope, and presented herself before Brian. "Yes, sir, you wanted me?" She positioned herself in such a way that enabled her to watch both Brian and Hope.

She's afraid of me. Satan or me. Why should she be afraid?

"We need you to ride with us to the town," Brian explained. "When we meet with Kan you will be useful in our negotiations."

Myra bit her lips and shoulders sank. "I wish I knew how to help, Sir, but I think not." She looked at her clawed feet. "They hardly know me."

"Nevertheless," Hope answered firmly, "you will ride with us." She extended her hand. "Here, sit in front with me, Satan has plenty of room." She grasped a claw. It felt warm and soft. Hope pulled Myra up. "Let's move, Brian, it's late."

She lagged behind Brian and tried to engage the girl in conversation. Hope felt shivers running up and down the slim body nestled in the saddle before her. She decided to come straight to the point.

"What's the matter, Myra, afraid of me or the people in the town?" she asked kindly. "I know it can't be Satan." Hope stroked the horse's neck.

Myra paused a long time before answering. When she spoke, it gushed out in a rush. "No Mistress Hope. It is you and this great beast. You are both so," she paused, groping for the right word, "awesome."

"What?" Hope reared her head back. "That's the silliest statement I've ever heard. Why would you say that?"

Myra blushed but replied, "No, truly. You and Sir Brian. Of all the peoples of the valley, only you two are brave enough to lead an army against the demon king." She said as an afterthought, "You are matched for each other."

Hope blushed this time and changed the subject.

"Brian says you lived in this town, your relative rules. You still have family there?"

"Oh, yes," Myra replied, "although I doubt anyone will remember me. I was no more than a baby when my parent left and fled to Mictian."

"Why did she leave?"

"I am uncertain," Myra said. "My father was human, she, a half-breed. Maybe when my father died she decided I would fare better among the people of the valley, since I am three-quarters human anyway." She stopped, trying to recall details. "My father had a brother living in Mictian. He owned a small plantation, but when we located his home, we learned he had died and a neighbor bought the land."

Hope laid a hand on the poor girl's shoulder. "Oh, that's terrible. Couldn't you buy it back?"

Myra shook her head. "We had no money, and did not know how to farm anyway. My mother could not find work, and we found ourselves with no place to live. When Sir Brian discovered our plight, he furnished a job for my mother in his kitchen and allowed us to live in his tower. She died two years ago."

"Oh, I'm sorry." Hope remembered when her parents died, but at least she still had Diane. This poor girl had no one. "It must be hard to be so alone."

"Oh, no," Myra exclaimed, twisting around to address Hope. "Sir Brian treats everyone he employs so nice, like kin." She said thoughtfully, "I guess we *are* his family, here in the valley. He even made sure I had schooling in letters and numbers," she said proudly, "and I am learning how to work a loom, so I will always have a trade."

Hope watched the back of the man riding before her. "Yes, he is a good man."

She sped up. "How do we do this?" she called to Brian, "Walk in and announce ourselves?"

He looked skeptical. "Not a good idea unless we wish

187

to die, or be imprisoned. We stop at the main gate, tell the sentries who we are, and ask for Kan. If he appears, fine. If not," he raised a hand and dropped it, "well, we explain to the guards, or whoever shows up, what we are doing and hope for the best."

The sentries closed the gates when they reached the city. Brian stopped and called out, "We seek Kan. I carry important news for him."

An armor-clad soldier called back from a tower, "What news? We will inform him."

Brian frowned and shook his head. Hope answered, "We do not speak with underlings. Tell your leader to meet us here for civilized conversation. This is a matter of life or death to your city, and for his ears only. We shall wait." She folded her arms and reclined in her saddle.

The guard snorted, vexed, and conferred with a companion. Both withdrew. After a long time, the massive gates swung wide and Kan stepped out. Six spindly legs supported the body and head of a human. Two claws passed for arms, while Hope knew without asking, that the segmented tail with the wicked barb at the end produced venom.

"Who summons me with important messages?" the demon sneered, his tail curling and uncurling in agitation.

"I am Sir Brian of Mictian," Brian announced proudly, raising his hand in a sign of peace. "Both our lands face invasion by molochs and demons from the south. We raise an army to repulse this host. If they are not stopped, all the towns and valleys of the north will be destroyed."

The tzitme stared at Brian and Hope with loathing and shook a claw. "This is news? You waste my time, foolish humans." He made as if to leave.

"Wait." Hope spurred Satan forward. "Don't you care what happens to your town? We need your help. You need ours. Whatever men you have, demon, or half-breed, we will use." She waved to the troops waiting in the distance. "As you see, warriors have already been given, but we need more if we're to defeat this Ose moloch."

Kan paused and swung back with an expression of irritation. He peered past their party to the small group of soldiers. "You call that an army?" he sneered. "I will summon the females from my city with brooms to chase that rabble away."

Hope seethed inside at the arrogance of this demon. Incensed, she yelled, "Even your kin flock to help us. Are you a coward?"

The tzitme scurried forward, arms up, pincers snapping. "This is no kin of mine," he shouted, stretching a shaking claw toward Myra. "She is the misbegotten half-breed of my brother's folly." His claw moved as if to snap the girl in two.

"Uncle," Myra choked.

Hope reached for her sword.

Kan stopped short.

The tzitme was silent, his rage spent. The pincers still snapped, but Hope could tell less from angry than thought. At last, Kan grumbled, "I see you will not withdraw unless I supply you something. A few catapults and the crews to operate their mechanisms should serve. Who leads this army, you?"

"Sir Brian and I," Hope said. She lifted her chin, waiting to see if he would challenge that statement.

The tzitme ruler snorted but remained silent.

"After here we swing to the valleys heading east, acquiring more soldiers," Hope continued. "If the towns wish to survive, they'll contribute soldiers, too."

Hope's determination was beginning to infect Kan, although the ruler loathed admitting it. "If you raise a thousand men before you meet this southern army, you will be lucky," he replied with cynicism. He choked out his next remark. "Nevertheless, I shall send runners to the towns

189

beyond this one telling each of your need. What you do though is folly. You are all doomed." He silently trudged back into the town.

From Kan they collected four catapults and twelve operators. After ten days of hard marching, begging at every settlement and valley they crossed, the tzitme's prediction proved correct. Their army numbered seven hundred, most half-breeds, few with any military experience. As they neared the end of the mountain range, they surveyed their force soberly.

Hope worked tirelessly to train their small force, the great black stallion becoming a familiar sight as she pounded along the line, teaching, cajoling, and barking out instructions. Long after everyone rested, she marched through the camp, haggard, muddy, but determined to create the best fighting force possible. The admiration of Brian, who drove himself as hard, spurred her on. Her one driving thought was, *what would my father have done?* with the ever present reminder if she failed, not only were the valleys and cities doomed, but Apophis would remain a prisoner in his small room forever.

"We must stay together," she warned the soldiers, marching between the smaller squads of warriors she conclude were appropriate. "Fight as a unit, move forward and backward together."

Hope devised simple bugle calls for retreat or advance, and as they marched, had the soldiers practice the maneuvers over again.

"They are not enough," Brian stated. "Even though Ose brings a mere portion of his army this way, these few will not suffice."

Hope was thinking the same thing. She asked, "Is there no one else to call to our banner?" She looked into his face. "Surely you and Eldridge are not the only wizards on this world. Wouldn't some of your comrades help?"

"You are right," answered Brian quietly, "but few live

and none close by. They are old, a mere one or two born in each generation." He stared off into the sky and watched a flock of birds winging their way east. "In my time I was the sole one born with the power, and I am...broken."

Hope grimaced, his bitter words cutting into her like a knife. "Don't speak that."

Brian shrugged. "It is true. You have seen it yourself."

"You speak the words and make it so," Hope accused. She gestured to their troops practicing a maneuver. "They don't have the slightest idea what they're doing, but at least they believe in their worth. You should do the same." She reached out, patted his arm, and said in a gentler tone, "I have grown to know you, not only as a man, but also a warrior. When the need is the greatest, your power will stand by you."

**

The next day they reached the last valley. Hope gestured to the pass. "After this there is no more," she said. "Let's ride in and hope for the best."

Brian sat awkwardly in his saddle and replied, "I told you, they will render us no aid. We should not waste our time." He waved their column on.

"Hold it." She signaled the troops to halt and gave Brian a look. She wasn't to be dismissed so quickly. "It doesn't hurt to ask." A bright smile lit her face. "Who knows, right? Anyway, we'll be no worse off than we are now."

Brian held up his palms and dropped them in defeat. "If you insist," he replied glumly.

The army made camp. She and Brian galloped to the mountains, locating the faint trail leading to the valley. The path showed signs of neglect, in some spots weeds sprang up to Satan's rump. "These people don't travel much do they?" Hope said as they skirted a fallen log blocking the trail.

"They are a closed people," Brian answered. "Their

farmers and craftsmen have nothing to trade. The valley provides the inhabitants with everything they need. For that reason this land has never been attacked and the ruler does not fear invasion." He pursed his lips. "I know what will happen when I ask Robert..." His voice ceased as he slumped in his seat.

"Who is Robert? The king?"

"The Prince Regent," Brian replied woodenly, "and my brother."

"You have a brother who's a prince?" Hope gasped. "You didn't say you had a brother. I'm sure he will help us. Why did you say he wouldn't?"

Brian slide farther down on his saddle. "I told you I was the second son of a second son. Robert is my elder sibling, and the bane of my existence."

"Nonsense," Hope chirped. "You should have said this before. He is your closest blood. He will provide assistance." She pictured it in her mind. More soldiers on horseback, wagons full of catapults. *It would happen.*

They reached the top of the pass. Guards scrambled out of fortresses with crossbows leveled. They recognized Brian, and with a grudging nod, waved Hope and he through. Hope felt an itching on her back, as if the bolts still trained on them as they hastened down the trail.

"My father was a prince," Brian said to himself as much as to Hope as they traveled to the brooding castle, "so the titles and estates he owned passed to Robert when he died." Brian laughed to himself. "All I inherited was my father's ability as a wizard, and that hasn't done me much good."

A valley stretched out surrounded by the rugged mountains. Smaller than Mictian, it appeared more crowded because of its size. Hope thought Mictian was more beautiful, she doubted she would enjoy living here.

"How did your brother come to rule in this valley?" Hope asked as they neared the castle. She noted the hulking pile of granite was not as grand as the fortress in Mictian.

"He married the eldest child of the king," Brian said. "I do not know how it works in your world, but here the eldest, no matter woman or man, rules. The king is old, his wife is dead. Robert will one day be sovereign. When he left, it was the best day of my life."

They reached the castle gate and Brian called out, "… I hail Sir Brian, I visit Robert if he is in residence."

The guard nodded. "He is indeed, Sir Brian. Enter and be welcome." They ambled forward into the courtyard.

Hope was puzzled. *Why did Brian hate his brother? Surely, it wasn't because he'd received the family wealth? That was common, even in her world.*

Guards ran up to take their horses as Hope and Brian dismounted. "Why do you dislike Robert?"

Brian gritted his teeth. "As the elder it was necessary for him to instruct me at times, however his *'instruction'* consisted of criticizing everything I did. Nevertheless, since he was older and more experienced, I never surpassed him in anything."

"Of course," Hope said, puzzled "What was the problem?"

"When it came to magic, though, he did not train me, although his criticism never ceased. In fact, it increased and turned bitter. He declared that if the ability had grown in *him*, he would have been the greatest wizard in the world. On me, the power was wasted. My every mistake was blamed on my own stupidity."

This is where he gets his insecurity from. A guard escorted them to the main hall. *Is this how Diane felt?* Hope admitted to herself at times she could be bossy, but the admonishments always meant to instruct, not hurt. Did Diane see it that way? She decided to have a good heart-to-heart talk with her sister if, no, *when*, she regained her own world.

In contrast to the run-down appearance of the castle,

gay banners and works of art lavishly decorated the great hall. Brian's brother, Robert, reclined on a throne. A smirk crossed his face as they strolled to him on his raised dais. A fair-haired man, perhaps Rehana's age, sat next to him. As they approached, the young man broke into a smile and rose.

"Brian," he exclaimed in real pleasure and hopped from the platform to shake his hand, "it has been too long since I've seen you." The young man's blue eyes regarded Hope. "Who is this beautiful woman? Have you taken a bride?" He grinned at Hope roguishly.

"No bride yet, Alfred, maybe one day," Brian guffawed back. "This is Mistress Hope, my comrade-in-arms." His gaze sought Robert.

Hope extended a hand for Alfred to take. Instead, he bowed low and kissed her fingers. "Mistress Hope, I am happy to have you in my father's hall."

Hope blushed and shot Alfred a sideways look. "Your father...?"

"Alfred is the son of the king," Brian explained.

"So Brian, you greet everyone else but forget about me?" Robert called out. In contrast to Brian, Robert was short and skinny, but he displayed the same dark countenance. His eyes burnt into Hope.

"Not at all, Robert. I was ambushed." Brain strode up to the dais and mounted it, hugging the older man. Hope walked slower with Alfred trailing behind. She presented her hand to Robert. He accepted it briefly with a slight bow.

"Where is the princess?" Brian glanced around the hall. "I wish to greet her, too. I have not seen the lady since you wed."

Robert's lips tightened. "My wife was not feeling well today and has retired to her chambers," he replied. "A sickly woman. Sometimes I wonder why I married her."

Hope noticed Alfred frown, his jaws tightening, but he

194

said nothing.

"I am sorry to hear that," Brian replied with regret. "Please send her my regards."

"I will tell my sister you asked," Alfred said, before Robert replied.

Robert ignored Alfred's remark. "So brother, what brings you to *my* kingdom? Is this perhaps a social call?" He bent forward and scrutinized Brian with interest.

"I–I have come seeking your help," stammered Brian. "As you have heard, I traveled to the Southern Plains…"

"Oh, is that you raising all the fuss?" Robert leaned back in his throne and crossed his legs. "Yes, we received a rider from Mictian, warning of a raid," he chuckled. "I paid it little mind, and if I had known you spread this rumor I would have shown it less." He waved his finger at Brian. "You know how excited you become at the slightest thing. I thought you had grown out of this habit by now, but I see I was wrong," he lectured. Robert said to Alfred, "Remember this if you ever happen to rule. Those of little ability always try to transform themselves into something bigger than they are."

Brian ground his teeth and sputtered, "This is not a game, Robert, I have seen for myself…"

"Please," Robert snapped and waved him off. He said to Hope, "Did my brother inform you he is a great wizard with the ability to see and do many things?" He chuckled again. "No doubt, he has conjured these monsters from thin air to demonstrate how important he is."

Hope burned to scream at this imbecile, the battle rage she reserved for monster longing to emerge. She tensed, hand reaching for her blade, a mother lioness ready to protect her cub. *How dare he humiliate Brian in this manner?*

Shaking, she restrained her rage. *He's one nasty little toad, but we need his help.* "Your Majesty," she said, "If you'd seen this demon army, the devastation, women and children tortured. You must give us soldiers…"

"You too?" Robert addressed Alfred again whose eyes had darted between Brian, Robert, and Hope. "You see, they run in packs. Mark that also." He issued a deep sigh and shook his head at his brother. "Dolts will strip you bear with nonsense, and apologize with foolish grins."

Hope's face clouded white with fury as anger exploded like a volcano. "Let's go Brian," she grated between clenched teeth and grabbed his sleeve. "You were right. We will receive no help from this oaf." Turning to Robert, she said, "One day you will regret your words, and pray your brother was here."

As she stormed from the hall with Brian by her side, Robert's mocking laughter echo in the air.

They walked their horses to the gate, and Alfred appeared at the main door.

"Brian, wait." He rushed over, embarrassed. "I am sorry for what happened in there. If it were for me to decide…"

"I understand," Brian said. "I place no blame on you." He shot Hope a look of reproach. "I knew from the first this would be a waste of time. I should never have ventured here to begin with."

They mounted. Alfred strolled alongside as they rode to the drawbridge. "Your brother rules this valley with an iron fist," he explained. "It does no good to complain to my father. He is sick and confirms everything Robert does."

"Robert forced people into doing what he chooses," agreed Brian.

"It is worse than that," the young man exclaimed. "He has raised the taxes on the poor and spends the money on himself and a few of his cronies. He claims the largeness is to keep the nobles happy, but they were content enough before your brother married my sister. Every time I ride from the castle, I see people struggle to survive. It shames me."

Brian cursed under his breath and the veins in his temple stood out in stark relief as a great conflict raged inside his mind. "If your father refuses to act, how about you or your sister? Have either of you tried to persuade Robert to be kind with the people? Explain that his power rests with them?"

They approached the exit to the castle. The faint screams of Robert demanding the steward fetch more wine reverberated from the hall. Alfred winced.

"I have argued with Robert until my lungs ache," he declared in frustration. "Your brother replies I am too young to understand the ways of rule. My sister has tried to reason with him, but it useless," Alfred slammed his fist into his palm. "She is not sick. She hides and cries."

Brian grimaced. It broadened into a snarl. "As my brother declared, 'remember this if you ever rule'." He laughed disparagingly at his own joke. "You see? Sometimes Robert does issue good advice."

"You have not lost your sense of humor," Alfred replied, smirking. "Before marching to battle, will you meet Rehana again?"

"I wish it were so, but fear not," Brian replied soberly. "From here we seek the demon army and will not stop until they are defeated." He grinned at the younger man. "When I see Rehana, however, I will tell the princess you send your thoughts."

Alfred beamed. "Warmest thoughts, if you know what I mean."

As they exited the valley, Hope said, "Your brother is the most despicable man I've ever met." All her dreams crumbled. The great expectations of receiving additional men vanished in a heartbeat. How could this Robert treat his flesh and blood that way?

"It has always been thus," Brian replied. He gripped his reins tighter until his fists shook. With a sigh he said, "We still have the problem of what to do with our little army." He looked hard at Hope who refused to give in. "We cannot win," he said softly.

The moon floated in the sky. Below, the flickering lights of campfires shone, dotting the plain.

Hope sighed. "I know, fight and hope for the best, I guess. What else is there to do besides run? Our scouts say Ose's army will close on us in two days. If we decide to retreat we must start now." She watched Brian carefully to see his reaction.

Brian's jaw muscles tightened. "No. We did not gather this army to run. Besides," he put his head back and laughed, "if we fled, eventually we would hit the sea, and then die anyway. It is better to fight now and yes, hope for the best."

The resolve in his voice put new strength into Hope. She marveled how she could kill dragons, run a large farm, yet felt so inadequate when it came to leading an army. Brian took everything in stride. Nothing fazed him. He reminded Hope of her father, until the pain of Apophis's birth crushed him.

Brian would fight, and she would battle with him until the end. It didn't matter if Ose won battles, maybe even the war. They would not falter. The idea was not to die, keep together, and hope events changed the odds.

Brian saw the fire in her eyes. "You have a plan?"

"The beginnings of one. Retreat is not a bad idea," Hope mused. "We can't let it develop into a rout. We have to maintain a force in the field."

The camp was asleep, except for the guards, as they picketed their horses and sought their sleeping quarters. Brian had a small pavilion, which served as both their headquarters and chambers. Although they rarely shared it together, one sleeping while the other watched with the army, it was a haven away from the worries of the march. Hope enjoyed it when Brian slept there with her. His gentle snoring made the quiet of the interior less frightening.

The inside was pitch black. As they settled down, Hope remarked, "I heard Alfred asking about Rehana. Are they close, maybe more than friends?" Rehana never mentioned the young man, in fact, now that she thought about it, Rehana never spoke anything about the men in her life.

Brian's voice drifted out of the darkness. "They met at Robert's wedding. The princess infatuated him. Rehana? Who knows? Many young sons of the nobility seek her favor. She is a beautiful young woman, even of temper, and whoever weds the girl will one day rule Mictian beside her as king. My cousin smiles at all, but she is quite shy."

Hope giggled to herself. The princess was anything but shy. She drifted off to sleep thinking of Rehana and Alfred in bed, and then fantasized about her and Brian making love and married. They fought together, relied on each other for strength. Was that part of marriage? She fell asleep thinking of her, Brian, and Apophis living a normal life in his tower.

***

The next morning they broke camp and marched ahead. Hope and Brian scouted forward, searching for the best place to stand against the advancing demon army. They found it, a steep rise with a long slope.

"This will do," Brian said. He rode along their imaginary line.

"We must put our cavalry on the edges to protect our flanks," Hope cautioned.

"Should we keep men in reserve?" Brian asked. "I learned in the arts of warfare, troops are retained in case of a breakthrough."

Hope laughed and waved at the small army. "What men? You and I are the reserves."

"We have time. Let us deploy the men and start digging trenches." Brian made a long sweep along the top of the ridge. "They can throw up dirt and make earthworks."

"Good. If we hold this position for one day, we'll withdraw in the early evening."

Brian stopped riding, his mouth dropping in surprise. "I knew you contemplated retreat, but why if we are not overwhelmed?"

"Why?" Hope frowned. "To preserve the army. Our warriors might stop the demons on the first day, but the second? We don't have enough soldiers to win, however if we withdraw at our own choice, we can continue that indefinitely. As long as we preserve our force, Ose's troops can't unleash their full strength on the valleys and towns. If nothing else, it will allow the people more time to escape." She flashed a smile. "Who knows, maybe something will happen in the meantime to let us win."

Brian surveyed the battlefield once more. "Well, at least, it will provide us a chance to make peace with the gods. It is a good plan."

Chapter Thirteen

"*W*ake up."

"Huh?"

The last few weeks engulfed Hope in a blur. "What's the matter, another attack?" It couldn't be. They'd marched for two days, falling back to this position in good order. Hope, Brian, and a small party of half-breeds, fought continuously to buy precious time to allow their army to escape.

Hope groped for her sword and rose from the filthy mat of reeds. The reek of death and caked blood covered her. "What's happened?"

Myra stared; Hope's stark appearance sending a shiver of fear through her slim body. "We captured an enemy scout, Mistress Hope. You left orders to notify you or Sir Brian if we did." The girl tore her eyes away from Hope's dire visage and mumbled, "We could not find Sir Brian."

The speed in which her body tensed surprised Hope. *Brian missing? Not that she needed him,* she told herself, but the worry of his death always hovered. She ignored the panic and willed herself to relax.

"No doubt he will show up in his own good time," Hope mumbled. She tried desperately to collect her dazed senses. "Thank you for waking me."

The young half-breed assumed the duty of Hope's aid-de-camp, fetching clothes, food, and drink as needed, rarely leaving Hope's side since the fighting started unless ordered to do so.

Hope yawned. "Bring the prisoner here, I want to interrogate him." She covered her mouth and tried to focus. Dizziness hit and she teetered until Myra reached out a supporting hand.

"I have dama brewed. If you wish I will fetch you a cup." Myra waited expectantly.

It took a moment to realize the half-breed had spoken. "Thank you. Bring that first, maybe it'll wash this taste out of my mouth." Hope managed a grateful smile, and wondered how she would have survived this war without someone like Myra.

The girl brought a goblet of steaming liquid, retreated a step, and waited in quiet observance. Hope gulped thirstily and felt the alcohol and spices raise her to sharp awareness. She inhaled deeply, nodded. "All right, let's get this over with."

Myra ran to notify the guard her mistress was ready. Hope licked her lips and wished Brian was with her. He didn't leave the camp without informing the officer in charge. Maybe he *had* said something and she'd forgotten. The days blurred together, it was like fighting dragon after dragon with no rest in between. She didn't know how much longer she could continue.

Two sentries heaved the prisoner in. She pulled her wandering mind back to the present and the duties at hand.

At first, it was impossible to tell what the demon was. Dirty, bruised, and bleeding from a dozen rips on its body, this thing must have been dragged horseback by one of the forward rangers. "Is it dead?" She toed the creature with a foot.

A soldier grabbed the monster by the skin on the back of its neck and lifted. The demon's eyelids blinked. "No," the man replied. "Not yet." He dropped the creature. "You," he ordered. "Mistress Hope wishes to speak with you."

The creature twitched, the chest rose slightly, and the head elevated. It was a cherufe. "Pleasss-e?"

Hope asked one of the guards who netted the demon, "Where did you capture this thing?"

"Found him in the no man's land between our camps, "Mistress Hope," the guard replied. " We did not know if he was a scout, or attempting escape from the enemy army.

When we discovered him he tried to run."

A twinge of joy flared in Hope's chest. Desertion had become a major problem with the demon soldiers as they progressed farther into the Northern Plains and Hope's small force continued to oppose their advance.

"He was alone?"

"As far as we know. We searched the area, but retreated. Baitals flew overhead and we feared they would dispatch a patrol."

"What happened to him?"

The soldier shrugged. "It refused to return with us voluntarily."

Normally Hope would be angry, but she understood the soldier's feelings. They watched their comrades die for the last month by the score, only a few hundred of the original army remained. Of those, most suffered wounds inflicted in battles. The hatred, fear of the demon army, ran deep. Revenge tasted good. Hope debated whether to discipline the half-breed for his treatment of the prisoner, but decided no. It was useless.

She nudged the creature. "You, how many advance?"

The cherufe groaned. "Do not know. Some stay to attack town."

That sounded right. In the retreat, they passed a small half-breed village the day prior. The demon army would have stopped to raid and loot. That was their practice since this war began. Fight Hope's army, halt to rape a town or valley, battle with her small force again. She and Brian utilized these opportunities to either rest or counter-attack.

As Hope's strategy of slash and run continued, however, the demon army abandoned assaulting the larger, well defended, places of habitation. Unable to protect itself in the rear while battling in front, Ose's army now concentrated on the poorer settlements.

"What do they plan?"

"Find. Attack. Kill all." The demon's head fell back

on the dirt. Pain filled its voice. "Pleasse?"

Hope understood what the demon wanted, but she was not finished with it yet. "When?"

"Day after, must gather troops."

This poor creature spoke nothing they did not already know, but it confirmed what the scouts reported. They had one more day of blessed rest.

The cherufe bled profusely. Its blood oozed in a puddle. Hope peered closer at the devastated face. One of its eyes was shattered.

"*Pleassse?*"

Hope drew her sword. For a week, she had not cleaned the blade. Dark stains covered the weapon from tip to hilt, and the runes carved into the metal etched in crimson. They'd stopped wiggling at each taste of blood. Hope supposed the weapon grew tired as well. The jewel in the hilt however, still glowed, but instead of gleaming white, the gem pulsed red like the eye of an angry dragon.

The cherufe nodded.

Hope's sword plunged down.

She wasn't even aware if it was her or the blade which made the death stroke. It didn't matter anymore.

The cherufe released a low chirp, a bubble of crimson dripping from the ruined mouth. Hope brushed matted hair back and scrubbed at her forehead. "Get that thing out of here," she ordered the guards. Not bothering to wipe the blade, she slid it back into the sheath.

Her eyes were moist.

A bolt of lightning streaked across the sky. It had rained for two days. Hope didn't know if it was night or day. She scanned the area, spotted Myra standing, waiting for instructions, and asked, "Has Sir Brian reported in yet, or sent word?"

She stepped forward. "He was out inspecting the line, Mistress, that was why we did not locate him, but he has ridden in. Should I fetch him?"

"No," Hope decided, letting out a deep breath. "Let him rest if he desires, or work his healing magic on those who still need it." With practice Brian's confidence in his ability had swelled, and he'd become their chief surgeon besides his duties as deputy commander.

The young half-breed nodded. "As you will, and yourself Mistress? Will you go and rest?

"I want to inspect the line also," Hope decided. She trusted Brian entirely, and the officers, but as long as she was awake she felt obligated to check the fortification they'd built. "If Brian is still awake when I return I will meet him." she gave Myra a curt nod and stalked off toward the front.

The warriors waved in silence as she passed. Hope raised an arm for a victory salute and kept walking. She was happy to see the men relaxed, but alert. After an hour viewing the muddy trenches, she hiked to camp and found Brian. He talked in low tones to a moloch with a horn broken at the tip, the captain of the watch.

"You may go," she told the officer. She snagged Brian by the arm and waited for the moloch to march off. "Our scouts captured a prisoner," she said.

"What is wrong?" He instinctively turned to reassure himself their defenses and surrounding area was secure. Fatigue etched on every inch of his body. He'd driven himself even harder than Hope and it showed. His cloak hung in tatters around his body, gaping rips in a dozen places, sliced to shreds from sword strokes. Mud caked his face, the rain carved rivulets on his cheeks as it fell.

"Nothing," she hastened to say, "but he confirmed what our scouts recounted. No fighting tomorrow." She scowled at the sky. "Whenever tomorrow is."

Despite the assurance in Hope voice, Brian's expression remained colorless. He nodded as if he knew it already.

"I scouted forward to the enemy line," he said. "It is

205

guarded, but in the distance I saw that half-breed village burning and the noise of fighting. Ose's army is busy, but not with us."

Panic overwhelmed Hope. She might have lost him. She pushed this thought down by will alone, a fierce sense of protection filled her chest. She would *not* lose Brian. She looked around for Myra seeking moral support. The half-breed had withdrawn.

Despair turned to anger. She was being irrational, but couldn't stop. "You went where?" Before he replied she exclaimed, "That was stupid. What if you'd been caught, or worse, killed." She waved her arms in the air to keep from striking someone. "The ocean is to our backs, we have no place to retreat anymore, what am I supposed to...?"

Brian shook her gently by the shoulders, his eyes crinkling in response to her condemnation. "You worry too much. No one captured me, did they? If the demons killed me now, or during an attack, what does it matter? The army still has you."

A chilled wind rattled Hope's body. "You put too much faith in my ability." She took a deep breath and tried to match his light attitude. "Is it time to pray?"

Brian chuckled. "Before the last battle, then we say goodbye to this world, hello to the next, and we fight to the death."

Hope cursed herself. "So the war has narrowed down to that." She curled her hands into fists and growled under her breath, "Who was I to think we could organize a free company on our own and fight demons?" She paced. "This was my idea from the first, dragging you along, pretending to know all the answers. I was wrong."

Brian stopped her pacing, holding her shoulders. "You have undertaken more than possible, never realizing how lonely a life of command is when the safety of comrades is involved."

Hope gulped back tears that came all too frequently in

her exhaustion. "My father never mentioned this," she whispered. "The few times I asked about commanding a free company he'd poo-pooed and answered, 'It takes practice, that's all'.

"The farm wasn't like this," she said with a hopeless laugh. "If I misjudged planting, we always had reserved stores to hold us over. When killing dragons, all I worried about was myself." She stopped, and thought about what she wanted to say next, but her words had legs of their own. "If you die, Brian, the whole load transfers to me. You would be gone from me."

She felt regret, too. This life held so much more to do. She would never see Diane again, or bring Apophis to this land. Never marry, have more children, or settle down.

Brian saw her shivering in the rain. He put the remains of his cloak around her and held her hand. "Let us go, it is becoming dark. We both need a good night's rest."

"Is it evening?" Hope gazed at the sky. It hadn't changed. "When I lay down it was night. Did I sleep the whole day away?"

"Nonsense," he scoffed, "a few hours at most, but you do require sleep. Come with me, I have a treat for you." He led her away from the rest of the soldiers to a secluded spot bracketed by tall trees. "I had our pavilion erected." He grinned. "No fighting till day after tomorrow, and I left word with the officer of the watch not to disturb you unless we are attacked. You can slumber the night and wake when you desire."

Myra was standing at the tent flap, a smile on her face. Hope walked forward as if in a dream. "I had your gear moved over," the young girl said. "We set up a table for you and Sir Brian to dine. The cooks have discovered a few herd animals that escaped from the town. They made a stew." She drew the tent flap aside. "Rest well."

Hope gasped; she'd completely forgotten. "If anyone has escaped from that village we must..." She tried to break away from Brian, hurry to the army, and order riders out. A hand jerked her back.

"There are no refugees," Brian said. "The town was too small. Ose's army encircled the place."

"Oh." She pushed the thought from her mind. Thousands had died already. They'd *warned* the village to evacuate. She'd done her best.

The room was dark except for two candles placed on the table with a steaming cast iron pot nestled between them. In the corner, a bucket of tepid water sat alongside a washbasin.

The sight of the water made Hope realize how dirty she must be…and the stench. Long ago, they had dismissed washing as an unachievable luxury, not even hands and faces. They never found enough time. Even the scent of her vanished as she'd grown used to the odor. Now the smell overpowered her.

"When did you make time to do all this?" Hope asked in wonder. She dashed toward the water and started a quick bath, stripping off clothes and scrubbing away as many weeks of blood and filth as possible.

Someone, probably Myra, laundered a shirt and pants. They smelled of smoke from drying, but she slipped both on anyway. When finished, Hope hurried to the table where Brian ladled out large bowls of stew, fragrant with chunks of meat in a thick broth.

"I had Myra arrange it after my inspection," Brian replied. He dunked a chunk of black bread into the stew, his white teeth ripping off a bite. Hope did the same, laughing, as the food settled happily in her stomach. Before she realized it, the bowl was empty and the bread gone. Brian reached for the pot. "More?"

Hope released a contented sigh. "No, not now, I'm full."

Brian rose. "Then I leave you to a good rest. I will wake you in the morning."

"I thought you had set this up for both of us," Hope blurted unable to keep disappoint at bay.

"I do not want to disturb you." Brian shrugged. "One more night in the rain will not bother me. Such is the life of a warrior." He flashed one of his smiles. "Besides, does it matter?"

Hope pictured Brian huddled over a campfire with his cloak wrapped around him to keep the drizzle off. "It matters to me," she said firmly. "There is ample room for two. I see no reason why you should sleep in the cold and wet, while I'm here snug and dry."

"If you insist," he said.

Hope unearthed covers, undressed, and slipped under their warmth. Brian stripped, did a quick wash, and slid in beside her. "Good night," he whispered.

The inside of the tent was warm. Underneath the blanket, Hope sensed the heat radiating from Brian's body, detected his faint pungent smell. Her body responded to each inhale and exhale of his breath. Next to him, their shoulders touching, Hope felt a hungry yearning. She perceived his tenseness, too.

"Someone needs relaxing," he said softly. "Roll on your stomach."

Brian's statement was so unexpected Hope obeyed without questioning why. His hands massaged her neck, rubbing, his naked calves pressed against the inside of her legs. She winced at his roughness at first, but then wiggled in delight as the tight muscles loosened.

"Oh, that feels wonderful," she whispered.

"Good." His thumbs dug into her shoulder muscles, back and thighs, his hands squeezing and pushing as they moved lower.

He ended by rubbing her feet, fingers working into her arches, bending and stretching each toe.

She reached back and touched him.

"Hope?"

"Don't talk."

The world outside disappeared as she twisted on her side and drew him close, hip to hip. She threw one leg around his and held him tight as he buried his face in her neck. Hope moaned, her mouth seeking his.

Their lips met and he crushed her to him, and then pulled away to nip her ear, his sharp fingernails scratching her back from shoulders to buttocks. A low scream of pain and delight escaped her and Hope tugged and rolled, pulling him on top.

Brian's lips and hands moved over her body, spreading calves wide as he planted kisses on Hope's legs and feet. His mouth traveled upward again, broad shoulders lifting thighs as he tasted her, and for a moment, she was lost in pleasure.

Hope's hands grabbed his shoulders, fingers hooking under his armpits. "Now," she whispered, yanking him up on her. "I want you now."

He entered in one quick hard thrust. She closed around him, her body arching upward. Their bodies started moving together, at first slow, and then faster and faster. Hope's breaths came in rapid grunts, her hips swirling and pushing as flesh rubbed against flesh.

Brian's mouth pressed into Hope's neck. Faintly she heard his deep gasps in her ear as they grinded together.

A tingling started between her thighs. Hope tried to hold it off, to stop the feeling inside from exploding. Her legs tightened, shivers ran up and down her body, time stopped.

Brian pounded deeply into her one more time. She felt him pulsing as an intense wave surged through her body. Grunts became screams. Explosions of ecstasy erupted, transforming them into a raging beast. They locked together, two animals as one, twisting and turning in their own lust and passion.

The grinding slowed to a gentle thumping. Hope's

fingers firmly embedded in Brian's shoulder muscles. Their breathing quieted. Her heart beat against his.

Brian kissed her. "Relaxed?"

Hope kissed him back. "Much. I needed that."

"Good, so did I." Brian nuzzled her neck and bit an ear. "Now we will both sleep well tonight."

"Uh, huh," she murmured.

Brian rolled and she rolled with him, still locked tightly around his body. Hope snuggled her head into his chest. "Best sleep I'll have for the rest of my life."

***

Sometime during the night, she woke. She was still nestled on Brian's chest, his soft breath caressing her neck. An impish expression of delight crossed Hope's face and she reached down, taking him in a callused hand. She squeezed lightly and felt him harden between her fingers.

"Again?"

"I'm not finished with you yet." She put one palm on his chest to hold him down, and brushed her lips against his.

Brian laughed as she threw her leg over his hips and mounted him. Seizing his shoulders, she started a slow rocking motion, back and forth, bending forward to kiss his mouth again. Brian cupped her hips, trying to match her movement.

The pace quickened, Hope's hair whipped around as she pressed hard to him, guttural cries of pleasure issuing from her lips as she built to climax.

A violent explosion detonated inside. Hope plunged down one last time as Brian's hips crashed up.

Hope felt she must break, split in half by the violence of their meeting. She fell forward, spent, hair tangled as if blown by a hurricane.

Barely able to move, she rolled away weakly. "Now I am done with you," she murmured as he held her in his arms. Brian pulled the blanket up over their naked shoulders and she fell asleep.

***

When she awoke, Brian was missing, but the place next to her was still warm from his body heat. Hope sat up, stretched and yawned, a smile touching her lips, remembering their lovemaking from the night before. She dug out clothes and dressed slowly until muffled shouts from outside the pavilion raised hackle on her neck.

Snatching her sword belt, Hope buckled it on quickly and hurried outside.

The clouds had dissolved, the sky streaked in pink fingers from the afternoon sun. Brian stood half-dressed, screaming orders to the soldiers as they scurried forward toward the front line.

"What is it?" Hope said to Brian, although she knew the answer already.

"They have arrived," Brian replied grimly. "Word was delivered by our scouts. Ose's army will be here tonight. We fight first thing in the morning."

Hope steeled herself and looked up into his face. "This is it then."

Brian stared down and nodded. "Yes. Tomorrow is the day we die."

Chapter Fourteen

They deployed their army that night. In the predawn darkness a low rustling whispered, as if a hive of bees were disturbed. Hope kept charging up and down the line, checking, adjusting the perimeter, and praying.

Brian passed her, galloping the other way, surveying the troops also. "Are we ready?" he slowed and called out.

Sweat dripped down her face, clouding her vision. Hope cursed and hastily wiped it away with her arm and yelled, "Yes, I think so. Wait." She dashed back to a wagon, searched around, and returned with a bag. She tossed the sack to Brian. "Eldridge's pills. Hand them out to the troops."

"Are you going to take one?" Brian shook the bag.

"No. If by some chance we live, I want to function afterward. I'll survive without his magic."

Brian grinned, saluted, and hastened away.

The noise of bees expanded into an angry growl like some gigantic beast on the prowl. On her right, Hope saw Brian take a stance on his horse behind the trenches. She patted Satan on his neck and whispered, "Okay, boy, it's time to start work." His muscles quivered in anticipation, tenseness ran through his body as he prepared to fight. She moved to the left of the line.

They waited.

A red glow spread over the horizon and Ose's army rolled toward their position, a sea of demons ready to sweep anything from their path. Moloch Lore Masters stood behind the troops, lashing the most reluctant with red balls of power to move faster.

The first wave of demons crashed into their fortifications and stormed over the top. Hope fought for her life.

Two molochs leaped past the trenches. Hope jumped

Satan forward. The horse reared back, flashing hooves striking one demon in the head, while Hope bent low, swinging her sword and catching the marauding demon across the neck.

Satan bucked, lashing out with his hind legs at a demon who hurled a spear at Hope. She tumbled from the saddle as the missile flew past her shoulder. Hope sprang up and a half-man, half-lizard thing, bowled her over in an attempt to run through the line. She whirled her sword and caught him across the shins. He howled and tumbled under the feet of the troops rushing to fill the gap.

Scrambling up, she leaped to the top of the berm. With a wild cry of joy, Hope hacked off the horns of a moloch trying to gore her. On the back swing, she smashed another on the side of the face with the hilt of her sword.

Above the din of the battle, Hope heard loud cursing from the left. Brian crouched there, dueling with two moloch Lore Masters. Red balls of fire shot from their staffs, while Brian's golden rays blasted each out of existence. His face locked in concentration as his beams came slower.

A third Lore Master joined his comrades and Brian's light faltered.

Hope sprinted and dove forward, knocking Brian aside as blasts of energy struck the spot he'd stood on. She struggled up and hurled her short sword at the nearest moloch, catching him in the throat. The remaining two Lore Masters leveled their staffs at her.

A golden blast of power transfixed the pair. The molochs shrieked, stiffened, and collapsed.

Brian was on his knees, wand out. For the moment, they were free of attackers.

A cry rose from the fortifications. One of their captains raced their way. "An army approaches from the south."

Hope jumped over the trench and clawed to the top of

the earthworks to see for herself. A crawling line of soldiers loomed on the horizon.

"To the *north*. More converge on us." Brian gestured to their right flank.

Good gods, Hope thought, twisting back and forth, staring in horror as the three armies merged on her small force. *Where are they all coming from?*

A bolt zipped overhead and she swung her attention back to the demons. "Brace yourselves, they're attacking again," Brian shouted. A wild look of desperation flashed in his eyes. He gripped his wand in his right hand, his sword in the left.

Hope leaped off the berm. "Satan, where are you?" She searched desperately for the horse.

"Here, Mistress Hope." Myra stood behind her, Satan at the ready, the young half-breed clutched a bloody short sword in her claw. Blood covered her tunic from a gash in the side.

Hope dashed back and leaped on the horse, screaming orders to anyone who would listen. "Circle the flanks. We can't let those armies surround us." She dug heels into Satan's sides and galloped to the left, determined to charge the new army singlehanded if necessary to stop the horde from overrunning her people. Myra raced in their wake; half-breeds within earshot leaped to the call and converged on her.

"Hope, wait." Brian yelled, gesturing. "They are not attacking us. They march against Ose's army."

Hope pulled up short. "What the...?"

Both new forces curled inward, aiming at the enemy's flanks. Ose's army had stopped their attack and begun retreating, drawing into a defensive position to protect themselves from being routed.

Above the southern army flags flew, foremost a bird of prey clutching a spear.

"It is Mictian," exclaimed Brian, "but who are...?"

"No time," Hope shouted back. With a grim look of savagery, she raised her sword over her head. "Now it's their turn." She swung the blade in a wide circle for all the troops to see, and pointed it directly at the demon army. "CHARGE." At her shout, she leaped Satan over the palisade, and without a backward glance, galloped straight for the enemy line.

The next few hours blurred in Hope's memory. The startled demons stared in disbelief as Satan crashed into their ranks. Hope swung her sword until her arm ached and she winced trying to lift the blade.

Scenes of the struggle flashed around Hope. Severed arms and legs trampled as man and beast raged over the body parts. Half-breeds and demons locked together with belt knives at each other's throats, screams of the dead and dying echoing in her ears.

At one point, Hope remembered jumping off Satan's back to haul bodies out of the way. The pile was too high for the stallion to leap over safely. She slipped on red mud, regained her footing, mounted again, and charged a band of molochs trying desperately to escape the slaughter.

By the time night fell, Hope found herself slumped in the saddle, with no one else to fight. The killing lust vanished, breath issued in short gulps, and her soul drained of hate for a time.

The bloodstained visage of a man emerged from the gloom. "Are you all right?" Brian asked.

He looks as bad as I feel, or do I appear the same to him? "Fine, I think," she whispered back. "Is there more fighting?" She hoped not. All around were bodies.

Brian rubbed his haggard face, smearing red and dirt into a bloody mask. "No, for now it has ceased." His voice was dead. "The leaders of the armies are preparing a council of war. They wish you there."

Hope moaned. Her muscles protested as she sat straight. All she wanted was rest, better yet, dig a hole, crawl inside, and close the entrance.

"Let's go, Satan," she wacked the horse on the rump. "One more battle to fight." The stallion whinnied and with slow, painful steps, trudged after Brian's mount.

They ambled to the rear. Still in a daze, Hope asked, "Did we win?"

"I do not know. I think so," Brian replied dully, "at least this battle. Ose's army is in full retreat. That is what the council is about. Should we pursue?"

"Should we pursue?" Hope repeated, puzzled. She must have heard him wrong. "Of course we should pursue. Why wouldn't we pursue?" She paused. "Who are they, by the way, these strangers I mean?"

A huge barn fire burnt in the darkness. Hope lifted her head to see who congregated. Men, half-breeds, and demons assembled in a great semi-circle, voices raised in argument.

Brian's eyes met hers. He flashed a brief smile. "Who cares? King Gregory leads the humans from the valleys. The rest," he paused and lifted his hands, and then dropped both onto his saddle, "I have not the slightest notion."

Limp banners scattered throughout the crowd. More than a score by Hope's count. Each one represented a town or valley that was present. Prominent in the front sat King Gregory, and next to him to Hope's surprise, rested the tzitme ruler, Kan.

"Well, you have been located at last," boomed Gregory, rising as they entered the circle of light. "We thought you died in the fighting." A series of shouts from the humans echoed for her as the king sat again.

Hope dismounted and her knees buckled. She steadied herself on Satan's flank. *Hold it together, this won't be long...I hope.* She gulped air, straightened her shoulders, and strode forward. "I thank you for you timely rescue, Your Majesty." She peered past Gregory, "and yours, too, Kan. Without your help we'd be dead right now."

A flicker of smugness passed over the tzitme's face, but he hissed back, "We did not do it for you, human, but to protect ourselves. Ose's army has ravished far and wide across the plains, and if we did not attack, our towns and villages would fall next." He shifted, casting an eye to Gregory, and did not look comfortable.

Let's finish this fast. She noticed how ill at ease the demon ruler acted. Hope already foresaw trouble for this temporary alliance.

"I was told we gather to debate the wisdom of chasing the enemy," she said swiftly. She searched the faces sitting in the circle. "If it has any meaning, I vote yes."

Kan rose and advanced to confront her. With a wave of his claw he shouted, "I vote *no.* The demons of the south are defeated, scattered to the wind as chaff winnowed from grain." He paused and surveyed the men clustered around his side of the fire. "I witnessed too many of my own kind killed today. From the south, yes, but still my kinsmen. No more should we fight." Murmurs of agreement arose, mostly from the demons.

King Gregory's face burnt red. He sprang up and strode angrily to the barn fire, challenging the tzitme leader. "No sir. Now that we have these southerners on the run, we must continue the attack and exterminate the devils. The valleys have suffered too, but if we do not strike now, they will invade in greater numbers, I wager." He stroked his beard in aggravation. "Fight or the deaths we suffered today will be in vain."

Cheers arose from Gregory's side of the fire.

Hope saw two of everything. Her muscles felt like hot coal rested on the inside of her bones. She concentrated hard to return her vision to normal. Summoning what strength remained, she stalked in between the two arguing monarchs.

"You're both right." She looked from Gregory to Kan. "No one should continue the war who hasn't volunteered.

Let's all sleep on this and decide in the morning. The fighting is over for today anyway, and we need time to rearrange our men when we continue."

A few assents from both sides penetrated the hammering in her head. Hope sighed. The farce of a meeting had finished. She wavered away from the fire to Satan and clung to his saddle.

Gregory shook his head, undecided. Kan scowled and waved his pincers in disgust. Brian hurried to Hope, wrapping his arm around her before she fell.

"This woman is right," he shouted at the two rulers, glaring at each. "Both valley and town have fought hard today, and we are not thinking with clear heads. Tomorrow comes soon enough and the enemy will not venture far in that time. Those who wish to continue the battle can do so then."

When he heard no answering dissent, Brian led Hope and Satan away. "Thank you," she whispered. "I couldn't take another minute of that. If they kept arguing, I would have collapsed."

Brian stroked her dirty back and held her close. "You have accomplished more than enough already," he replied in a soft voice. "There is no need for you to referee among the victors also."

"All I want to do is sleep."

"Our tent is back there," Brian gestured toward the rear, "but I think, riddled with arrows." He helped Hope into her saddle. "I brought warm blankets, though, and Myra has set up a camp for us with our troops." He gathered Satan's reins, and that of his horse, and let both away.

Cries of welcome rang out as they made their way to their own men, but all Hope noticed was Myra perched next to a fire, behind which stood a tarp stretched across two bushes with blankets underneath. She staggered forward and lunged in, falling asleep at once.

***

When Hope woke, a white fog extended across the camp in every direction. She crawled from beneath the covering, wrinkles etching her brow from a worried frown.

"You are awake." Brian lounged on a rock by a fire. He tipped a caldron, poured a mug of hot dama, and carried the cup over. From inside his cloak he produced a packet of travel rations and handed that to her also. "Feel better?"

"Much." She snapped off a piece of the dried brick, crushed nuts, berries, and meat pounded together, and chewed, washing the food down with a draft of the dama. Before she realized it, she was licking her fingers. "More?"

Brian strolled over to a pack and dug around. "As much as you want," he said, drawing out three more of the tightly wrapped meals. "You did not eat at all yesterday, you must be famished." He handed a new block over and squatted by the fire, patting a stone next to his. He tore open a packet for himself. "Sit. Eat. When you are ready we meet with King Gregory and Kan."

"Oh, by the gods, no," Hope moaned. "I thought it was a bad dream." She rubbed her forehead and gave him a pitiful smirk.

"Oh, by the gods, yes," replied Brian. He scowled, ripped off a bite to eat, and chewed the morsel savagely. "I hope Kan and Gregory agree on some decision, for or against pursuing yesterday's victory." He glanced around the camp; many of their soldiers relaxed, most wounded in the recent battle. "We need the day's rest, and I must attend to their healing, but we cannot delay long."

"Whatever that tzitme decides, we will continue to fight," Hope stated. She braced herself to mediate this newest war, stuffed her mouth with food, and gulped more dama. "I'm finished," she announced as she pushed herself erect, "let's go."

King Gregory waited with the rest of the lords in their own separate camp. Large pavilions of red, green, and blue

220

transformed the landscape into concentric circles of colorful mushrooms, with Mictian and a few of the most important valleys in the center.

Hastily constructed benches made a horseshoe, the nobles sitting, Gregory perched on his own seat. When he saw Hope and Brian, he beckoned them over to sit by him. "You look fit," he commented.

"Better than yesterday, anyway," replied Hope with a smile. She gazed around at all the pavilions with their flags flying in the morning breeze. "How did you...?" She waved at the assembled men.

Chuckles rippled through the crowd. Most of the lords were young, some not long out of their teens. The king sputtered. "You may thank my daughter, Rehana, for this army."

"Rehana? How in the world...? What did she do?"

The king beat on the arm of his chair with his fist and laughed again. "That girl. After you left, and it became apparent none of the valleys would lend assistance, she leaped on a horse, commanded an escort, and rode from castle to castle."

"She *did?*" Hope's eyes widened as she listened to the king's astounding story.

Gregory grinned. "Rehana is of age to be married, and has many suitors among the princes of the valleys."

Hope noticed wolfish grins displayed on the young men, who were close enough to hear the king speak.

"She informed each if he desired her favor he must raise an army and help you," the king finished, waving at the assembly. "As you see, many wanted her attention."

"Well, I'll be," Hope exclaimed, stunned. "When we return to Mictian I must thank your daughter." *And I know just how.*

Alfred was with the nobles. The young prince waved to her and beamed. Erected next to him was a banner with the crest of his valley. Hope noticed a scarf tied under the flag that look suspiciously like one she remembered Rehana wearing.

"Have you decided yet what you will do?" Brian asked.

Mumbles of agreement arose from the nobles. Gregory nodded. "We have elected to pursue the demons to the end of the mountain range, where the hills meet the Southern Plain. After that we cannot go. Our lines of supplies will not stretch that far, and our men must attend to their homes and gather in their crops."

Hope was disappointed, but she said, "It's a good plan," but she cautioned, "You realize, of course, that you leave yourselves naked for invasion again. This is not Ose's sole army. He has hurled a mere portion against you."

Her words generated a worried buzz from the younger nobles. The king grumbled mournfully, "It is true, no doubt, but we cannot attempt more at this point." He slapped his palms on his knees and stood. "Let us see what this tzitme lord has to say. Perhaps he will lend support or good council."

Kan, however, was adamant in his desire to abandon battle and take his men with him. His one concession was to allow any warriors who wanted to stay and fight, to do so.

"I cannot stop my people," he hissed, shaking a claw at the half-breeds and demons surrounding him. He said in a loud voice, "Remember, though, you are murdering your own kind."

"Well, that was plain enough," Hope said to Brian as the meeting with the demons adjourned. They wandered back to their own camp. "The valleys fight by themselves for the balance of the war."

"It is more than we had before," stated Brian. His lips moved wordlessly as he counted the men bivouacked, preparing to continue the assault on the enemy. "We have five times the warriors we started with, and if any of Kan's people stay, we will have more. When we began, it was with the hope of stopping Ose, not defeating his army. We have achieved our purpose."

"Yes, but I'm wondering why Ose did nothing to reinforce his army, or if he will." Hope put a finger to her mouth, puzzled. "I don't picture him having a defeat on his hands like this and doing nothing. Unless…"

"Unless what?" Brian asked. He waved to three drivers bringing wagons from the rear. He gestured to the left, right, and pointed to his feet.

"Unless, his captains are afraid to send word to him. Perhaps they fear his wrath."

"I do not think that is the case," Brian replied. He tossed his gear into the wagon. "More likely he is still consolidating his rule over the south and cannot spare the men."

"What happens when he does?" Hope asked.

Brian was still busy packing more tackle. Hope started saddling Satan. Brian looked up from the blanket he was rolling into a bundle and replied, "Then we will fight again. As King Gregory said, we are doing all we can at the moment. The men we started with are mostly dead. We have exhausted our provisions, and once the danger is past, I doubt the valleys will supply more men or food, unless another army descends on our doorsteps."

"No doubt," Hope murmured. Worry flooded her. She'd pushed the men and herself as hard as possible, but had not eliminated the danger. The valleys earned a limited win. That was all, not the victory she hoped they'd achieve in the end.

Hope finished readying Satan and wandered around, a puzzled expression on her face. "Where's my gear? I don't see it anywhere."

"I had Myra ride back and pack your things up," said Brian. "It is on one of the wagons. Which, I do not know." When he saw her expression, he chuckled. "Do not worry, we will straighten out everything along the way. Right now it is more important to start this army marching again before the demons decide to regroup."

"What am I supposed to do...?"

"Have no fear," he answered with a wicked smile. "You have me to keep you warm at night while you sleep."

Hope returned his grin with a light fistful of knuckles in his ribs. "We'd better locate those blankets by nightfall," she warned with mock seriousness, "otherwise neither one of us will get any sleep."

As they fought and marched back up the length of the mountain range, their troops encountered little resistance. Ose's army had fallen apart. The remains were in full retreat, deserting horses, wagons, and those unable to maintain the pace, to the mercy of the lords from the valleys.

After a brief battle beyond the entrance to Mictian, King Gregory ordered, "Brian, Hope, you have earned yourselves a rest. Take the men who have fought with you from this valley and relax for a few days. You may rejoin us later."

Hope looked at Brian. Their eyes met.

"A hot bath..."

"...and hot food."

"Best of all a soft bed without mud, bugs, or rain," finished Hope with a laugh.

"I will gather our men," Brian exclaimed and dashed off.

Alfred was near and overheard their conversation. He approached King Gregory and asked, "Sire, do you think it possible...?"

Gregory stared at him. Amusement flickered on his lips. "Maybe I might spare you for a day or two." He turned stern. "Only for a day or two, though. Understand me, young man?"

Alfred exploded into smiles. "Yes, Sire. Two days, no

more, I promise." He sped away to load his horse.

"He has important business in Mictian?" Hope asked.

Gregory nodded shrewdly. "Rehana."

"Oh."

Of the hundred who followed Hope and Brian from Mictian valley, twenty remained. Myra was one. The young woman managed to stay close to Hope even when battle raged and her mistress galloped away to fight on her black stallion. Hope began taking the tzitme half-breed into her confidence, confiding wishes and fears depending on how the war raged. By now, the girl had grown into a friend and sympathetic confidant.

Hope longed to tell the young woman about Apophis, unburdening herself of the guilt of keeping him hidden, and discussing how half-breeds fared in this world. The secrecy engrained for so long kept her mute.

As they left for the valley, Myra scrambled up into her usual position behind Hope in a wagon packed with Hope's gear. Hope spied her and waved the girl forward, extending a hand. "Ride on Satan with me," she said. "It'll pass the time." She helped Myra up into the seat.

"Is it true we are going home?" Myra asked.

"Yes, for a few days to relax," Hope cautioned. "There are still battles to be fought and won."

Hope heard a disappointed sigh. She added, "If you wish, you may remain in the valley. You've struggled harder than most and no one will fault you for not continuing. I'll tell King Gregory myself."

"Oh, no, I will stay by your side," Myra exclaimed. "I wished the fighting was concluded, that is all. I thought perhaps you and Brian were going to Mictian to wed."

Hope spun Myra around to face her. "Where did you hear that nonsense?" she demanded, shock and disbelief in her voice. "Whoever said that must be out of their mind. Sir Brian and I are not discussing marriage."

"No one had to say anything, Mistress," Myra replied,

the conviction in her voice frightening Hope. "I have seen how you two act when you are together, and the way Sir Brian gazes in your direction after you stroll into sight. I yearn for a man to want me that way." She whispered, "I have heard the moans of your lovemaking at night, and..." She stopped in awe.

Hope released the girl. Brian *loved* her? That much? Yes, they fought side by side, coupled. Brian was kind, a good man. He made her laugh – but marry him?

"Well, that is far into the future, maybe," Hope replied stiffly. She stared at the back of the man riding in front of her. "Brian has voiced nothing of this to me, and I certainly never spoke to him."

The thought of actual marriage frightened her. At times, Hope fantasized about living with him, sure, but that had always been play in her mind. Now she pictured herself settled in Brian's tower, transforming the rundown keep into a home with a prosperous farm, and happiness fluttered in her chest. Nevertheless, Brian might desire her, and she wanted him, but what about Apophis?

Alfred passed Satan to ride next to Brian. Hope spurred the stallion and fell in beside the two.

"Sir Brian," the young man said, "I sought to speak with you alone before now, but I never had the time with the fighting."

"I with you also," Brian replied. "I wondered how you managed to assemble men for this battle." He flashed Hope a sideway look with a wink. "After the last meeting with my brother, I imagined we would not see anyone from your valley till the war was over."

Alfred's expression went blank. "No one told you then? Robert is dead."

Brian pulled up short, his face white. "What? How?"

"Ose's army attacked the valley. We were unable to hold the demons at the pass," explained Alfred, his voice wooden. "My father, sister, and your brother died in the

226

fighting at the castle."

"How did you escape?" Hope was rattled. Predicting this might happen in a fit of anger was one thing, but she never dreamed Robert would die. It wasn't her fault. It was his own folly, but somehow the weight of guilt fell on her

"A small band of soldiers and I managed to break through their lines at a weak point at the rear of the fortress. Even so, the battle was sharp. We stole horses and gathered what people we ran across before the rest of the valley fell." His voice was hushed, reliving the struggle in his mind. "We hiked mountain trails until we came to Mictian," he said. "The women and children are there now, but the men wanted to fight with me."

"Robert and I were never close," Brian muttered, "still, he was the last link to my family. He is, was, my brother. I will miss him." His fists clenched tightly white on his reins.

Hope put out a hand and touched his arm. "I'm sorry," she whispered. She looked across Brian and said to Alfred. "I regret your loss, too. What are you going to do now?"

"Now?" Alfred cleared this throat, his voice shading deeper. "Continue fighting, win back my valley, and rebuild. What else?" He sat straighter as the full weight of his new responsibility hit him. "I will need a queen," he muttered.

Hope had a sudden pain to see Diane again, hold Apophis in her arms. The two men next to her refused to mourn the loss of their families aloud. Wetness dripped down Hope's cheeks. She cried for them.

***

In the afternoon, Brian called a halt at the foot of the mountains. Nearby, a shallow stream wandered out of the hills to flow across the plains.

"Why are you stopping here?" Hope saw no reason. Mictian was on the opposite side of the hills, and the pass was in clear sight.

227

"We cannot reach the castle until late tonight," explained Brian, scrambling off his horse. "Even traveling on mountains roads you know well, it is still dangerous in the dark." He studied the terrain. "There are bands of demons from Ose's army hiding who have escaped our wrath. I do not wish to lose any of our party now fighting in the dark." He regarded the soldiers around him with affection. "It is better to camp here this evening and first thing in the morning continue."

Hope shrugged. It made no difference as long as they weren't fighting. She wished to have a proper scrubbing, but one more day wouldn't hurt. She'd grown accustomed to been filthy, the dirt and blood coating her body seemed natural now.

The rest of their troop set about collecting wood and preparing a noon meal. A few of the soldiers erected small tents and organized a defensive perimeter for the camp.

Brian and Hope brought their mounts to the water and filled their canteens.

"This will allow our people time to clean themselves," said Brian. He gestured to the soldiers. Even though they had not fought in several days, the grime of the war clung to them as it did Hope and Brian. Dust covered their bodies, many wore battle torn tunics held together by threads. "They can wash their clothes and make themselves presentable for their loved ones, take a bath if they wish."

The swift flowing mountain stream held no appeal for Hope, but it was better than she was use to during the war. "I suppose I should clean myself up too," she replied. She surveyed her grim appearance. "These breeches will stand by themselves once I take them off," she joked, "unless they collapse under the weight of the dried muck and blood."

She reached down and felt the water. It was freezing cold and muddy from the soldiers sloshing around on the rocks watering their horses. With a groan, she started to strip.

Brian took her elbow. "For you, I have a surprise." He tugged her away from the fridged stream and climbed on his horse.

"What?" Hope clambered onto Satan. "Where are we going?"

"Wait a minute." Brian leap to the ground and strode to a supply wagon, lugging back two skins of wine, and a wrapped package of food. "In case we become lost," he joked, remounting.

Brian galloped for the mountains. "Hurry," he shouted back to her, "I wish to show you something."

They rode up a rocky slope. When the grade angled too steep, Brian dismounted and tied his horse to a tree. "From here we walk," he said.

"What on earth...?" Hope exclaimed as she looped Satan's halter next to his mount. Brian was already moving and she hurried to catch up. They scrambled over boulders, entering a crack in a cliff. Brian acted so mysterious she found herself smiling.

"Is this a shortcut into Mictian valley, or have you unearthed a path to the underworld?"

"I discovered this place when I was hunting by myself," Brian explained. He held out a hand and helped her along the fissure. "It is secret to me."

The rock under their feet vibrated from some force moving beneath the rock. "Why is the ground shaking?" Hope asked. It felt too much like an earthquake for comfort. "I hope this crack doesn't close and crush us."

"Underground river," replied Brian. He squeezed her hand. "You will understand in a moment."

They emerged into a small canyon no more than a hundred feet long. Across from the fissure, a waterfall cascaded down the cliff wall, falling into a crystal pond. Hope couldn't tell where the water stopped and the grassy bottom began.

She halted in amazement. *"Beautiful."*

"This is not all," said Brian, still tugging her along eagerly. "Let me show you the rest." He guided her around the edge of the canyon until they stood on a ledge at the base of the falls with the pond at their feet. "You want to bathe?" Brian said with a wicked grin. "Remove your clothes." He stripped.

Hope mouth widened in astonishment and began taking her clothes off also until she was completely naked.

This water will be like ice. A breeze blew under the waterfall, sending a chill down her spine. *He brought me here, though it was a sweet idea. I'll smile and jump out as fast as possible.*

Brian prodded her shoulder, pushing forward. Hope braced herself for the cold she knew was coming.

Water pounded like a hard rain. She sputtered and gasped, "It's *warm.*" Hope cupped her hands over her eyes trying to see. "Why is it warm?"

An arm encircled her waist. "Back this way." Brian steered her toward the cliff face where the flows diminished to a mist. He stuck her palms on the wall. "Feel."

The rock radiated with an internal heat.

"Hot water is squeezed up from the earth below," explained Brian, "and mingles with the cold water from above."

Hope learned by moving from one spot to another she could choose her own temperature and intensity. They wandered along the cliff until she discovered a spot where the shower caressed her body like a warm soft glove, and let the water wash through her hair and trickle along her back and legs. Eyes closed, she let out a small groan of pleasure, and relaxed completely.

Brian walked up behind and wrapped his arms around her waist, his hard body pressed against her back. "The pond is warm too," he whispered. "The sun reflecting off the rocks heats the water." He kissed the crook of her neck. "This is your present for winning the war." He saw a smile. "Enjoy it?"

"I never knew a place like this existed," Hope murmured. "Only one thing could make it better."

"What is that?"

She braced her hands against the rock and opened her legs. "Make love to me."

"I must fetch you to this spot more often," Brian chuckled as he cupped her hips.

***

A long time later, they scampered down to the pond. The water was indeed warm. They washed their clothes and left them on a rock while they bathed.

Hope swam to the far end of the canyon and climbed up on a rock. She tossed her head back and stared at the sky, letting the sun shine on her face. Above, hanging from vines, were clusters of fruit.

"Brian, look at this." Hope reached up and gathered a bunch. She began stuffing her mouth.

Brian paddled over and scrambled up alongside her. "What is it?"

Hope spit out seeds and swallowed. *"Grapes."* They were small and sour, and the best thing offered to her taste buds in months.

"Pick as many as you want," Brian laughed. "I will go fetch the wineskins and rations." He called over his shoulder before diving into the water, "Meet you back at the clothes."

They lay on their stomachs in the warm sun, ate grapes, munched on the dried food, and washed both down with the wine.

Hope smiled suspiciously at Brian. "Did you plan all this?"

A solemn expression passed over his face. "Yes, My Lady, even to the planting of the grape vines."

A warm sense of belonging filled Hope when he said, 'My Lady'. A languid smile crossed her lips. She liked that expression.

After their clothes were dry, they dressed, collected their horses, and took a leisurely trip back to camp.

"Brian? I think this is the best afternoon I've ever had," Hope said. Emotions raced around inside her. She gazed back at the mountains. The sun was painting the sky red as it sank out of sight.

Hope studied Brian's outline in the firelight as he moved around camp checking on the men. *Was this what love felt like?* She didn't know. She had never been in love before.

***

Guards at Mictian greeted their party with eager questions when they reached the pass. Brian shouted, "It will soon be over. King Gregory has defeated Ose in the north."

Cheers rang out in the towers. One sentry yelled back, "It cannot conclude fast enough. Thank you, Sir Brian, Mistress Hope, and you, too, Alfred."

A bird flew from the tower, carrying a message to the castle announcing their arrival. They entered the courtyard amidst howls of approval and the blare of trumpets. Queen Adrinna rushed out to greet the soldiers.

"We shall have a banquet," she declared, her face threatening to shatter, she smiled so hard. The queen hugged Brian and Hope, broke away and shouted to the rest of the soldiers, "In your honor. Most of the men have left to fight, but the women and men who remain want to hear your stories."

Brian sent Hope a questioning glance. She responded with a slight shake of the head. "Please, it is late," he begged. "A meal, a bath and a soft mattress is all we require for the night."

"But…" The queen's lips sank.

Hope inspected the troops lined up patiently waiting. Even though they had tried their best to clean up, the men were still dirty, dressed in tattered rags, with deep wear lines on their faces. A majority of the soldiers expressed a desire to do nothing more than seek their homes and families.

"Brian is right, Your Majesty, we would not be good company. The hour is late and you couldn't arrange a proper celebration now, anyway. Many of the men wish to see their wives. Tomorrow after a good night's rest, we'll be much more mood for rejoicing."

Adrianna pouted but relented. "So be it. Steward? STEWARD. Find chambers for any of the warriors who wish it and lay out food. Send runners to the neighbors and escort their families here. Tomorrow we feast."

Rehana ran out of the castle door, gasping for breath, Maralene trailing close behind. "Hope, Brian." She threw her arms around both in a hug, and then sighted Alfred.

Rehana paused, stunned. "*Alfred.* You have returned." Oblivious to the rest, the princess broke into a silly grin and leaped into his arms.

Hope smirked knowingly at Brian. "I think Alfred has attained his queen," she giggled. The young woman and man held each close around their waists, gazing into each other's eyes.

Brian put his finger to his lips. "Let us not disturb the two. I am sure we will see both later and receive all the details. Now however," he pulled her away by the elbow, Hope still watching Alfred and Rehana, "food, bath, and bed, remember?"

After eating, Hope retired to her chambers. Two husky men carried a bathtub in and filled it with steaming hot water. When the servants left, Rehana entered.

"Rehana." Hope embraced the younger woman and planted a quick kiss on her lips. "I wanted to talk to you when we entered the castle but I saw you were busy," she giggled at the princess with a mischievous smile, "Very busy."

Rehana blushed and wrapped her arms around Hope's neck in a hug. "When Alfred led his people to our valley I had a chance to know him better." She whispered into Hope's ear, "Much better."

"Oh, yes?" Hope raised an eyebrow, and pushed the girl's arms away. "I am still filthy from our long march." She pointed to the tub. "The bath is big enough for two, and the water is still hot. Join me and let's talk about what's happening between you two."

They disrobed and climbed into the tub, facing each other. "Oh, this feels wonderful," Hope sighed, ducking down into the water up to her chin. Rehana ran a foot up the inside of Hope's leg and tickled. "Stop that, you dirty girl," Hope snorted. "Wash yourself first. I think you are covered in boy humors." She tickled Rehana back.

Rehana snagged a bar of coarse yellow soap from a tray, built lather, and reached out, rubbing the suds on Hope's shoulders and chest. Hope grasped her arms and drew the princess closer, placing a long, slow kiss on her lips. "That's for raising an army for us," Hope breathed into Rehana's ear. She caressed the girl's face. "Whatever caused you do that?"

The princess settled back in the tub, face red. "I foresaw no one would support you, and had no desire to let you and the rest of our people go to your deaths." She shrugged her bare shoulders. "Many men have come to my father's castle pledging their love for me. I could never decide among all the suitors, and wanted to see how far their love extended, so..." She flashed Hope a smile "...you received an army."

Hope took the soap and washed the girl's arms and body, and then seized Rehana's foot and worked on her legs. "From what I saw this afternoon, *I* think you have chosen," she teased.

Rehana squirmed as Hope ran the soap up the sole of her foot, along the inside of the calf, to the knee. "I think, yes," she said shyly. "He makes me feel so," the princess hugged herself and sat up straight, "I do not know. What is it to be in love, with a man, that is?"

Hope lounged back and place Rehana's foot in her lap. She played with the girl's toes as she thought. Finally, Hope replied, "I guess you want to be with that person forever, and can't dream of not living without him."

"Is that the way it is between you and Brian?" Rehana asked. "I heard rumors about you and him from the soldiers and I thought, well, you know."

"Maybe." They depended on each other, were ready to die for each other. Her own world was a dim memory now. At times she had problems picturing Apophis and Diane's faces. Nothing mattered except finishing the war and Brian. "I think so," Hope replied slowly. "Yes, that is the way it is with us."

"Tell me how it feels." Rehana hugged herself and stared at the ceiling. "I mean, being with a man. No one has ever told me, and I am embarrassed to ask my mother."

Hope remembered the time with Brian at the waterfall. "It's wild and fierce, or soft and gentle," she said at last, "fun with someone you love and care for."

"Is that what you and Brian experience?"

Hope thought back to the occasions they'd made love. Yearning swelled to hold Brian tight. "Yes."

A shiver ran up Rehana leg. "I hope it will be as wonderful with Alfred and me."

Hope kissed the princess's foot. "Oh, honey, I hope so too."

After Rehana left, Hope dried slowly, inner turmoil about Brian and herself crystalizing into sure knowing.

A rap sounded on the door. Hope draped a towel around her neck. "Rehana? Did you forget…?"

Brian entered. "I see you found that bath," he said,

gesturing to the tub and wet floor. "Feel good?"

The hot bath and talk with the princess left Hope feeling more than good. The thoughts about this man caused shivers of happiness to radiate through her body. She couldn't resist throwing her arms around Brian's neck, placing a deep kiss on his mouth. "Very." A playful grin flashed across her face. She walked backward, dragging Brian along, until they collapsed on the bed laughing.

She giggled in delight as Brian entered her and they coupled. The laughter turned to moans as their passion mounted. Hope tossed her head, noticing the door was ajar a crack; the princess Rehana was peeking in, her mouth agape in wonder.

For a second, their eyes locked. *Yes, little one,* she hugged Brian fiercely, *this is what it's like.* An intense spasm burst inside and Hope howled in pleasure, closing her eyes, body tightening around the man on top of her.

When Hope was able think clearly again, she checked the door.

Rehana had vanished.

Chapter Fifteen

The next day Alfred left to rejoin the war. Hope and Brian descended the castle stairway, hand-in-hand, to the courtyard for a last goodbye until they met him later with the army.

"Stay safe." Hope reached up on toes and planted a peck on the young man's cheek.

"Tell, King Gregory we will return within the week," Brian boomed, clasping Alfred's hand in a shake.

"I will," Alfred assured him. The young man's lips widened in delight and a tender expression crossed his face. Rehana was hurrying out of the castle toward the trio. Hope thought the young woman had been crying, but now a brave smile spread across her face.

She ran to Alfred and threw her arms out. He reached down and swept Rehana up in a kiss, setting her gently back onto the paving stones. "Hurry to me soon, warrior," she breathed, "with your shield, or on it."

He replied with a wicked smile and exclaimed, "Nothing will keep me away now that you are mine."

Rehana blushed and retorted, "I know."

Alfred laughed, waved, and wheeled his horse, galloping over the drawbridge.

Hope watched the young man ride off, and swung her attention to Rehana. The princess had a smile painted on her face, and carried herself differently than in the past. Hope wondered if that minx fled from the doorway to Alfred's bed. She snagged Rehana and whispered, "Did you...?"

Rehana sighed. "It was."

Brian overheard their conversation and exclaimed, "In that case I am sure this war will finish soon. Alfred will confront all Ose's army to embrace you again."

Rehana studied her shoes, red-faced, and murmured, "I am sure I do not understand what you mean, cousin."

***

Four days later as Hope and Brian prepared to leave, a rider pounded into the castle. "It is over," he announced, leaping from his saddle out of breath. "King Gregory and the rest swept the field of the remaining demons in one last battle. He returns now."

The next day the king led a procession of exhausted soldiers down the valley road. An overjoyed crowd trailed in his wake, emptying out the farms of people as the valley poured from their homes to greet him.

He entered the yard. Gathered behind him, a line of prisoners stumbled in shackles. Hope recognized the lead demon as the moloch Lore Master, who was one of Ose's trusted advisors, but now his shaggy skull glistened from shearing, the creature's horns severed at the skull, and his head bowed in shame.

"We captured the general of the army," Gregory declared with satisfaction. "He will sit at the base of my throne and be my servant until he dies."

Hope crowded forward with the rest. "Has he told you of Ose's plans?" she called out. "Does the demon entertain thoughts of attack again?"

Gregory replied, "No. I have not had time to interrogate him properly yet." He shouted down to the moloch with sour pleasure, "If you wish to live and not have your days cut short, you will, though. I am sure you will."

The moloch kept his head bend and contemplated the paving stones with grim determination.

Brian strolled over and stood next to Hope. "When the king questions him, I will make sure we are there," he reassured Hope. "Are you still set on leaving?"

During the last few days since she found time to relax, Hope realized months had passed since she'd been home, much longer than ever before. What was worse, the question of Ose's intention to invade her world remained

238

unresolved. She feared though, whether he knew of the portal's location or not, too much risk was involved to leave it unsealed.

When she announced this, Brian's face went stony and he mumbled something about that being her decision to make. No one had to tell Hope he wished she'd stay with him, his expression explained everything. More than anything, she wanted to remain, but had yet to tell Brian about Apophis, and didn't know how he would react.

Rehana appeared. She searched the warriors accompanying Gregory with increased concern. "Father, where is Alfred?" she exclaimed at last. "Is he with a different party?"

The king smiled at his daughter. "No. He has taken his men home to start rebuilding." When he saw the expression on Rehana's face, he added, "He sent word to you, however. He said when construction on the castle was well underway he would travel here."

Rehana stared off into space, lips parted. "I will go to him," she whispered. "Yes, in a few days I will leave."

Her father shook his head. "You cannot. The demon army destroyed the castle, burnt the houses down. Where would you stay? The valley is in ruin."

His daughter laughed. "I will sleep in the mud if necessary, but I will not allow Alfred to stay by himself without someone at his side." Some difference in her voice made the king look sharply at her. When Rehana saw his expression, she added, "Besides, what does a man know about the proper layout of a stillroom or kitchen? If I am to carry his keys one day, I must know where all the locks are."

"Hmm...I see you are determined." Gregory issued a soft chuckle. "When you are ready, I will see what craftsmen to send with you. We cannot have a future queen sleeping in the mud."

The crowd wandered back to their own tasks as King

Gregory dismounted and entered the castle. Hope watched Brian as he picked up a stable boy, a five year old half-breed, whose mother worked as a seamstress, and carried him piggyback to the barn.

Since their return, Hope had the opportunity to observe Brian in his own environment. Both servants and nobles loved and respected him, except for the crusty old Baron Wolf, who didn't seem to like anyone. Brian never uttered an unkind word to anyone. The more she witnessed, the more she fell in love with this man.

She kept reminding herself sharply she was a hired hand. Dragonkiller, brought to this world for one reason.

Does Apophis cry for me at night?

Even that thought didn't solve her dilemma.

When not busy with the few tasks necessary for everyday living, Brian would sit with Hope for hours, revealing his hopes and dreams, asking questions about hers, and learning of her world as Hope fell deeper into his.

Grim faced guards led the Lore Master general and other prisoners to the dungeon. Hope turned bleakly to Brian. "We have yet to determine if Ose knows about the gate to my world. If he has, I must find some way to close it." A sinking sensation filled her chest.

Then I will lose my son or lose you.

She gripped Brian's hand. "If I can't, I must warn my people, and discover a way to rally the land after he invades. You see, either way I ride."

"I have not the knowledge," Brian admitted, "of how to destroy the gate, and without the help of the valleys there is no way of stopping Ose. Perhaps Eldridge," he muttered. "Tomorrow we journey to him, if you are willing, and ask." His eyes held steady on her. "It is too bad we cannot devise a plan to permit the doorway to remain open. Our worlds might become friends, and you could visit at will."

Hope sought his gaze, lips parted. "I would enjoy nothing more than to stay here." Her heart and mind raced to uncover a way to obtain both dreams. Nothing surfaced; she felt weary. "I mean, with our worlds becoming friends, that is."

That night Hope cried herself to sleep. Even when Rehana tried to cheer her up, nothing helped. She cursed the unfairness of it all. The princess might declare what she wished with no repercussions. Hope couldn't. She felt trapped. Duty to her world and love for Apophis, pulled one way, her desire to stay in this land with Brian urged her to remain.

***

In the morning, they left to find Eldridge. The wizard exhibited no trace of pleasure at their appearance. "You two again?" he shouted, his brows knitting when he discovered Hope and Brian sitting on his doorstep. "Am I to be plagued by visitors every few months that have nothing better to do?"

"Sir," Brian shuffled his feet, "we have need..."

"You have need? YOU HAVE NEED," he roared. Eldridge scowled at them both. Hope heard his teeth grinding together in an effort not to yell anymore, visibly suppressing his anger. "You may enter, Sir you have need, but you will have to wait. I am busy."

The wizard spun on his heels with a swish of his robes and stalked back into his cave, not verifying if they accompanied him or not. Hope and Brian shrugged at each other and skulked behind, making sure they caused as little noise as possible.

In the middle of the cavern, a huge cast iron cauldron bubbled away. Eldridge sauntered over to the kettle and peered in. "Now where was I?" he muttered, shooting a dirty glance at his visitors.

Beside him was a bench containing different colored jars resting in the middle. He surveyed each and seized one, a small ruby colored urn, pouring the contents into the pot.

The steam changed color to a light red. Humming,

241

Eldridge selected a container with a smiling demon lid and dribbled a few grains of chartreuse powder in. The steam shaded green and smelled of fresh rain.

"Perfect," the wizard exclaimed. With a low groan, he straightened while holding his back, and awarded them a reluctant scowl. His agitation had moderated. "Sit," he commanded. "What is so important you must disturb me?"

Hope explained what they sought.

"Hmm…" Eldridge closed his eyes and pressed his fingers together. "I have long pondered how to close this portal if need be," he said.

"Really?" Hope said in surprise. "Did Brian tell you about…?"

"The doorway between our worlds?" Eldridge busted out laughing. "Who do you think told him when he ran to me asking about it? How do you suppose he located it, eh?" The wizard nodded to himself. "It has long been known to us who deal in the nether realms." Intrigued by their request, the old man raised a hand and suddenly paused. "Wait here, I have something." He sprang up and hurried away.

"Do you think he has a potion that will work?" Hope whispered to Brian as she watched the wizard disappear into a back room.

"He said so, we shall see." Brian's eyes shifted to the cauldron. The green steam emitted had deepened to black; the putrid odor of rotting vegetation filled the room. Dark motes shot into the air. "I hope he hurries, though."

Hope tugged on his sleeve, licked her lips, and started to rise. "Should we say something?"

"Uh, Eldridge?" Brian shouted out.

"Yes? I said I would be right back," the wizard yelled a reply from the chamber.

"Your pot, it is…" The steam, now blood red, held angry grey streaks mixed in. The motes faded, replaced by sparks. The wizard emerged from the room carrying an iron canister. He glanced from their faces to the pot. With an angry curse, he dropped the container he held, rushed over to the table, and tore out his wand. With three passes, the cauldron quieted.

Hope had been on the verge of dashing from the cave before an explosion occurred. She hesitated and watched Eldridge instead.

"What are you brewing?" she asked. She craned her neck to peer into the pot.

The wizard fished around inside with his wand, withdrawing a steaming woolen cloak. "My laundry," he replied, matter-of-fact. "Today is wash day." He wrung out the garment, shook it, and hung the cape on a peg to dry. Hope and Brian exploded in laughter.

"Funny, is it?" Eldridge snarled. He walked back and picked up the canister. "Magic is fashioned in all shapes and sizes," he lectured. "Some used for good as you observed. Alchemy such as I hold," he shook the container in their faces, "constructed to destroy. I expect you will not label this one as funny."

The canister was featureless iron, except for a long green fuse coated with beeswax extending from the side. Hope reached out and touched the surface with a finger, and withdrew it quickly. "What is it?"

"Most powerful magic," replied Eldridge grimly, setting the container on the bench. "Ignite the fuse with your fire striker and run," he warned. "A great detonation will occur. The blast destroys whatever is near. If placed in your portal, the bridge between our worlds will be terminated."

"This little box will accomplish that?" Hope reached out again and this time ran her hand along its length, gaping in dread.

"Assuredly," replied Eldridge. "Guard it well, and do not discharge it until you have nothing else to lose."

Brian accepted the canister and cradled it in his arms.

"Thank you, Master Eldridge, this is more than we hoped for." He stood and glanced at Hope, and then to the wizard. "We must hurry. I wish to stay and talk longer, but the king expects us as soon as possible."

Hope rose also. "King Gregory has captured the moloch general that led Ose's army," she explained, "and we made him promise not to start the interrogation until we're present."

Eldridge nodded. "I understand. Go, this war has been a nasty business. I am glad the killing is over."

Apprehension built inside Hope as they sped back to the castle, and she didn't understand why. In response to her fears, she urged Satan to greater speed until they galloped through the night, Brian's mount hard pressed to keep up.

She glanced behind at him. Was Brian the reason for the dread? The time was drawing near to make a decision. She now possessed the means of closing the portal if necessary, and Brian had not uttered a word about marriage.

Hope remembered the time of their arrival. Brian remarked he needed a good overseer for his farm. Did he assume she'd run his estate, and be his whore on the side without wedding her? She knew him better than that, but wished she understood what his heart contemplated.

"Hope, slow down," Brian shouted in her ear. "That great beast of yours may be able to maintain this pace, but my horse cannot."

Satan glistened in sweat, foam dripped down his mouth.

Hope slacked her speed. Brian's mount was shaking, exhaustion displayed in the tremors of its body. "Sorry, Satan felt my need and responded. It is always thus."

"Both will need a good watering and rest when we reach the castle," Brian replied. "They have undertaken too much of late."

Hope and Brian pounded over the castle drawbridge. An excited steward rushed to greet their entrance with relief. "Sir Brian, Mistress Hope, I am glad you are back. The king has left word for me to wait for you," the man exclaimed. He gasped, trying to catch his breath.

"Has he started questioning the prisoners?" Hope said, fearing they were too late. She protested to Brian, "I thought you asked him to wait until we attended?"

The steward gulped air and continued, "No. He has not begun, but he wishes to start the interrogation of the moloch general, and to fetch you upon your approach. Gregory declared he would delay, but not long. Come..." the man tugged on Brian's sleeve "...we must hurry. His Majesty grows impatient."

The steward escorted Hope and Brian a twisting way through the corridors into the bowels of the castle. Sputtering brands set in brackets on the wall lit the passage. Hope wrinkled her nose as the reek of mold and old death assaulted her. A creeping sensation crawled along her spine. *I wouldn't want to be on the receiving end of what happens down here.*

The man hustled them into a large chamber. King Gregory, Baron Wolf, and an old gentleman Hope knew simply as Egbert, stood impatiently waiting. Strapped to a table in the middle of the room lay the moloch, hands and feet secured with ropes that led to rollers with handles and ratchets. Prominent in display was a brazier filled with glowing coals.

"About time," snapped the baron. He crossed his arms and declared, "We expected you this morning. If we knew you would be this late I would have urged his Majesty to start without you, no matter what you requested." He said to the king, "Let us begin, Sire. We have wasted enough time with this craven coward."

"Tut-tut," admonished the king mildly. He smiled at the moloch. "Now that we are all assembled, I see no need for haste, is there? Egbert?" he asked the old man, "Are you in a hurry? If yes, let us proceed when you are ready."

Hope saw the old man around before, usually resting in the garden, smiling at the flowers, or playing with the children. She thought he was an old pensioner of the king, kept around because he had no family to live with. His value to Gregory became all too clear as the tools displayed in the chamber showed his real function.

"I am in no hurry, Your Majesty," replied Egbert gently, "but I notice the good baron is." He made a slight bow to Wolf and issued a tired sigh. With a groan and muttering about his old bones, he ambled over to the table. "Let us see, now," he murmured, "where to begin?" He studied the rack the moloch hung on. "Ah, yes, I remember now, I left these ropes loose until the fair lady and gentleman could attend." He bestowed a toothless smile on Hope.

The ropes were bowstring tight. Egbert walked to each ratchet and cranked them tauter. Hope heard popping noises.

The moloch screamed.

Hope felt sick. Killing was part of life, but always swiftly, never with malice or anger. Stonings were bad. What was about to commence horrified her. This was as repelling as anything perpetrated by the demons during the war.

"Perhaps you care to ask him a few questions before we start, Your Majesty?" Egbert inquired. "I must prepare my tools, in any case." He fondled a branding iron, measured the head against the chest of the moloch, and shoved it into the coals. The prisoner grimaced with terror.

"Beast, does Ose plan to attack us here in the north again?" Gregory leaned over the moloch. "Speak fast before Egbert is ready." The old man was humming to himself. He held up a small saw and checked the sharpness of the teeth with his thumb.

"Do not, please, I was not told," the prisoner whimpered. "I do not think so."

The king said to Egbert, "Equipment arranged?"

The old man glanced up from a pick he was examining. "What, Sire?" His mouth dropped and he hurried back to the rack. "Sorry, Sire," he apologized, "these are new ropes and I never found time to stretch each properly. They have loosened." He quickly turned the crank a few times on each ratchet. Hope heard cracking. "There, that is better," exclaimed the old man. "What was it you asked, Sire?"

The sounds of the moloch screaming drowned out the king's answer.

Egbert touched the ropes and nodded. "Perhaps I never told you, Your Majesty," he said. "When I was a young man, before I came to work for your father, I studied with the molochs." He patted the demon general on the shoulder. "Your people are inventive at persuading information from their friends," he sighed, "but I think I have outdone my master. We will see." Egbert blinked and waited for a reply. When none was forthcoming, he ambled back to prepare his equipment.

The heat from the coals in the small room was stifling, the smell overpowering. Sweat dripped down Hope's back and sides, staining her shirt dark. If Egbert thought he had surpassed his teachers in torture, she had no desire to stay longer than necessary.

"Your Majesty," Hope said, breathing hard, "may I ask a few questions?" *Let's finish this quick, before I vomit on the floor, faint, or both.*

"Of course, Mistress Hope," the king replied. He waved his hand and backed up, making room for Hope by the head of the moloch, "Go right ahead."

"If Ose didn't reinforce you, and isn't planning to invade again, why did he dispatch his army to the Northern Plains to begin with?" Hope snapped. "He's not that stupid to waste his men, or arrogant to conclude we wouldn't fight back." She appraised the progress Egbert was making. The old man had withdrawn his branding iron and was inspecting the head. The rod glowed cherry red along half its length. The moloch followed her eyes in terror.

"A feint," the demon screamed as Egbert stepped forward. "Ose thought to keep the valleys and towns in fear. He marches his troops to a new realm."

Egbert approached closer, whistling, holding the branding iron high.

"What place? Speak."

"I do not know," screamed the moloch, white saliva dripping down his chin. "A secret domain he claims is his. Somewhere in the hills north of here, Ose never told anyone its exact location. He said a path would lead to a part of his new empire." The branding iron hovered over his chest. Egbert gave Hope a questioning look.

She held up a hand. The old man sighed, disappointed, and withdrew a step. Hope said to Brian, "It's the portal. I must hurry. It could already be too late." As she spoke, she spun away, rushing to the door.

Brian said to King Gregory, "Sire, If we may, excuse us, there is need."

Gregory nodded. Baron wolf said, "A few more questions." As Hope hurried along the corridor, terrified screams rang her ears.

Hope ran blindly ahead and discovered herself squinting in the strong sunlight of the courtyard. Where was Satan? Time remained to rush to the portal, and set off Eldridge's magic before Ose struck. She blinked hard, searching for her mount.

The stable.

Hope sprinted in that direction, all else forgotten.

"Wait." A hand grabbed her sleeve from behind.

"What?" Brian was running beside her, worry on his face.

248

"You cannot rush off. You have no supplies, you do not know where to go, or how many people you face."

Annoyed, she glared at him, but realized he was right. She couldn't recall the route the first time attempting to leave. What made her think she'd find it now? It had taken three days to reach Mictian from the mountains. She remembered the river, the island, but before that? Hope tried to think. They had emerged from a grotto, but there must be dozens of similar ones scattered among the hills. Could she navigate across the plains to the right one? What if Ose had already marched his troop through, or the portal guarded...?

"I'll have to take that chance." She tried shaking his hand off. "Let me go, I've wasted enough time." She struggled free and continued to stride toward the stable.

Brian unerringly followed. "I am going with you. It is suicide to attempt this alone."

Satan was in a stall, munching hay. Brian shouted to the startled groom, "Bring travel rations, quick, and two canteens of water. We ride." He said to Hope, "Do you wish a new mount? Your horse has run for four days without a rest."

Satan nickered and swished his tail. Hope laughed. "He's always ready to go." Her saddle and gear rested in the corner, waiting to be stored away, along with Eldridge's magic. She readied Satan. "Remember, I'm not as heavy as you. For this one, carrying me is as if running free."

The stable boy scurried back balancing wrapped packages and two leather canteens in his hands. Tucked under his arm was a skin of wine. "Will this be enough, Sir Brian?" He passed the rations and water over. "I have fetched this, too." He held out the wine. "I did not know if you want..."

"We will take that, also." Brian cut him off short, snatching the skin. "Tell the horse master I have taken one of his charges."

They set off. Hope kept generating plans for action once they reached the hills. It all revolved around the moloch. If Ose had not attained the portal yet, the solution was simple, enter the gateway and destroy it after exiting. If he already posted guards at the entrance, attempt a mad dash and try to win through.

A pang of disappointment surged through Hope. She would never settle in this land with Apophis no matter what Brian asked now, but no alternative proposed itself. Her world needed protection.

All that day, and well into the night, they raced. Hope refused to slow their pace until Brian sharply informed her killing themselves would not make reaching their destination any easier.

On the second evening, when it became too dark to see, they slowed to a walk. Satan stumbled and Hope conceded it was time to stop and rest. As they made camp, Brian gestured to the northeast.

"Fires."

Barely visible on the horizon, Hope detected lights of a large army resting for the night.

"Ose," Hope whispered. She stood and ran to Satan.

The horse hung his head down, shivers of fatigue tore down his body, lather matted his sides.

As if reading her thoughts, Brian said, "He needs rest. Your mount will carry you until he dies, but we still have a long way to travel." He gestured to his horse. "My animal is jaded also. Neither have had proper watering since we left the castle. Even if yours does not die, mine will."

Tension mounted in Hope's chest, radiating down to her abdomen. "Do you have any more of Eldridge's bola pills?" *Feed Satan a few and keep on riding. He recovered last time. He will survive.*

Brian's expression spoke the answer.

Hope released a groan of hopelessness. "Then it dissolves into a race tomorrow."

At false dawn the next morning, they awoke and rode. Soon, the hills materialized over the horizon.

"To the right," ordered Brian. He waved his arm at a series of low mountains. A black spot stood between the brown and green of the landscape. "You see that tree burnt by lightning? That is the way."

Hope checked over her shoulder. Like army ants on the march, Ose and his soldiers approached.

They passed the blasted tree, attained the trail leading to the portal, and started a slow ascent. Yawning high above, the mouth of the grotto waited, which led to the cave.

Two molochs stood guard.

"We'll have to fight." Hope drew her sword.

"The one on the left is a Lore Master," Brian said. "I am better able to deal with him. He is mine."

As Brian uttered these words, the molochs discovered the two. The Lore Master leveled his staff, realizing they were not part of Ose's army. Brian raised his wand. Red and gold fire met in a fierce blaze of light.

Hope leaped off Satan and sprang under the inferno, racing up the hill to engage the remaining moloch as he slid down the trail to attack. The guard's momentum carried him into her, and they both crashed onto the path with the clattering of their blades.

On hands and knees, the moloch swung with his long horns. Hope lashed out and kicked him in the face as she scrambled to her feet. She chopped, catching the demon on the side of his head as he tried to rise. The blade severed one of his long ears, leaving the fur stained red. With a roar, he clambered to his feet, waving his sword in the air.

Dust billowed around them as they battled. From somewhere Hope heard detonations as Brian and the Lore Master dueled. The moloch she engaged howled in pain and rage. He gripped his sword two-handed and charged.

251

Holding her weapon straight out, Hope dove forward beneath the chopping sword of the demon. Instead of having her skull cleaved in two, the hilt struck a glancing blow on the top of her head as her blade sliced into the stomach of the demon.

The moloch screamed again, clutched at Hope's sword in panic, bewilderment on his face. He staggered three halting steps, tripped over her, and crumbled.

Hope reached up and touched the top of her head. She drew away a handful of blood. Dazed, she pushed the body of the moloch off. Staggering upright, she jerked the blade from the demon and searched for Brian and Lore Master.

The two still fought furiously. Hope gulped air, raised her sword, and screaming, rushed the moloch.

The Lore Master jerked around with a snarl of contempt. In scorn, he flicked his staff, shooting a bolt of power her way. Hope ducked and the fire struck the blade.

The gem blazed hot, searing Hope's hands. Instead of exploding, sparks erupted from the tip, altering into an incendiary blaze of light. The sword pulse and the power of the staff, magnified a hundred fold, rebounded on the Lore Master.

Hope heard a blast, saw a flash of light, and the moloch vanished.

The explosion blew Hope off her feet. A gray haze filled her vision, little streaks of lightning flashed before her eyes. The next thing she knew, Brian was kneeling on the ground, holding her firmly with his arm. "Are you all right?"

She blinked, trying to remove the dazzle. "I–I think so." She held the sword up. The gem had stopped glowing. The blade was unhurt. "What happened?"

"I do not know," Brian replied in shock. He reached to touch the blade, thought better of it, placed his hand on her shoulder. "That was strong magic, ancient magic."

The Lore Master's blasts burned most of Brian's tunic

away. Char marks covered his body. He bled from a dozen different wounds. Reflected in his eyes, Hope saw he held the pain in check by willpower alone.

"You're hurt."

"You too." He touched the side of her head. The blood from the wound had congealed in her hair.

"I will mend," she murmured. "We both will."

A sad smile crossed Brian's face. "You had better go." He gestured across the plain. "Ose is almost upon us."

A dragon flew high above the army. Apep. Directly below in a sedan chair Ose screamed at his men to run faster.

"Can you stand?" Brian asked. He extended his arm and helped Hope erect. "Go. Hurry." He still held his wand in his right hand. He withdrew his sword with the left. "Take Eldridge's magic through the portal. Destroy the doorway from the other side. I will hold off the soldiers."

Brian walked away, confronting the plain and the oncoming army of demons. Hope heard determination in his voice, but before he turned, she saw hopelessness cross his face.

Hope made a decision.

"I will not leave and permit you to die alone."

Chapter Sixteen

Brian swung and exploded. "You cannot. If we both stay, you will perish. Why would you want to stay here and die?" He pointed up the grotto in exasperation. "Go!"

"Nonsense," Hope lied. She strolled forward and tugged his hand. "Ose is almost here. Help me set Eldridge's magic."

Satan waited patiently for Hope, the magic death still secured to his back. They carried the cylinder up the grotto, and placed it inside the cave. Hope embraced the sense of freedom she only knew while fighting dragons. Diane would care for Apophis. *She is more of a mother to him than I've ever been.* A twinge of guilt that her sister would also have to run the farm tugged at her, but Diane knew how. Hope trained her sibling well.

Hope kept shooting glances in Brian's direction as they walked down the path. He hadn't spoken this whole time. His face was a study in contemplation.

To break the silence, she said, "We'll both confront Ose. When the time is ripe, we'll ignite the fuse, and as Eldridge said, 'run'." She flashed Brian a chipper smile, although she understood the words she uttered were nonsense. "At least that moloch will know he was in a fight."

Brian remained mute, but he scrutinized Hope's sword with intense interest. Finally, he mumbled, "It responded to the Lore Master's power. I wonder if it will answer to mine as well." He snatched Hope's arm and pulled her along. "Let us hurry to the plain, I want to attempt something."

They ran down the path. Brian grasped the hilt of the sword and withdrew the blade from the scabbard. "Stand aside," he ordered. "Anything could happen. It will be dangerous."

Hope backed up a few paces and watched with more

curiosity than fear.

The weapon swung awkwardly in Brian's hands. He held it out, tip up, and touched the gem with his wand.

Nothing happened. He muttered a few words under his breath in a language Hope didn't understand, and gold spark shot from the rod to the sword. The gem glowed faintly, but that was all.

"No good," he grunted at last, an expression of defeat on his face. "It will not obey me."

The first of Ose's advanced troops had attained the foot of the trail. Brian said urgently, "It was worth a try, but now ignite the cylinder before it is too late." His lips set into a grim line. Behind the forward soldiers, howls and strange cries echoed from the plains as the demons sighted Brian and Hope.

Brian strode forward, wand out. "The cylinder, Hope, ignite it, now," he ordered.

Hope didn't listen to him, she was thinking furiously. *What was different, except for Brian's magic, instead of the Lore Master? Why work for demon witchcraft, but not the human?*

"Wait." Hope jerked the sword out of his hands. "I was holding the blade when the moloch's power struck. Try again." She held the weapon in the air as before.

Brian shrugged, dubious but desperate to try anything. He extended his wand; the tip emitted a slight twinkle of yellow, touching the gem lightly. The gem glowed and died. A shallow flush of heat warmed her hand.

"It's not enough, Brian," Hope shouted. She rattled the blade in his face. "*Again.*"

Brian nodded, inhaled deeply, and gave her a hard look. "Let me know when it is enough."

This time a line of sparks spun from his wand, building in intensity as Brian increased the output by notches. The hilt of the sword flared hot in Hope's burnt palms.

Power erupted from the blade.

Running toward the soldiers, she cracked the weapon, lashing the demons. They wilted like melting snow.

The sword pulsed with energy in her hand. Hope squeezed the hilt, letting the power flow up her arm.

"More."

"Hope, your hands."

She stared in horror. Red blisters covered the fingers from the heat. She gasped as pain hit and dropped the blade.

Brian scooped the weapon up, his right hand clutching both wand and sword tightly together, touching at all points. He wrapped his left arm around her waist and hugged her close. Hope gazed at him, not understanding what he planned. Brian smiled down and muttered, "Perhaps if our bodies touch, this will work as well."

At the fall of the lead demons, Ose's soldiers stopped in fright, no beating from the Lore Masters strong enough to persuade the beasts farther. The molochs cursed the monsters, and ran to the front, staffs leveled. They made a slow advance.

Hope threw her arms around Brian's neck. "This is the best I can do," she murmured. "Hurry."

Brian smiled and squeezed her. He shouted more strange words and sparks flew out of the sword, sweeping over the Lore Masters. They crossed their staffs creating a red shield. The glimmers from the blade intensified until they built a solid beam of light. The demon screen flashed through the spectrum. With a high-pitched whine, the moloch barrier exploded in a bust of fire.

For the moment, they were safe, but Ose's main army arranged themselves for an assault.

Brian started a chant. His arms clenched, and sweat trickled down his face. He threw Hope an imploring look.

She answered his plea with a small smile. "Anything I have is yours to receive, wizard."

He drew power as he had twice before.

Energy sprang from her, leaving Hope gasping. She clung tighter to Brian in a fierce embrace and let him pull the life force from her body. He closed his eyes. His chanting grew louder, and shifted back into his own tongue.

Golden smoke arose from the clenched wand and sword, transformed into flames, and streaked up Brian's arm. He didn't notice. His chants transformed into shrieks. He screamed, "Aktzin and Chac, Dongo and Jokuta, Adad and Jofur. Hear my prayer...*I summon thee!*"

The air around Hope and Brian stilled. Sounds muffled as if a blanket smothered the earth. Hope's last remaining dregs of energy trickled out into Brian. He, in turn, crushed the wand and sword harder until the fire blazed up to his shoulder.

The sword evolved into a lance of flame. Lightning pulsed into the air, a beacon piercing the stars themselves. Hope and Brian collapsed to their knees, drained of power.

The heavens answered Brian's plea.

Thunderheads rushed in. The sky boiled. The day blackened to night. A pattering of rain fell, changing into a torrent of water that made it impossible to see more than a few feet ahead.

The rain froze to hail. Fist size chunks of ice pounded the earth, chattering like a wild animal as it cracked and broke. The crashing built into a roar. Hope covered her head to stifle the noise and protect herself.

When she thought nothing could surpass the violence, bolts of lightning streaked between the clouds. The air glowed like the sun. Flashes of brilliance transformed dark into light and back again.

Blasts of thunder exploded and the lightning crashed down, leaving smoking craters. The earth itself rolled. Hope would later swear dark figures strolled in the clouds carrying maces, clubs, and hammers, hurling bolts of fire at the army. The plain descended into a heaving maelstrom of destruction.

Cowering, Hope and Brian fell on their faces, terrified by what they witnessed.

Hope was unsure how long the holocaust lasted, this wrenching of the earth. Minutes? Hours? Each time she dared look up, the sky still churned, the sight making her ill. She clung tight to Brian, burying her head under his arm at every boom of thunder.

The hail filled the craters, steam boiled up. The fog covered the savannah in a blanket of death.

Eventually the rolling stopped. The thunder died to faint grumbles. Hope drew a sobbing breath and lifted her head.

In the distance cyclones twisted away. Above, the clouds scattered, swept from the sky leaving a blue firmament that spread across the heavens. What drew Hope's attention, however, was the plain.

Where the flat savannah once stretched, muddy lumps of dirt blossomed, erected by the ripping of the earth. In places bones protruded, the skeletal remnants of Ose's army. Nothing stirred.

"Brian, we did it."

She heard no answer.

"Brian?"

The man beside her grimaced in pain, his right arm charred to the shoulder. Ashes slipped between blackened fingers, the remains of his wand. The sword he clutched was unharmed, but the pommel's glow was dead, the blade lifeless.

Brian tried unclutching his hand, his eyes mere slits. "I cannot let go," he hissed.

One by one, Hope pried his fingers from the blade and pushed the sword away.

"So you think you have won?"

Wings beat above their heads, shattering the silence. Apep landed. His massive skull twisted until his snout was parallel with Hope and Brian. He hissed, "You have rendered me a favor, humans. With Ose dead I rule his kingdom." He reared up, fire trickled from his nostrils, his voice glowed in malice. "It is a pity to kill you."

"How did you manage to survive?" Hope tried to sit up, discovered she was far too weak, and sank down. She pointed a shaky finger. "No one could live through that."

This time a blast of fire shot into the sky as Apep bellowed in laughter. "Fool, I am a dragon. When the storm approached, I flew above the clouds. Do you think this is the first tempest I have ridden out?"

"You are wise, indeed, Apep," Hope said. *Stroke him. Keep the snake talking. This one likes to brag.* Aloud she shouted, "How can you rule? That was Ose's kingdom. He conquered it. The captains he set in place and the people serve him, not you."

Apep gave the equivalent of a dragon smile. "Stupid human, am I unwise? My plans were prepared long before this." He lifted his head in pride and preened. "Behind each conquest I let it be known I spoke for Ose. He was too busy killing and expanding his territories to recognize what I did. Eventually he relied on me to deliver his communications to the towns he conquered." The dragon extended his talons. "Now all obey me, apart for the dragon council, and I shall deal with those fools in my own good time."

Apep furled his wings and waddled closer. Hope eyed her sword. The strength slowly seeped back into her muscles. Did she have enough to snatch the blade and attack? She flexed arms and legs.

Brian pushed himself to his knees with a groan cradling his burnt arm. "You will never rule. The peoples of the Northern Plains and valleys will see to that," he declared stoutly. "We have defeated the army of Ose. We will destroy yours as well."

Apep swung his head to regard the human with scorn. "They will be no harder to subdue than the lands of the south," he scoffed. "I am not as foolish as Ose, who listened to my words, and divide my army to waste troops on a useless attack. When I strike, it will be with the full force of my soldiers. I will destroy the Northern Plains and conquer this new world."

Brian watched Hope out of the corner of his eyes.

She shifted her attention to him and then to the dragon. *He knows what I'm doing. Keep Apep occupied.* Hope stretched her legs out.

As if their minds merged, Brian said, "You will never find the portal, only Ose knew of its location," he waved to the plain with his good hand, "and Ose is dead."

Apep regarded the remnants of the demon army. "Where do you think Ose learned about the tunnel between our land and this new world?" he hissed.

Hope dug the tips of her boots into the dirt, pushing with legs, and sliding inches closer to the blade. "You told Ose about the gateway?" she said. "I thought none but Ose knew the location of the gate."

"You humans are dim-witted," sneered the dragon. "I mentioned the legend to the moloch and how the dragons feared that place. He searched and stumbled upon the portal." He chuckled at his own cleverness. "The knowledge of the hidden place was lost, but now it is revealed." His nose snorted fire in the direction of the trail leading to the grotto. "You see how clever I am? This was part of my strategy, also."

Hope seethed inside. *Keep bragging, snake, and you'll see how dead you are.* She edged closer to her sword.

Apep puffed his chest out with pride. "After the moloch entered, I decided to seal the portal with fire and trap him there, until his kingdom was firmly in my control. Then reopen the cave and negotiate with him at my leisure."

The blade was close enough to grasp. Hope slid a hand forward through the muddy earth. Fingers closed around the hilt of the sword, legs tensed to spring.

"You think I do not notice what you attempt, female?" Apep hissed. His jaws gaped wide. "Now we finish."

Hope lunged. Brian staggered to his feet and charged. The sky darkened and a blast of fire engulfed Apep. A shadow passed over his head and a new dragon swooped in between Apep and the humans.

"The council has watched and decided, traitor," Bane said. He flapped his wings and raised his head high. "Your time is done."

Apep hissed. His eyes sparked red. "You. Be gone, child, while I deal with these humans, then it is your turn. The council has no authority over me. I rule."

Bane puffed himself up and stood his ground. "My mother says otherwise. The council is united. We side with the humans of the valleys and the free peoples of the plains."

Arrogance filled Apep's voice. "I will march my army over the council and destroy you all," he boasted.

Bane stepped closer to the older dragon until they were face to face. "Not so. You possess no soldiers. As we speak, the council has disbanded the Kingdom of Ose. Our people land and kill your tyrants. Each town is free of his rule, and yours. They do as they please."

Standing together, Bane had grown in stature since Hope observed him weeks ago. While still not at full size, his muscles rippled with youth and vitality, his scales glistened, the skin underneath deepened to a dark green.

In contrast, Apep projected a picture of decay, dull and faded, with faint wrinkles crossing his worn hide.

Apep blew a fury of fire into the air and charged Bane.

Their chests clashed. Necks intertwined as both struggled for chokeholds. Razor sharp teeth snapped at exposed throats, trying to end the encounter quickly. The younger dragon reeled toward Hope and Brian, collapsing under the sheer bulk of the older.

A hand tugged on Hope's collar. "Back," Brian gasped, "or we will be killed." Trampling feet and swinging tails sent flying debris in all directions. "We must take shelter or they will crush us." He staggered backward, dragging her along.

Bane regained his footing. With a twist of his head, he broke free, flailing his wings to stop from toppling backward again.

Brian tried to seek the safety of a boulder while still yanking on Hope. He tripped, both floundering, as Bane's tail swept over their heads. Hope wavered up and grabbed Brian's burnt arm, attempting to raise him also. Brian screamed. Hope ignored his pain and shoved a shoulder under his armpit. Using her sword as support, they tottered to safety.

Bane and Apep separated, each sizing up his opponent in wary agitation. Both heads rose and wings stretched as they hissed defiance. With a leap, Apep soared into the sky, Bane flapping hard in pursuit. They circled higher and higher like two fighters searching for an opening. Flames belched out. They collided, powerful rear talons ripping at the belly of the other. Sharp forelegs raised, ready to lash out at any opportunity.

"Can you walk?" Hope searched Brian's face. Pain etched in every line of his body.

"If I have too," he grunted back. He stared up into the sky. "Who do you think will win?"

From above, a keening wail echoed. A black dot trailing smoke plummeted downward, another, spiraling slower, shadowed.

"We will soon learn," Hope replied grimly. She watched the falling body. "If it is Apep, be prepared to fight. Again."

The dragon hit the earth. Flames rippled along the wings. The smell of burnt flesh filled the air. The victorious dragon glided to a landing next to the body, scorch marks and blood covering head and back, one front leg nearly bitten in two. The long neck rose to the sky and a screech of triumph issued from his mouth.

Bane snorted fire from his nostrils. "This one will spread his deceit no more," he declared with satisfaction. "I will ensure that." Hope noticed again the red swelling under the dragon's throat, enlarged now to bursting.

Bane approached the body of his late opponent. Flame issued from his mouth washing over the corpse and centering on the head. Scales and flesh melted away. The fire changed from red to white, disappearing until all that showed was the shimmering of the air. The skull exploded into nothingness, leaving the blackened stub of the neck.

Hope and Brian emerged from behind the boulder.

"Thank you," Hope called out. "You've saved our lives."

Bane dipped his head low in a bow. "You are welcome, but that was not my main intention."

Brian leaned against the boulder to steady himself. "Regardless, it was a timely rescue, but why did you come, to fight Apep?"

Bane issued a chuckle deep in his throat. "No, that was my good fortune. I shadowed to learn the location of the portal to close it. The council has ordered the doorway sealed. None of our children shall ever wander back into that evil place. I will terminate it now." He breezed past Hope and Brian, waddling up the trail.

"Not yet," shouted Brian. "Hope must pass through."

Bane halted. He regarded her with interest. "Why? You enter a terrible world, full of hate and misery. Who would seek such a place?"

"That is my home," stated Hope in a quiet tone. "My family lives there."

"Really?" Bane cocked his head. "That is a shame."

Brian whispered, "Stay here. I still need someone to

teach me how to farm."

Hope's eyebrows rose. "Is that why you want me to remain, to be your steward?"

"I wish you to dwell in this world and be my wife," he proposed softly, "if you will have me."

Hope's first impulse was to say yes. She swallowed. "I have a son, a half-breed."

Brian startled. He attempted to say something, but nothing came out.

Hope glanced at Bane and then stared steadily into Brian's eyes. She hoped to phrase the next sentence different, but she said, "It was rape."

Brian laid his hands on her shoulders. "If I cherish the son, do I receive the mother?" Brian searched Hope's face.

"Yes."

Bane listened to this exchange with interest. He said, "What do you now propose to do?"

"Will you delay a few days, please?" Hope pleaded. "We must ride to my valley, and then we will return. After that, do with the gate as you wish." She waited expectantly for his answer.

"If you insist," Bane grumbled, "but be quick. I have reached maturity and must win a cave of my own. I do not want to abide here forever."

Hope put two fingers to her mouth and blew a shrill whistle. From a rift, a whinny answered. Brian's mount emerged, shepherded by Satan, who nipped at the flanks of the reluctant horse herding the animal their way.

The horse shied from the stench of dead dragon and blood. Brian hobbled after his mount, snatching the reins with his good hand. Hope blinked. Was he capable of riding?

"Are you okay?"

Brian inhaled. "Even if I were not, I would leap at your command forever, Hope Nearwood. Yes, I am fine. Once we achieve your home land, I have salve in my pack, and I still know healing magic, even if my wand is destroyed." He touched her tunic. Red blotches showed through. "I think you will need fixing too."

A rumble issued behind the two. Bane squatted, his muzzle pointing toward the cave.

"We'd better hurry," Hope whispered. "Someone is growing impatient."

The path through the mountains was warmer than Hope remembered. When they'd left fall had set in. As they progressed into the lower levels, the green grass of the valley announced spring commencing.

***

Satan increased his pace as they approached the manor house, the stallion prancing in anticipation of being home. Hope felt the same way. She kept casting glances at Brian as she rode beside him, wondering what he thought.

"This is all your land?" Brian marveled as they transversed tilled fields ready for planting.

"Nearwood land," she confirmed. Hope considered taking plants back to Mictian. The climate was warmer in Mictian than here in the valley. She wondered if seed from this world could germinate in Brian's land.

Hope laughed. If what grew in her belly was any indication, they would.

As they passed a field of newly sprouted winter grain, Brian exclaimed, "If my farm prospers half as well as yours, I will be a happy man indeed."

Hope laughed. "I will make sure it does."

Gazing around, Hope admitted, Diane had performed well with the spring planting. Rows plowed straight, neat and even, the young shoots, erect and tall.

The servants at the house halted in surprise as they approached. Cries of recognition started and then stopped as they realized Brian escorted her.

"It's all right," she assured the head groom as he took their horses and shot a suspicious glance at Brian. "Is Diane

265

here?"

"Yes, Mistress Nearwood," he nodded to the manor house, "inside."

Diane worked in the back office when they entered. Hope heard the door slam and the clicking of boots as the young woman hurried along the hall to see who waited. She halted in shock when Hope and Brian burst into view.

Diane shifted nervously, unsure what she confronted. "Hope, you've returned. We thought you were…Who is this?"

"It's all right, he knows everything." Hope's face lit up. "We are to be married."

Diane gasped. She fell silent and then rushed to Hope, engulfing her sister in a tight hug. "Oh, by the gods, I am happy for *you*." She started to cry. "I imagined you were lost, you've been away forever. I never dreamed you'd bring a man. Where have you been? I mean, I thought…"

Hope held Diane at arms-length, laughing and crying. "Slow down, Sis. First of all this is Brian." Hope narrowed her eyes. "I've been in another world."

Diane goggled, mouth dropping, debating a greeting. Brian settled the matter by advancing and placing a kiss on her cheek. "I am happy to finally meet you," he said.

Diane blushed and smiled back. "I'm glad my sister found you. I never thought…" she turned to Hope "…is it true? You're getting married? You were in a *different land?*"

Hope gritted her teeth. "Yes, and I'm returning."

"But the farm…?"

"I'm taking Apophis with me."

Diane looked straight ahead. "This is so sudden. He's in his room." As if in a dream, she spun and walked down the hallway. Brian and Hope tailed silently.

They entered. Apophis had his back to the door, sitting on his toy box, staring out the window between the curtains. When he heard Diane, Hope, and Brian enter, he stood and faced the trio.

"Mommy?" He stepped forward, not believing who was there. His face lit up and he rushed to embrace her. "MOMMY." His forked tongue flickered in and out with excitement. Hope fell to her knees and held him close.

For the first time Apophis noticed Brian. He pointed a clawed finger. "Who is he?" The child pressed closer to Hope.

Brian knelt until he was head level with Apophis. "I am a friend of you mother's." He flashed one of his grins. "Do you like to ride horses?"

The boy put a finger to his mouth. "I ride," he admitted, "but at night. I'm not allowed to be outside during the day." He looked at Hope and Diane for confirmation.

"Would you want to come with your mommy and me to where I live? I have plenty of horses to ride all day long if you wish." Brian raised one eyebrow and winked. "There are boys and girls to play with too, and a stream to go fishing. Sound like fun?"

Apophis shifted from one foot to another in delight. "Gee." Again, he checked with his mother and aunt. "If that's okay with you."

Diane started crying again. "Of course it's all right, baby." She knelt and hugged Apophis.

"We must hurry," Hope said, standing. "Pack his things. Apophis, take what toys you want. We can't bring too much," she cautioned, "one or two."

"I thought you'd be staying…"

Hope shook her head. "No. The doorway between worlds is to be closed." Diane nodded silently, dealing with all the sudden changes transforming her life. "Do you want to leave with us? Once it's sealed we'll never return."

"I…" Diane paused, weighing options. "I will stay in this world, on the farm." A slow smile crossed her lips. "I met a man also, a merchant. He heard the property next to ours was for sale. He traveled here and found out we'd bought it already. He wanted to know if we'd sell."

"A merchant?" Hope said, surprised. "Whatever would he do with a farm?

Diane shrugged. "He wants to settle down. Said he was tired of traveling all the time. He's wealthy from trading and desired a home and family. He seemed nice. I'm to discuss the sale tomorrow with him."

"I bet he was young and handsome?" Hope interjected with a grin.

Feet shuffled along with a nervous titter. "Very, handsome that is, about your age, I guess. He asked to visit today and go riding, check the property. I told him no, I'd meet him in town." She glanced at the boy. "Apophis, you know, but now…"

"Good luck."

The sisters embraced. No words passed between them. They'd said goodbye a hundred times before and realized this was for the best.

"Is there anything to gather before we leave?" Brian asked. "A keepsake maybe?"

"I don't think so." Hope thought. "Yes, wait a minute." She rushed off. A moment later, she reentered the room carrying a bundle and the jar of rubies. "My dowry," she announced with a silly grin, holding up the gems. "I can't go into a new world penniless."

Brian reached out and hugged her to him. "You bring more, woman, than all the jewels in the world could buy. What is in the package?"

"Oh." Hope ruffled Apophis stiff hair. "My father's chain mail, for when this one gets older."

***

Bane still waited by the path when they returned. "Well, it is about time," he announced. Apophis shrank against Hope when he saw the dragon, though Hope had warned him what to expect.

268

Bane's long neck snaked down. "I will not hurt you, little one." He sniffed the boy. "You smell good."

The red at the bottom of his throat was prominent. Hope asked. "What *is* that?" She pointed at his neck. "I noticed it before. Have you hurt yourself?"

"This?" Bane pawed at his neck with his foreleg. "That indicates I am a mature adult, ready for mating." He paused, thinking. "First I must find a lair suitable to my new status. I cannot live with dragonets."

Hope had a sudden thought. She said to Brian, "That dragon we killed. You said sometimes valleys propose alliances? Do you think...?"

"Bane, if you are searching for a home, we know of an empty cave in the mountains of Mictian valley," Brian called out. "It is yours to make a den if you wish."

"I will seek the place out," agreed the dragon. "Now I must destroy the doorway. Beware." He waddled up the path toward the cave.

Hope, Brian, and Apophis dashed out onto the plain.

"Brian, Eldridge's magic." Hope twisted around with a sharp cry. "We forgot to warn Bane."

Brian looked back also. An explosion rocked the hills and a huge cloud of dust rose in the sky. A few moments later, a dark shape winged overhead in the direction of Mictian valley. "Do not you remember? Dragons are immune to magic."

"Mommy? What was that noise?" Apophis was straining to see the cause of the disturbance.

"Don't worry, baby," Hope said. She hugged him close. A warm sun shone on the prairie, and the breeze blew on her back, hurrying her along. "That was an old door closing, but we have a whole new world to explore."

Social Media Links:

Twitter: https://twitter.com/artyny59

Facebook: https://www.facebook.com/pages/Arthur-Butt/1528729850734703

www.ingramcontent.com/pod-product-compliance
Lightning Source LLC
Chambersburg PA
CBHW051146030726
47504CB00004B/1061